Praise for

When the Sandpip

"Hats off (red, of course) to Peggy Darty for penning such an interesting, fun filled, and inspiring cozy mystery. She has captured perfectly the friendship, camaraderie, and humor exemplified by the ladies of the Red Hat Society. I can't wait to buy my copy!"

—Jo Ann Cole, Queen Mother, Circle City
Sassy Sisterhood

"Forget that trip to the beach this year. Just escape into Peggy Darty's latest novel—and you'll be there. Mystery, romance, inspiration, and the authentic atmosphere of Florida's Emerald Coast will leap off the pages and into your heart."

—Joyce Holland, *Northwest Florida Daily News*

"*When the Sandpiper Calls* by Peggy Darty is a story as intriguing as the author and her work. I've been a reader of Peggy's books for many, many years, and she never disappoints. Once again, she has drawn me into a story from the beginning with the delightful character Christy Castleman, uniquely herself yet able to interact with persons of all ages and walks of life.

"Peggy wastes no time getting into the mystery that makes this novel a page-turner. She presents interesting characters, all with their own special personalities that delight and charm me as a reader. Summer Breeze is a delightfully cozy setting, perfect for the unsettling crime to be committed. Peggy combines action with emotional and spiritual journeys in a masterful way. Don't miss this intriguing story told by one of my favorite authors."

—YVONNE LEHMAN, author of *Coffee Rings*,
director, Blue Ridge Mountains Christian
Writers Conference

When the
Sandpiper
Calls

When the
Sandpiper
Calls

A Cozy Mystery by
Peggy Darty

WATERBROOK
PRESS

WHEN THE SANDPIPER CALLS
PUBLISHED BY WATERBROOK PRESS
12265 Oracle Blvd., Suite 200
Colorado Springs, Colorado 80921
A division of Random House, Inc.

Scripture taken from the *Holy Bible, New International Version*®. NIV®. Copyright ©
1973, 1978, 1984 by International Bible Society. Used by permission of Zondervan
Publishing House. All rights reserved.

ISBN 1-57856-904-4

Library of Congress Cataloging-in-Publication Data
Darty, Peggy.
    When the sandpiper calls : a cozy mystery / Peggy Darty.—1st ed.
        p. cm.
    ISBN 1-57856-904-4
    1. Detective and mystery stories—Authorship—Fiction. 2. Female friendship—
Fiction. 3. Women authors—Fiction. 4. Florida—Fiction. I. Title.
    PS3554.A79W47 2005
    813'.54—dc22

                                                    2005011652

Printed in the United States of America
2005—First Edition

10 9 8 7 6 5 4 3 2 1

For David and Drew with all my love

Acknowledgments

I owe a debt of gratitude to many people in the creation of this book.

First, I want to say that Summer Breeze is a fictional community nestled among the beachside towns stretching from Panama City Beach to Fort Walton. I love each of those places so much that it became impossible to choose one over the other.

Thanks to my friend Nancy, who pointed me to the perfect spot.

Hats off to Denise, JoAnn, Vivian, and all my fellow members of the Red Hat Society. You've been generous in letting me move you around and incorporate you in one setting. And you've been terrific friends.

At WaterBrook I was blessed to know Don Pape, former publisher, whose kindness and encouragement made every writer feel special. Many thanks to Dudley Delffs, my editor, whose intelligence and expertise make every writer better, and thanks to Shannon Hill and Carol Bartley for editorial suggestions and assistance. Thanks and a hug to Ginia Hairston, the charming lady who handles marketing and publicity with an efficiency that amazes me. Thanks to sales and the great staff in all these departments, as well as the art department, and especially Kristopher Orr, who designed the beautiful cover.

And thank you, Steve Cobb, president, for making all this happen.

Finally, I would like to thank my husband, Landon, who thought of the title and offered ideas and suggestions. To Lan, Steve, and Darla, our wonderful adult children, and our terrific daughters-in-law, Susan and Lucy, and of course our grandsons, David and Drew—thank you so much for blessing my life and encouraging me to keep writing.

Monday, February 16, 2004

H ellooo, Mystery Lady!"

Christy had just stepped out of her car onto the concrete parking lot of Frank's Steak and Seafood Restaurant. Hoisting tote bag and purse, she turned with a smile, knowing who owned that voice.

"Hey, Bonnie. It's good to see you."

Bonnie Taylor sat behind the wheel of her 1990 baby blue Cadillac, her dark face framed by the open window. Beneath the window, *How Sweet It Is* swirled in red cursive across the door.

"Wait a minute, honey." The long blue car floated past and turned into the parking spot in front of the No Parking sign.

The door flew open, and Bonnie unfolded from the car, a huge red purse swinging from her arm. It always amazed Christy that a woman almost six feet tall and well over two hundred pounds could move with such grace A feathered red hat and purple pantsuit announced her attendance at the Red Hat luncheon with her chapter, Sassy Snowbirds of Summer Breeze.

The chapter had originated with a group of ladies from Canada and the northeast who wintered in the Florida Panhandle, bringing news of the Red Hat Society from their hometowns. Their red hats had captured the attention of locals, and as a result, the ladies of Summer Breeze had joined Sassy Snowbirds in spreading fun, friendship, and good deeds.

Christy reached up to give Bonnie a hug, inhaling cinnamon and cloves. It was fun to hug Bonnie because she always smelled of spices from her famous pie kitchen. "Bonnie, I assume you saw the No Parking sign."

"Yeah, but my knees are hurting today, so I take special privileges." Her lips spread in a wide, wicked grin. "I'm big. I'm black. And I'm a woman. Frank's afraid I'll yell discrimination. Or he's just afraid of me, period."

Christy laughed. "I don't think Frank's afraid of anything."

"Heard you were our guest speaker, so I made a special effort to be here. But hold on a minute." Bonnie's hand shot into the huge purse and whipped out a compact, popped it open, and held it in front of Christy.

Christy faced her reflection and winced. Her mascara was smudged, leaving a glob beneath her left eye.

"Here." Bonnie handed her a Kleenex.

"Thanks." Christy scrubbed the smear, leaving a red mark instead. She blinked, peered into the mirror, and surveyed her reflection with a critical eye. Her blue eyes seemed too big for her oval face, and her lips looked too thin. Well, not thin exactly. Just not full enough. And the pink gloss felt sticky on her lips. Nerves—she just had a case of nerves.

Which was why she had lost a page from her carefully typed speech.

She smoothed her brown hair, a layered cut that twirled around her face and waved to her neckline. Sun streaks were natural, but those who hadn't known her long thought she paid a hairstylist for the look she took for granted.

Otherwise she appeared normal. But she didn't feel normal. She hated making speeches.

She sighed, thinking it wouldn't be the first time she'd had to wing it. She looked up at Bonnie. "Better?"

Bonnie grinned. "Now you look terrific."

"You should see me when I crawl out of bed. I worked hard for this." She waved a hand from her face down the straight, pink linen dress.

"You'd look good in a straw hat and overalls, but listen…" Bonnie paused, glancing around. "This may not be the best day for your speech."

Christy stuffed the Kleenex in her purse and surveyed the crowded parking lot. "Why is that?"

"Some of us are upset with Marty. You know Marty McAllister, the Realtor?"

"Sure. I bought my house from her. What's up?"

"Marty volunteered to find us a small office where we could plan our get-togethers and such. She invited us to her house for dinner last night. Couple of the girls canceled other plans, and I made pies. The house was dark, the doors locked. She didn't even leave us a note. Instead of Marty, we were greeted by her big dog, overfed and overfriendly. He knocked me down and gobbled up the lemon pies before we could stop him."

"Oh no!" Christy tried to look horrified, despite a humorous flash at the picture of Bonnie overcome by Marty's Saint Bernard, lapping up lemon pie. Then she thought of the perky, five-foot redhead whose driving ambition had won her Realtor of the Year. "Does Marty belong to your organization?"

"No. She's just hoping to make some money on us."

"Woo-hoo!" The voice of Aunt Dianna reached Christy as she and Bonnie climbed the steps of the rambling, white stucco restaurant. They waited for her to catch up.

Aunt Dianna was in charge of this month's program and had invited Christy to talk about writing. The publication of Christy's first mystery novel had been a success; she was now completing the last two chapters of her second novel.

"Hey, Bonnie." Dianna smiled, then turned to Christy. "And how's my wonderful niece?"

"Fine. And you look great."

Dianna struck a pose for them in her wide-brimmed red hat, red feather boa, and purple dress. With auburn hair and a friendly smile, she had captured the attention of a guy parking his Harley. As he climbed the steps, he turned to stare.

"Aren't you a bit overdressed?" he teased, looking at Dianna.

Christy caught her breath, wondering how her aunt would respond. She had always been the spark in her father's family.

"No, I always dress well. But I need your jacket."

Determined to be a good sport, the guy whipped off his leather jacket and handed it to Dianna.

Bonnie nudged Christy. "This'll be good. If anybody's still poutin' with Marty, Dianna will make them forget it."

"She'll do her best."

Fascinated, Christy followed the two women and the Harley guy into the driftwood lobby, past the decorative palms and hanging ferns, through the arched doorway of the party room. A lively group of ladies gathered around the tables, decked out in their charming red hats of all sizes, all shapes, all designs.

"Dianna, what in the world are you doing?" Maryann called. Maryann was the pretty blond Queen of Sassy Snowbirds.

"Do you like my outfit?" Dianna twirled, showing off the jacket.

Every face broke into a smile, and then laughter cascaded over the room as she gave a bow, removed the jacket, and returned it to the Harley guy, who chuckled as he shook his head at the group, then disappeared.

Dianna motioned to Christy. "Just take a seat beside me at the head table. Maybe we can get this crew settled down."

Christy left her tote bag next to the podium, then joined her aunt. Her eyes scanned the crowded room, then she gazed at a painting on the wall.

An artist had expertly captured their beachside community with its sugar white sand, emerald waters, and pastel beach houses set behind white picket fences. Studying the painting, Christy thought about their cozy little seaside village.

Summer Breeze stretched from the Gulf of Mexico back to Highway 98 in the Florida Panhandle. Sandwiched between some of the more affluent communities along the Emerald Coast, Summer Breeze belonged to its inhabitants in a special way with neighborly front porches, community barbecues, and church socials. It was a place where everyone knew everyone else and helped when there was a need.

Maryann welcomed everyone, acknowledged their special guest, then announced there was only one item of business to discuss.

While Christy stared at Maryann, pretending interest, her mind shot back to her early morning trip to Shipwreck Island and the antique bottle she had found half-buried in sand at the shoreline.

She glanced at the tan tote bag that contained books to pass out. Beneath the books, wrapped in tissue, lay the bottle—with a frightening note tucked inside. She still hadn't figured out if someone was playing a joke on the mystery writer...or if she should have stopped to show Big Bob, the local deputy.

"Does anyone have suggestions for our float this year?" Maryann asked, pulling Christy back to the moment.

Maryann began to describe a float that she and Dianna had seen at the National Peanut Festival. She thought it would be fun to have a Sassy Snowbird float in the Fourth of July parade.

Various opinions were discussed, and Christy tilted her head, pretending fascination, while she made a mental dash back to the island. She had been headed to her car when she spotted a lone sandpiper pecking at something green in the sand. At the sound of her footsteps, the little bird lifted its head and softly peeped.

She approached, and the sandpiper flew across the sand like a motorized toy. It stopped a comfortable distance away to observe.

She leaned down and gently wedged the green bottle from the damp sand, brushing away the grit. Back at home she had pried the cork loose and read the startling note...

"Hey, lady!" Valerie Moore, the town's favorite hairstylist, took a seat beside Christy. She was wearing purple jeans and a matching sweater, with a red cowboy hat tilted at an angle on her strawberry blond head.

"Hello, ladies!" Frank La Rosa's voice boomed over the party room.

All red hats turned in the direction of the burly, rough-cut owner. Tall and broad, he had black hair, a big, square face, and a spare tire around the middle. Along with good food, Frank offered perks to his regular customers. Today's perk was one of his ice sculptures, skillfully designed and sprayed red to resemble a red hat. *Oohs* and *aahs* flew around the room as he placed his masterpiece in the center of the table. With a few sharp tools and a block of ice, Frank could create a work of art.

"You gals are doing a super thing for Ellie Pearson," he said, smiling at the group, "taking food and running errands while she recovers from surgery."

"Thank you, Frank," Maryann replied. "Has anyone talked to Ellie?"

Dianna leaned over to Christy and whispered, "Thanks for coming, doll. Did you hear what Marty did to us last night?"

Christy recalled what Bonnie had said and nodded. "She stood you up?"

"I couldn't believe she would do us that way." Valerie entered the whispering conversation. "So I called her boss at home last night. Carl said Marty came to the office around noon yesterday and picked up keys to a beach house in Destin. She had an appointment with a Miami businessman and his girlfriend."

"The one who got so mad at her last month?" Dianna inquired.

"According to Carl, Marty wanted to make amends by showing him a couple of great buys."

"Dianna and Valerie, what do you two think about a float?"

Both turned to stare blankly at Maryann, who had a teasing grin on her face. It was her tactful way of shushing the buzz from their end of the table.

"I say we do it!" Dianna replied emphatically.

Seafood salads were placed before the ladies, and everyone dug in. Christy picked at hers long enough to be polite. Then she laid down her fork and touched the linen napkin to her mouth as Dianna went to the podium to introduce her.

Christy gently slid the speech from her purse. One page drifted to the floor. Being way too short to suit herself, she knew if she tried to reach down and retrieve it, her head would end up in the plate. She decided to forget about the typed paper. She knew what she had written, and she might even mention the bottle. And the note inside the bottle…

Christy grabbed her glass and took a sip of iced tea. Remembering the cowlick at her crown, she casually ran her hand over the back of her head, pressing her hair firmly in place while Dianna detailed the facts.

"Christy graduated from Florida State, wrote a best-selling mystery, and is finishing another while teaching fiction writing at Bayside Community College. She's active at Bayside Community Church, sponsoring fishing trips for the youth at Rainbow Bay." She paused for a sip of water.

A loud whisper sizzled through the crowd. "Anyone who can deal with Jack Watson is a saint. He may own the best fishing spot in Florida, but who wants to put up with him?"

Christy lowered her eyes, a rush of tenderness sweeping over her at the mention of Jack's name, the man who loved her like the daughter-in-law she might have been if only Chad hadn't… She swallowed hard, trying not to think about that now.

"…daughter of my brother, Pastor Grant Castleman, and his wife, Beth. So, everyone, please welcome our brilliant author, Christy Castleman."

Christy tried not to wince at Dianna's dramatic ending. Applause filled the room, bringing the familiar prick of self-consciousness when all eyes turned to her. Pushing her chair back, she rose beyond her five foot two to a respectable five five, which was why she loved heels. One spike heel ground into the paper she had dropped as she turned and walked to the podium.

She smiled around the group, trying to focus her thoughts. "Thanks so much for inviting me to come today and allowing me to talk about my favorite subject: writing. I've been blessed to live near Shipwreck Island, which allows me to dream up wonderful stories. I've been equally blessed to live in the wonderful community of Summer Breeze.

"But to tell you about my writing—I've always had a vivid imagination. However, it wasn't until college that I began to take writing seriously—when a creative writing instructor encouraged me to pursue my writing with the idea of getting something published. I began with short stories, but all I got from my submissions was a stack of rejection slips. One day I was gathering my overdue library books and noticed that all the books were mysteries. I wasn't reading what I was trying to write; I was reading mysteries. When I began to write what I liked to read, everything changed."

"Fascinating," Maryann murmured.

The word spoken softly beside Christy broke her concentration. Her mind went completely blank; panic began to swell in her chest. Then suddenly she thought of the bottle and decided to get some audience participation.

"Since mystery is basically about being a good detective, I'd like some feedback from all of you." She leaned down and picked up the tote bag. "I have books for you, but first I want to show you something." She lifted the wrapped bottle and held it up. "This morning I went over to Shipwreck Island. As I said, that's where I get my inspiration for stories of pirates, stolen gold, and murder."

"Excuse me," came a voice from the back, "but I'm new to the area. What happened there? Did a ship run ashore?"

Christy began to explain. "In the late eighteen hundreds, a Spanish galleon loaded with rich cargo got swept up in a powerful hurricane that drove the ship inward. Then as the hurricane gained momentum, the ship was hurled onto a deserted island that became known as Shipwreck Island. Over the years it has been explored and searched with metal detectors."

"In other words," Bonnie spoke up, "that hurricane blew stuff for a hundred miles, and folks still hope to find treasure and get rich. Nobody's been that lucky."

Christy agreed, and everyone laughed. "This morning at the shoreline, I found this bottle half-buried in sand."

Maryann, seated next to her, studied the bottle. "Says it was made in Scotland."

"Maybe the bottle came off the ship; maybe it's been lying on the ocean floor for years," Dianna suggested. "We had wind and rain yesterday."

Someone in the crowd spoke up. "Christy, I saw a bottle like that one in your mom's gift shop. Did you ask her about it?"

"Not yet. But what puzzles me most is the note."

No one moved for a split second. Then someone called out, "What note?" and everyone began to fidget.

Christy's eyes moved slowly around the room, watching carefully for any indication that someone was pulling a joke on the mystery writer. She met only interested, inquisitive faces. She sidled a look at her aunt. Dianna appeared to be as fascinated as Maryann. Besides, that type of joke wasn't typical of Dianna.

This was the kind of prank her younger brother would pull, then hide in the woods and watch with glee while she took the bait. But Seth was in Australia. And there were no footprints in the sand, as there would have been if someone had seen her white convertible, sneaked out to the beach while she was back in the woods, and left the bottle in her path.

"Tell us about the note!" an impatient voice prompted.

Christy hesitated, knowing she was about to ignite a blaze of speculation.

"When I got home, I found a corkscrew and began to work on the cork. It popped right out. And inside the bottle was this little piece of paper."

"Well, don't keep us in suspense!" Bonnie shouted. "What does it say?"

She looked from the ladies down to the small strip of paper. "It reads…'Call the police. Someone is trying to kill me.'"

A collective gasp ran through the group.

"Wait a minute. Wait…a…minute!" Bonnie sprang to her feet, startling everyone with her speed. "A tourist was murdered over in Panama City last week."

"That's right," Valerie spoke up. "One of my customers had eaten at the seafood place where he was found. A worker on the late shift found him in his car."

Christy took a deep breath. This was getting way out of hand.

"Well, I don't think this note has anything to do with that. Either this is a warped joke"—she waved the small strip of paper—"or…somebody threw it from a boat." She frowned. That didn't make sense either.

Chairs scraped over carpet and one toppled as the ladies crowded around Christy.

"Look!" someone cried. "The capital *C* is only half-formed. And there's that wide loop inside the *e*."

"Hey, Sassies!" Dianna pounded her iced tea glass against the table like a judge with a gavel, trying to restore order. "What are you talking about? Is someone taking handwriting analysis at the community college?"

"It's her handwriting." Peggy Sue emerged from the huddle,

her eyes wide beneath her Southern belle hat. "I made an offer on a condo, and she wrote up the contract."

"Whose handwriting?" Christy asked, alarmed by the panic spreading over the room.

Valerie pushed everyone aside to plop her handbag on the table. "Marty McAllister writes like a kid—half print, half cursive. I have a check from her that I haven't deposited." She scrambled through her handbag, dug out her wallet, and removed a wrinkled check. "Here, look at this." She unfolded the check and laid it on the white linen cloth.

Everyone stared at the childish-looking, print-and-cursive letters on the check. Christy compared the note and the check and tried to suppress her emotions. But Valerie was right. The *C* appeared to be exactly the same. And on the line that spelled out the amount of the check, the *e*'s in *fifteen* were dead ringers for the ones in the note.

"Well, what are we waiting for?" Bonnie towered over the group. "Come on, let's go!"

"Go where?" Christy's heart was racing. She'd had no idea that the little blaze she had hoped to ignite would go off like a stick of dynamite.

"To Shipwreck Island to look for Marty!"

"But Christy thinks the bottle washed in," someone spoke up.

"If it washed in, why did the cork pop out so easily?" Maryann asked. "And how do we know it washed in?"

"Hold on, everyone." Christy had regained her composure. "I

don't know if the bottle was tossed from a boat or if this was a cruel joke."

"Excuse me, ladies." Frank had been standing in the doorway, listening to the conversation, but now he was striding toward the table. "Marty stopped by here yesterday—I think it was just past the rush hour—and ordered her usual seafood salad. She told me when she left here that she was headed to Destin to show a beach house."

He inclined his head toward the bottle. "I heard you say there were no footprints in the sand, so it sounds to me like that bottle washed in from the ocean. Probably some bored sailor wrote it"— he shrugged his large shoulders—"who knows when?"

Christy nodded. "You could be right, Frank. Still, I think I'm going to show this to Big Bob. Can't hurt." Big Bob was the local nickname for Deputy Bob Arnold, who ruled the seaside community and answered to the sheriff in Panama City.

"Christy, take the check with you," Valerie said. "I may not want to cash it after all. It could explain why nobody has heard from Marty."

The ladies wandered back to their seats, sat down, and stared into space. Then Dianna reached over and touched Christy's hand. "What a strange twist to your speech on writing mysteries."

"I never got to the speech," Christy said. She lowered her eyes to the wrinkled note, the plea for help. Dianna was right. Her little talk about writing a mystery novel had taken a bizarre twist.

And now, it seemed, the real mystery had just begun.

Christy said her good-byes and excused herself after the luncheon as the ladies lingered over coffee. She had reached the front door when her aunt called to her. Christy turned. Dianna was hurrying toward her, looking down at her shoes, the way she often did while composing her thoughts.

"Hon," she said, laying a hand on Christy's arm, "could you do me a favor?"

"Never make another speech?"

"No, silly. Your speech was great, but I wish you'd drive over to Marty's house, see if she's home."

She studied her aunt's serious face. "Sure. If she is, you want me to tell her something?"

"No, just call me on my cell."

"Okay. Do you really think she might be missing?"

She folded her arms across her chest. "I'm not sure." She glanced back over her shoulder. "I'll explain something later."

"Fine. I'm on my way. But first I'm gonna give Big Bob a call."

Dianna nodded, then walked back to the party room.

Christy hurried to her car, beeping to unlock the door. Thrusting her tote bag and purse onto the passenger's seat, she opened the glove compartment, grabbed her cell phone, and dialed Big Bob.

"This is Bob." Suddenly the words were muffled, as though he'd placed his hand over the phone, but Christy heard every word. "Two eggs over light with grits. And an extra order of Shorty's hickory smoked bacon."

The sound of happy chatter rose amid the clatter of dishes.

"Bob? This is Christy. We need to meet."

"What's going on?" His deep voice rattled the earpiece.

"I want to show you something. Then we'll talk about it. If you're eating Shorty's bacon, you must be at Sunny Side Up." She was referring to a local coffee shop.

"I'll wait for you."

"Be there in five minutes."

One had to think fast to follow Big Bob, but she'd managed to track him in the past. If he wasn't chasing crime, she knew the places to look.

Christy started her car and headed for Middle Beach Road. True to her promise, in less than five minutes she had covered the short distance to Sunny Side Up. She reached for the bottle, then hesitated.

If Big Bob kept the bottle and note, she'd have nothing to ponder. She reached into the backseat for her digital camera. Christy opened the bottle, unfolded the note, and took a couple of pictures. She dropped the note back into the bottle and replaced the cork. She snapped three more pictures of the bottle, then returned everything to her tote bag, including the camera, and hopped out of the car.

As she entered the coffee shop, the aroma of fresh ground coffee and bursts of laughter greeted her. At the end of the long diner, she spotted Big Bob, seated in a booth with a couple of regulars.

As though she had just stepped onto his radar screen, he shot her a look, then sidled out of the booth.

He stood at least six foot five and was built like a Hummer. A large nose and wide mouth balanced a round face capped with short gray hair. Big Bob had a personal interest in keeping Summer Breeze safe since he and his wife Judy were raising five children here.

"Let's step outside," he said. "And this better be worth ruining my breakfast."

She ignored the latter comment and reached into the tote bag. "I found this bottle on a strip of beach at Shipwreck Island this morning. And I looked around," she added hurriedly, heading off a rebuttal, "but there were no footprints in the sand. No evidence anyone had been there. The bottle was half-buried right at the shoreline."

"So…what's the big deal?"

"The note in the bottle."

He leaned down for a closer look.

"Read the note." She handed him the bottle and watched as he yanked off the loosened cork and shook out the note.

Call the police. Someone is trying to kill me.

His gaze narrowed as he looked back at Christy. "Where's your little brother?"

"Backpacking in Australia. I don't think it's a joke, Bob." She cleared her throat. "I took this with me to Frank's restaurant, because Aunt Dianna had asked me to be the speaker at the Sassy Snowbirds luncheon. I heard that Marty McAllister had invited the ladies over for dinner and a discussion about a permanent meeting place. Yesterday she took off for Destin and didn't come home. She didn't call anyone to cancel the meeting, didn't leave a note. The house was dark—"

"If she thought she had a sale, she probably stayed over to wine and dine the buyer," Big Bob said. "Marty's a bird dog after the scent of money."

"Yeah, well speaking of dogs, Bonnie told me when they got to Marty's house, her big dog was running loose. Knocked Bonnie down and—"

"Knocked *Bonnie* down?"

"And gobbled up the lemon pies."

"Christy, where are you going with all this?"

She took a breath. This would be the hard part. "Two of the ladies claim the writing on the note is identical to Marty McAllister's."

"Aw, come on, Christy!"

"Valerie wanted me to show you this check Marty wrote at the beauty salon a few days ago. Fortunately, Valerie hadn't cashed it." She pulled it from her purse and handed it to him. "And Peggy Sue said the handwriting matches the signature on a contract Marty wrote for her."

He looked at the check, held it beside the note, and said nothing for several seconds. Then he turned and walked to his big SUV, unlocked the passenger door, and placed the items in a plastic bag.

"That island's pretty deserted, isn't it?" she asked, trailing him. "The lady who sold the ship house moved away, and nobody else has started construction. Of course, there's Buster down at the far end."

Buster was a recluse, the black sheep of the family who had owned the entire island, then sold off a few parcels. But no one had managed to root Buster out of the eight acres he inherited or the run-down bungalow where he nested with his fishing boat, the source of his enjoyment.

"Do you think Buster...," she began tentatively.

Big Bob hooted at that. "A bottle made in Scotland? Too classy for Buster. Looks more like somebody's trying to be funny."

He turned to face her. "I'll drive over there and take a look around, check on Buster. Then if nothing turns up, I'm heading into Panama City for a meeting at three. I'll take this"—he waved the bag—"and see what the guys over there make of it. Let's give Marty another day before everybody gets all riled up."

"Valerie said to keep the check. Maybe there are fingerprints on the check that would match..." Her voice trailed as she read the silent warning on his face. "Okay, I'm into your business, I know. But doesn't it seem weird that she would stay over in Destin and stand the ladies up? And leave her dog outside the fence?"

Big Bob tugged at the end of his broad nose, thinking it over. "Strikes me as odd that she wouldn't call someone, the way she loves to talk. Every time I've met up with Marty, she's had that cell phone attached to her ear."

Big Bob slammed the door, yanked his belt up over his bulging stomach, and shot a glance at Christy. "Okay, I'll let you know if anything turns up. Now let me finish my cold breakfast and get going."

"Okay. Sorry." Christy pressed her lips together, trying to hold back all the things she wanted to say. "Thanks," she called after him.

She hurried back to her car, wondering if the entire incident was a crazy prank that somebody would eventually explain or if a desperate soul had written the note, stuck it in the bottle, and thrown it from a boat.

She'd gone to Shipwreck Island to prowl through the woods beyond the beach, looking for the perfect place to hide a body. A pirate's body. She had snapped some pictures and headed out, satisfied she had the right ending for her novel. Then she'd found a note in an antique bottle with a message that someone was about to be killed. It was almost too ironic to wrap her mind around.

2

Christy sped toward Marty McAllister's neighborhood, resenting that Aunt Dianna had asked her to check on Marty. Why couldn't her aunt check on Marty after the luncheon? She had the time; Christy didn't. This very minute she needed to be at home working on her mystery novel. Her deadline loomed like a hurricane building up in the Gulf. But she had promised, and now she must make good the promise.

She turned onto Front Beach Road and gazed at the emerald waves rolling into shore. The night's rain and wind had swept the white sand clean. "Sugar sand," the tourist brochures proudly proclaimed. Along the way, sand dunes peaked like frosting on a cake, with a light wind ruffling the sea oats.

While this was still February, and yesterday had been rainy and cold, today was one of those beautiful days that made people happy to be living in Summer Breeze.

She knew where Marty McAllister lived, because she had gone to her house to make an offer on one of Marty's listings. The contract Marty had spread over her cherry-wood dining table was a standard typed form, and now she didn't recall Marty's signature on anything when she purchased her first home. Later she would root around in her business files and locate the contract that should have Marty's signature on it.

She turned into Marty's quiet neighborhood and slowed before the yellow frame house. She scanned the manicured lawn, then studied the house. Nothing was out of place on the small front porch overhung with a green scalloped awning. Behind the windows every blind was closed in perfect proportion. Almost too perfect, she thought.

If by some chance Marty was at home, she'd tell her...what? She'd tell her the truth: Aunt Dianna was worried about her. As she turned into the driveway, a persistent barking shattered the silence. She peered toward the back. She could hear the dog barking behind the six-foot white fence, gate firmly shut.

Had someone put the dog back inside the fence, or had Marty come home after all? She parked her car and got out, glancing right to left. Nice homes flanked the house, but no one was in either yard.

She noted the prominent display of an expensive security system. No one would be breaking and entering without the authorities hot on their heels. Leading up to the front porch, three narrow steps held a sheen of water and a frond from the palm tree. Wouldn't Marty, the meticulous housekeeper, sweep her front steps if she came home?

After picking her way up the steps, she went to the door and rang the bell. The mellow chime rippled through the house, and now the poor dog was barking louder than ever. She waited, listening. There was no movement inside the house, not that she had expected any. Clearly, Marty was not home.

She closed the door, turned and angled her heels over the wet steps, then retraced her path down the driveway. There was a single glass pane on each side of the double garage. She peered in. Empty. But that didn't mean Marty hadn't returned and left again.

The backyard was completely fenced, but she found a crack between two boards and pressed her face to the wood. She could make out the corner of a patio table, and near the fence, two large bowls held water and a mound of dog food that looked fresh.

She sighed, more confused than ever. Obviously Marty had been home. Her reputation of fussing with her friends might explain that she had, for some reason, stood up her dinner guests. But what about the handwriting that seemed to match the note she'd found in the bottle? That nagged at her.

She headed back to her car, picked up her cell phone, and dialed her aunt.

"Hello," Dianna shouted. Apparently the get-together was breaking up, and everyone was saying their good-byes and bumping chairs.

"She's not home. But her dog is back inside the fence, and there's fresh food and water in his bowl." Christy reported.

"Hmm."

"Maybe she stood you guys up after all. Anyway, I gave the

bottle, note, and check to Big Bob, and he's gonna drive over to Shipwreck Island and nose around. He thinks we should give Marty another day before we get, to quote him, 'all riled up.'"

"Thanks for checking, Christy," she said quickly. "Talk to you later."

Christy closed her phone and drove out of the quiet neighborhood. Her aunt knew something she wasn't telling.

She turned down the street leading to her mother's gift shop. She'd tell her about the antique bottle, but that was all. She didn't have time to go into details. Her mother would hear about it soon enough.

The Treasure Chest had been converted from a frame house that Beth Castleman had painted brown. She had put gold-colored hinged shutters on the windows and installed a brass door with a large gold key for the door handle. The concept worked, and now the shop resembled a giant treasure chest.

Within the shop, one could find a variety of items, some dating back to the seventeen hundreds. Had she stocked the green bottle from Scotland?

Christy pulled into the parking lot beside a white Lincoln Continental with Georgia license plates. The Treasure Chest drew lots of tourists, and even the locals dropped in to check out new finds. She hurried up the stone walkway and pressed the gold key handle. The door swung back as an antique bell announced her entrance.

Her mother was helping two older women near the back of the shop. With Beth's natural blond hair and fair skin, she clearly had Norwegian roots, and yet her Minnesota voice had blended with soft southern, rendering a nice effect. She was wearing a long-sleeved blue linen dress with tan pumps.

"Hi, Christy," Beth called. She turned back to the ladies. "Could you please excuse me for a moment? I need to speak with my daughter."

The ladies nodded, glanced toward Christy, then returned to their examination of a mariner's clock.

Beth approached Christy, gave her a quick hug, and looked her over. "I know why Olivia telephoned wanting your number," Beth remarked, in one of her trademark out-of-the-blue statements.

Christy blinked. "Olivia who?"

"Olivia Bomar. Owns Petite Possibilities. She's sending a model to the spring fashion show at the Panama City Mall. Wanted you to be her model."

"Mom, you know I don't do fashion shows! That's not my thing, and even if it were, I'm not tall enough."

"Don't get that defensive tone, Christy. I explained that you were finishing your novel. But I know why she called," Beth added, exemplifying her persistence with an idea. "You have your father's good posture and…" She cocked her small head and studied her daughter. "You just have a look about you that makes people take a second glance."

"It's probably when my cowlick stands straight up."

"How'd the speech go?"

"Okay." She opened her tote bag, removed the camera, and clicked to display her pictures of the bottle. Just the bottle. She pressed a button to enlarge the picture. "Mom, take a look. Do you stock these bottles? There's an inscription on the bottle. It was made in Scotland."

Beth lifted her bifocals from their decorative chain and perched them on her small nose. She viewed the pictures, then began to nod. "I stocked only one but sold it…sometime ago. Let me check my ledger. Why?" she asked, reaching under the counter. "Does someone want to order one?"

"No, I'll explain later. I don't want to keep you from a sale."

Beth pulled out the black ledger that detailed inventory and purchases and flipped through the pages, then paused.

"I sold a bottle exactly like that one on…Saturday, January 10."

"Sold it to whom?" Christy peered at the ledger.

Beth sighed. "I only record the names of purchasers on expensive items. The Scotland bottle sold for…thirty dollars, according to this."

"Mom, think hard. Who bought that bottle?"

Beth lifted a small hand to scoop her short blond hair back from her forehead. "I can't remember." She glanced at the desk calendar. "Most Saturdays are pretty busy with tourists. In fact, I'd guess a tourist bought the bottle. The locals usually do their shopping during the week unless they're entertaining out-of-towners."

Her mother was staring at the bottle. "Looks like there's something inside it." She looked back at Christy. "What is it?"

Did she really want to get into this now? She glanced at the customers, who were staring at Beth as though they wanted to ask her something.

"I don't want to horn in on your customers. We can discuss it later. I just wondered if you stocked the bottle and, if you did, who might have bought it. Can you recall anything about that Saturday that would jog your memory?"

Beth studied the ledger again. "I could go back through the other sales. But you know what?" She turned to another ledger labeled Expenses. She opened the tabbed section titled Payroll and ran her finger down the date column. A frown puckered the space between her brows. "That was the Saturday Lorie called in sick. I paged your dad at the golf course to help me."

"Then maybe Dad sold the bottle."

"Probably. I don't remember selling it."

Christy returned the camera to her tote bag. "Okay, now you'd better get back to those ladies," she whispered. "They look like they're getting impatient."

Beth whirled, her focus shifting back to her customers. "Be right there," she said, hurrying toward them. She called back to Christy. "Good luck with…whatever you're doing."

"Thanks." Christy dashed back to her car. Again she reminded herself that she needed to be home working on her novel, but her dad was the matter-of-fact type, and it wouldn't take long.

Two miles up, the community church perched on a narrow strip of land jutting toward the Gulf. The church replaced the lighthouse that had once stood there, but the church also served as a beacon of hope. Wanting a structure that suited the land, members chose a simple white clapboard church with a bell steeple, reminiscent of early churches in New England.

She turned into the parking lot and cut the engine. She withdrew the camera from the tote bag and headed toward the side door.

Grant Castleman sat behind his oak desk, head bent in concentration. Tall and well-built, with dark hair and eyes, he looked younger than his fifty-one years. Christy suspected that his positive mental attitude combined with regular exercise kept him young. He was surrounded by his "working materials"—an open Bible, an accompanying commentary, and a yellow legal pad filled with notes.

"I need a preacher," Christy called.

His head shot up, then a wide smile crossed his face. She wished she had a smile like her father's.

"You're in the right place. You look mighty pretty," he said, pride ringing in his tone.

She smiled, seeing the love in his eyes. At times like this she felt a stab of guilt for those years when she had worried and wounded her parents. "Are you golfing today?" she asked, noting the yellow golf shirt and navy Dockers.

A twinkle lit the dark eyes as he stood to give her a hug. "Maybe."

Each time she stepped into his strong arms, she could swear she drew goodness and strength from him.

"How'd the speech go?"

"Good. But something strange happened. I'll give you the short version, and you can relate it to Mom." Briefly she recapped what had taken place—finding the bottle and note, the comments from the ladies, her meeting with Big Bob. "I just left Mom's shop. When she saw these pictures, she thought she stocked a bottle just like it. And…she thinks you sold it that Saturday in January when you helped out. You can't see the inscription, but it was made in Scotland." She laid the camera on his desk with the little screen displaying the picture of the bottle.

He studied the picture and began to nod. "I did sell it! I remember being fascinated with the bottle; I'd never seen one quite like it, especially one that came from Scotland. A thirty-something woman bought it. I'd never seen her before and haven't seen her since. She had two rambunctious little boys with her. One of them bought an old pirate's mask; the other one was yelling for spy games. They were all over the place. I jumped to the shelf of breakables just in time. Caught a crystal sandpiper in midair."

Christy picked up the camera and clicked back to the note. "This was the note I found inside the bottle."

He read the message aloud. " 'Call the police. Someone is trying to kill me.' Wow! Those are alarming words." He looked at Christy. "The note could have been a joke," he said, voicing her thoughts. "Those little guys certainly looked capable of it. But there's also the possibility that it's not the same bottle. Did Beth stock more than one?"

"No. You know Mom and her ledgers. If there were other bottles in her inventory, she'd know it."

Silence stretched between them for a moment as the mental image of two little pirates—no, one pirate, one spy—taunted her. She sank into the armchair beside the desk.

"Dad, those little boys probably went looking for treasure at Shipwreck Island. And as a joke, they sneaked their mom's new bottle out and wrote the note on their school tablet. At least the wide-ruled lines resemble those tablets."

She sighed. "And now I've cranked up the rumor mill over a silly joke. Maybe Marty showed the beach house in Destin, then spent the night over there. I guess she forgot about her invitation to the ladies."

Her dad nodded, pursing his lips as he looked back at the bottle. "But," he emphasized the word, "if, by chance, Mrs. McAllister has mysteriously disappeared, you've alerted folks in Summer Breeze for a good reason."

"Yeah, but...she's been home and put the dog back inside the fence. And his bowls are full of water and food."

A dark eyebrow jumped as Grant glared at her. "Don't tell me you've been over there snooping around, young lady."

"Aunt Dianna asked me to check on her!" She fell back to the defensive tone she had perfected during her teen years.

He nodded. "So now you've given everything to Bob. Let him

do the investigating. I'll see him at the council meeting tonight. Want me to tell him about those little guys?"

She nodded. "Please." She was in no mood to have Big Bob barking at her again. Sometimes she wondered if he had ever forgiven her and Chad for rolling his yard. After a night of rain, the toilet tissue had been a soggy mess for Big Bob to clean up. That was years ago. People should forget about those things.

Her eyes strayed to the silver-framed picture holding a prominent place on her father's desk. Their picture presented the happy, loving family, with parents seated, looking composed and serene, and adult children standing faithfully at their sides. Christy didn't think she had changed much in the past year, but as her eyes rested on Seth, she knew there had been a significant change in him. But not everyone would see it.

Seth was a twenty-two-year-old version of his dad: brown hair and eyes, tall and slim. His face was more angular than his dad's, and he had inherited his mom's round chin, but there was no mistaking whose son he was. His features still held a boyish look, but the smile was strained, and the brown eyes seemed to look beyond the photographer, searching for…something. That gaze, more than anything else, reflected Seth's nature at the moment. Searching…for himself…and the life that suited him.

"Haven't heard from him in a couple of weeks." Grant was staring at Seth as well. "Have you?"

Christy had hoped to avoid this. She snapped her fingers. "I forgot to tell you. He called last night." She omitted the time of the call. "I had something to do and couldn't talk long." Like sleep. "He said to tell you he's doing fine and he'll call soon."

He frowned, studying her carefully. "Why would you forget to tell me that? Or your mom? You know we've been concerned."

"It was past your bedtime, and I didn't want to wake you. And with my speech and now this"—she indicated the pictures—"I completely forgot."

His brown eyes bored into hers. "Did he really call?" he asked in the tone of voice that you didn't mess with.

"Yes, he did." She looked him straight in the eye. She'd told him the truth; she just hadn't given the details. "He'll be calling you soon. Dad, I didn't mention that note to Mom because she had customers. You can tell her about it later."

"Okay. And I'm glad Seth called." He visibly relaxed, leaning back in the chair. The sigh of relief was small but clear.

"Well, gotta run. I'm in the throes of finishing my novel. The manuscript is due at my publisher's next week."

"You can do it. Just stay focused, and you'll make your deadline."

"Thanks for the encouragement." She made a show of peering at his desk clock. "Oops, I didn't know it was already three o'clock! Bye, Dad."

She wheeled and hurried out the door, having learned to successfully negotiate quick turns in high heels. She'd had years of practice while yearning to be tall.

"Christy." His voice echoed down the hall, and she turned to see him standing in the doorway.

"You forgot your camera."

Embarrassed, she rushed back and grabbed it from his hands.

"Thanks. Guess I'd better slow down." She gave him a sheepish grin.

Once out the door and down the steps, she reflected on Seth's midnight call. She had been in a deep sleep, having driven back from her grandmother's and then stayed up too late watching a rerun of *CSI*.

When Seth had called, she could barely hear him above the beat of drums, grinding music, and loud voices. "Call me tomorrow. But take into account the time difference," she had warned. She had hung up without asking him anything other than if he was okay. And he had responded that he was better than okay. And she hadn't liked the sound of that either.

She hurried across the parking lot to her car, looking at it with new appreciation. She had bought it brand-new two years ago to celebrate the publication of her first book. A convertible. She'd always wanted a convertible. She opened the door, slid in behind the wheel, and returned the camera to her tote. Since today was pleasant, she put the top down and let the cool Gulf breeze settle around her, calm her nerves, and feed her soul.

As she drove home, she thought about her dad's advice. Whether the bottle was a joke or whether it was real…she'd leave that up to Big Bob.

She turned into her neighborhood of pastel cottages set in neat squares of green grass. She had chosen a pale pink for the outside of the house, trimmed with clean white doors, windows, and shutters.

She turned into the driveway and cut the engine. She had bought the two-bedroom fixer-upper after returning to Summer Breeze. Then she'd thrust herself, heart and soul, into making it the safe haven she needed. And she had succeeded. She had converted the attached carport into a screened-in porch for plants and patio furniture. It was the perfect place for morning coffee or a cool drink on a warm evening.

She grabbed her tote bag and purse and was stepping out of her car as a horn blasted behind her. She whirled to see Jack Watson roaring into her driveway in his beat-up green truck. Perched in the passenger seat like a weathered old seabird was his cohort and partner in crime, J. T. Elmore.

Christy put her load in a wicker chair on the porch and smiled, pleased to see the two of them. As Jack shoved open his door, she thought of the comment she'd heard about him at the luncheon. Yes, he could be a bit difficult with some people, or call it eccentric, but just the sight of him lifted her spirits. At the same time, she felt the old pain clutch her heart, for he was Chad's father. But she thrust that thought aside and focused on the two characters unfolding from the truck.

Jack was lean and lanky, with thinning brown hair and piercing blue eyes. He wore a blue denim shirt that she liked, with jeans so frayed she wondered why his knees didn't poke through. On his feet were polished cowboy boots, a sure sign he and J. T. were up to something.

"Hey, pretty woman," he called out, reaching into the back of the truck to retrieve a small ice chest. He paused and glanced into the front seat. "J. T., you gonna get out and say hello? And clean off your glasses so you don't trip going up the walk."

Christy grinned at Jack. "What have you got? More important, what are you up to?"

"About five eleven. I could ask you the same thing. What're you doing in that fancy pink dress?"

She put her hands on her hips, pretending offense. "You don't like my dress?"

"Sure, I like it. I'm just used to seeing you in jeans and a T-shirt."

"I swear, Jack," J. T. hollered as he ambled up the driveway. "You're downright rude."

J. T. was a nubby little man who suffered with arthritis in his knees and tended to hobble more than walk. His baseball cap was so worn that the insignia of his favorite team was barely legible. He wore the cap half-cocked above wispy brown brows. Through the thick lenses of his glasses, the dark eyes gleamed.

J. T. gave Christy a crooked smile. "First pretty woman we've seen all day, and you go insulting her. Women don't like that."

Jack rolled his eyes. "How would you know what a woman likes? You haven't had one in forty years." He hurried up the walk toward Christy, lugging the ice chest, while J. T. dragged behind, muttering under his breath.

Christy laughed and looked from one man to the other. They'd been best friends most of their lives. Jack's wife had died years ago, and J. T. had married at eighteen and lost his wife to another man at twenty-six. She knew they got lonely and had their problems, but to ease their pain, they seemed to thrive on their constant bantering. She looked back at Jack, standing before her, holding the ice chest.

"Do I dare hope you've brought me some fish? Or shrimp?"

A wide smile filled Jack's craggy face. "I've got some fresh alligator just for you."

"But how did you know I was craving alligator?"

"It's not alligator; it's filleted grouper." J. T. glared at Jack.

"I knew that." She winked at J. T. "And thanks for filleting them for me."

The two followed Christy through the sun porch and into the kitchen. Jack set the ice chest down by the refrigerator, rubbed his hands up and down the sides of his jeans, then reached out to give her a hug. She got a whiff of the aftershave he hoarded for special occasions.

He released her and dropped his eyes for a moment. She could almost read his mind. He was wishing Chad hadn't hurt her so badly.

"Well," she said, looking from Jack to J. T., "I'd say you two have been to Belle's for some fried chicken."

"How'd you know?" J. T.'s eyes jumped behind the thick lenses.

"Aw, she probably smells the grease. But like I told Belle, fried food is healthy for people like J. T. and me. Give me fried chicken, mashed potatoes, and brown gravy. Add a hunk of greasy corn bread, and I'm happy."

"Then you should be real happy. You two have a seat, and I'll put on a pot of coffee. I want your opinion—"

Jack cut her off. "We can't stay."

"Yeah, we got someplace we gotta be."

"Oh really?" She looked at J. T. "Is it that back bay bar that features happy hour from noon till midnight?"

J. T. chuckled. "Don't guess you'd want to join us."

Jack whirled on him. "J. T., you know Christy shouldn't be seen with two old codgers like us. Not with *our* reputation," he added wryly.

She swatted his shoulder. "Don't say that to J. T. Or to me. I'd enjoy the pleasure of your company another day."

"Have you finished your mystery?" Jack was suddenly serious, and she remembered how he always showed interest in her writing.

"Nope. And I'm pushing a deadline. Aunt Dianna asked me to give a little speech at the Sassy Snowbirds luncheon today. That's why I'm out of uniform."

Jack turned to his pal. "Run for your life, J. T. If those gals are on the loose, we'd better take the back roads."

J. T. chuckled, pleased with the idea, and the two scuttled out the door.

"Thanks for the grouper," she called after them, watching Jack as he clomped down the driveway. He looked a little bowlegged in those cowboy boots when he tried to walk fast, but she could see he felt good today, and that made her happy.

She closed the kitchen door as the roar of his engine brought a rush of memories. Weekend trips to the Daytona 500 with Chad. Eating hot dogs with mustard dripping down her shirt. Moonlight swims. Kisses. Good times, bad times all mingling together.

Chad had been her best friend in junior high, her steady boyfriend in high school, her fiancé in college. It wasn't easy to let go of someone who had been a major part of her life for so long.

The roar faded, and Christy took a deep breath and looked around her house. She had painted the rooms in soft colors—the serene blue of the Gulf of Mexico, the lavender of the sky in late afternoon, the pale gold of the summer sun. She wandered down the hall, absorbing the colors and breathing a deep sigh as she began to relax.

Hardwood floors ran throughout the house, with throw rugs and a couple of expensive imports. She glanced into the second bedroom that she had converted into her office. Work always helped make the bad stuff go away. But she moved on to her bedroom to shed the dress and shoes.

In comfy drawstring pants and a loose T-shirt decorated with a recent tea stain, she was thrusting her feet in scuffs when the phone rang. She sank onto the bed, reaching for the phone. The caller ID showed Bonnie Taylor, and she smiled with relief.

"Hi, Bonnie."

"Hel-looo." Bonnie's melodious voice greeted her.

"Even if I didn't know you're a terrific singer, I would guess it from the way you say hello."

A deep laugh rolled over the wire. "Honey, I was born with the blues in my soul. Then I found Jesus, and the blues turned to gospel. I've been praising him ever since. Christy, do you think Marty wrote that note?"

"I'm not so sure anymore. Bonnie, I'm embarrassed to admit this, but that note may have been a joke after all."

"But...that check Valerie had..."

"I know, but Dad thinks he sold that bottle last month when he worked at Mom's shop. He remembers a lady—probably a tourist—with two rambunctious little boys. Maybe they went over to Shipwreck Island for a treasure hunt, and those little guys grabbed their mom's new bottle. Pretending to be pirates on the loose, maybe they wrote a note on their school tablet, stuck it in the bottle, and buried it in the sand."

"Well, maybe so. And I'm not really surprised that Marty took off like that. If you know Marty, you know she looks out for her-self, 'specially when it comes to money."

Christy fidgeted on the bed, absently tracing the oak leaf pattern on the quilt her grandmother had made. "Bonnie, I've put everything in Big Bob's hands, and now I'm staying out of it. Will you spread the word about those little guys and the possibility that it's all a joke? I *have* to finish this book." She decided to skip the part about the dog being inside the fence.

"I know, honey, and I'll let you go. I also wanted to say we enjoyed your talk today. I've been keepin' a journal for thirty years."

"Really? Journals, diaries, anything that makes a person write down their thoughts is a good thing. To me it's pure therapy."

"And a lot cheaper than some alternatives."

"Right," Christy laughed. "Bonnie, before I forget, the next time you bake one of your famous sweet potato pies, put my name on a big slice, please."

"You got it, girl. Take care."

She hung up, still thinking about the note. As she did, her eyes moved around the walls of the blue bedroom with its ruffled white curtains, white wicker dresser, and chest of drawers. Marty had sold her this house, and she loved it. Somewhere in her disorganization, she had that contract, and she'd look it up if, in fact, Marty didn't get back to Summer Breeze soon.

She had expected a call from her aunt. What was it that Aunt Denise had offered to explain later about Marty? Christy sighed. She had to let all that go and get busy.

She headed for the kitchen and opened the freezer and reached for a fun brand of coffee she'd bought at a shop in Panama City. And in the fridge she had a new flavor of cream to make it nice and rich.

After hurrying through the process and turning on the coffee maker, she faced the ice chest with the grouper fillets and smiled. When she finished the novel, she would make a nice dinner and invite some friends over. If she had any left. She tended to go into hibernation when she escaped to her fictional world.

After she had dumped the ice from the chest and washed it out, she took it to the sun porch, turning it upside down to drain. Then, with a tall mug of steaming coffee laced with cream, she headed for the room she referred to as her laboratory.

It was a nine-by-twelve room, with one large window at the rear looking out on the backyard. Sea prints and sketches of pirates and treasure chests flanked a huge map of Shipwreck Island. Her glance moved from the bookcases overflowing with books to the small shredder that huddled between her cluttered desk and her computer station.

A grin of satisfaction tilted her lips as she stared at the shredder, recalling her delight in shredding the rejection slips during the years she struggled to convince herself she was a writer. She had bought the shredder during a particularly bad time when her prized short story had been turned down by an editor whose letter detailed all the things wrong with her island story.

With tears flowing down her cheeks, she had grabbed her purse that very minute and headed to the office supply shop. She had wiped her cheeks and composed herself by the time she explained to the salesman what she wanted. He had shown her several types, but she chose the one that made the loudest noise. A shredder that seemed to enjoy what it ate.

In her office at home, she awarded the shredder a place of honor between her computer station and her desk. Smiling, pleased with her idea, she had taken the letter and shredded it, bit by bit. She added the envelope. A fiendish delight overtook her, and she shredded every rejection form stacked in the bottom drawer.

Since then, it had done wonders for her morale to shred things like copies of speeding tickets, splurge-sale slips, even a note from her mother to be nicer to Mrs. Halliburton when the woman always greeted her with personal questions, such as, "Don't you want to get married and have children?" While grinding up that note, she had entertained devious thoughts concerning the shredder and the nosy woman.

She shook her head. Sometimes she got a little crazy.

She hadn't shredded anything in a while, an indication that things were going well. She sat down at the computer and pulled up the file on her mystery novel, reading over the last couple of pages, orienting herself to her world of fiction. She trained her mind to recapture Shipwreck Island and the pirate's grave. Soon her fingers were moving slowly, then picking up speed as she glanced intermittently at her research notes.

At midnight she turned the phones back on, put the computer in sleep mode, and did the same for herself. She dragged down the hall, collapsed in bed, still in her clothes, and pulled up the quilt.

Christy rolled over in bed, wondering how long the phone had been ringing. She pushed herself up on her elbow and reached over to turn on the lamp. She checked the caller ID and read the prefix for Australia. Not again!

"Hello," she snapped.

"You don't sound too happy. You should be over here hiking Ayers Rock with me."

"Seth, do you realize what time it is? I told you last night to figure the time difference before you called. Tonight you're calling even later." She paused in the cold silence that followed.

She drew a breath, calming herself down. No wailing music in the background this time and no loud voices.

"Don't get me wrong." She made an attempt to be nice. "I do want to talk to you when I'm awake and thinking straight, but it's"—she squinted at the clock—"ten minutes after two in the morning."

"Sorry. But since you're awake, what's up in cozy little Summer Breeze?"

Australia was far way, but the sarcasm reached her loud and clear.

She raked a hand through her tousled hair and sighed. "Mom and Dad are fine, but you should give them a call. Check the time first."

"Give it up. I get your point."

She tried to be civil, a growing difficulty in the past year when it came to Seth. "I've been working hard to meet this deadline."

"Poor baby, busting her hiney to do the right thing."

"Yeah, well, I've gotten real attached to Ben Franklin. I like to carry him in my billfold, and on a good day, he spreads himself around in my bank account."

"Is money what rocks your boat these days? Christy, you ain't no fun anymore."

She winced at his slang. Who was he trying to be?

"Listen, I need to ask you something," he continued. "I've met this really cool girl from Sweden. Her name's Ingrid. I wanna play this just right—you know, not come on too strong, not let her know I'm interested, act a little indifferent."

"Sounds like the perfect plan for running her off."

"*What?* Girls like guys who act like they're not interested."

"No, they don't! I can't believe you're waking me up to ask how you can start a relationship with some girl from Sweden."

"You know what? I can't believe it either. Because that's the last thing you want. In fact, you're so afraid of losing someone again you've sabotaged—how many relationships now?"

"None of your business! But listen, little brother, you'd better take care of yourself. You're a long way from home and family."

"Now that I'm out from under Mommy and Daddy—unlike my big sister—I'm taking incredibly good care of myself."

"Fine. Then quit insulting me and go impress the girl from Sweden."

She slammed down the phone and flopped onto the pillow, wide awake now. Sabotage relationships? How dare he say that to her! If he had put those words in a letter, she would be shredding it right now.

Her gaze sneaked to the silver-framed five-by-seven nestled among a grouping of family and friends. She sat up in bed, staring at Chad's face as though she had never seen him before.

Green-gray eyes held the hint of laughter; dark blond hair needed a cut. Freckles skipped across his nose, missed the rest of his face, and sprinkled his shoulders. She remembered the sunburns, the way she had fussed over him, rubbing sunblock into his skin.

She studied the ever-present grin, as though he had just pulled off a great prank—and he probably had. But the shape of the face, the firm set of the lips, and the jutting chin all represented a younger Jack. Even at twenty-three, it was a boyish face that held a hint of mischief along with a promise that "Hey, I can be serious if I need to be."

She closed her eyes, wondering why she continued to torture herself. It was an old picture—she should put it away. For some unknown reason she couldn't bring herself to do that. Did she think that someday she would open the back door and he would be standing there, flashing that endearing grin? It was a grin that reached out and melted her heart, persuading her to forgive him anything, everything. And she always had. But he would never appear at her back door again, and perhaps that was why she kept him on her dresser.

"Why did you do it?" she cried, then bit her lip.

She had invested a lot of time and money trying to combat that anger, but occasionally she lost the battle. Glancing at her wrinkled clothes, she opened the chest of drawers and grabbed her pajamas. Dressed for bed this time, she turned off the lamp and settled down under the quilt, hugging her pillow. But she lay in the darkness, staring at the ceiling for another hour.

3

Tuesday, February 17

The first call came at eight, an hour before her radio alarm was set to float soothing music into her brain and bring her gently to wakefulness. She rolled over and glared at the slim white phone. The name of her friend Allie showed up on her caller ID.

Vaguely she could hear Allie's voice zipping through a message on the answering machine in the kitchen. The words blurred, with "Give me a call" being the most distinct. Allie always hopped out of bed at the crack of dawn to turn on the television and join the exercise lady for an hour of aerobics. After the aerobics Allie would sail on a current of adrenaline to her basement for a session with her weights.

Christy grimaced at the idea and closed her eyes, hoping to return to the sea of sleep. Not a chance. The brain waves were already rolling, tossing her conversation with Seth into her muddied thoughts.

Her head popped up from the pillow. She threw the quilt back and reached down for her furry house shoes. She studied the cute little ladybugs on the toes. She didn't need a third pair of house shoes, but these had called her name when she dashed through the mall to catch weekend sales.

In the bathroom she splashed water on her face and patted her skin dry on a yellow towel, one advertised as "thirsty." Yawning, she headed toward the kitchen, thinking of food.

No breakfast yesterday. At the luncheon before her speech, she had managed three or four bites of seafood salad that fought its way into her knotted stomach. An apple in the afternoon.

In spite of a hectic day, she had been able to clear her mind last night. Seized with inspiration, she had pounded the keyboard until late, letting up for a pit stop in the bathroom and another bottle of water.

Sunlight beamed through the kitchen window, and she smiled to herself. Food and a hot shower would do wonders. If she could forget what Seth had said to her.

She beelined to the shelf that held the mugs. An assortment greeted her, and for a moment she stared at the gift mug from Susan, her best friend who was off on a cruise. Against a white background a sassy-looking gal winked at her above the logo: Mystery Lady.

Definitely not sassy this morning. She reached for her rainbow mug; she needed a rainbow. She placed it beside the coffee maker.

During her final break for the evening, she had prepared the coffee maker to be ready with the flip of a switch. She flipped it and then headed for the cereals.

With cereal and bowl on the eating bar, she turned back to the refrigerator for milk, and her eyes strayed to the Keys-N-Things shelf on the wall. She stared at the sound-activated key finder. Seth's birthday present to her two years ago. She was notorious for losing keys. He knew her so well.

She sighed. Their once-close relationship had turned sour. She hated fussing with him. And she hated that he was not using that good mind of his in a more profitable way.

But...was there some truth in what he had said about sabotaging her relationships?

She pondered that as she dumped the cereal in the bowl and trailed milk over the top. She could sum up her dating life quickly and easily: a blind date disaster, then Randy who wasn't smart, Brad who was too into himself, and Matt who had no sense of humor. She gave a nod of satisfaction with those good-byes as she poured coffee into her mug and settled down to breakfast.

The phone on the kitchen wall rang. Christy peered over to read the caller ID, then answered.

"Hi, Christy, this is Dianna. What did Big Bob think about Marty's signature on the check?"

"Bob won't tell you what he thinks. Unless he's angry. But he was gonna check out Shipwreck Island and Buster, then take everything down to headquarters. I guess that counts for something. On the other hand, that note may have been a joke after all."

She told yet again the story of the bottle and the two little boys and took a generous sip of coffee. The caffeine streamlined her thoughts back to her aunt's promise to explain something about Marty. Before she asked the question, Dianna spoke again.

"One reason I called… This morning I stopped by Hal's to pay a bill, and he told me something troubling. He said Marty ordered ten pounds of shrimp for Sunday night, but she never picked up the order. If you order shrimp from Hal, you pay for it. With the price of shrimp lately, I can't imagine Marty forgetting. She was the Goddess of Greenbacks. Hal said he never heard from her, that he had the shrimp iced down and ready to be picked up at five o'clock. But Marty never came by, never called."

Christy thought it over, recalling what Bob had said about Marty's habit of using her cell phone. If she had taken off for a couple of days, why didn't she phone Hal to cancel her order?

Christy was hugging the phone between her chin and shoulder as she spooned cereal into her mouth. "That doesn't sound good." She took another scoop of cereal. With a trickle of milk sliding from her lips, she asked, "What were you gonna tell me later? Something you didn't want to bring up at the luncheon."

Another moment of hesitation. "Marty was seeing a guy who owned a white yacht. Luxurious, she said. Someone from Pensacola."

"And?"

"I think he's married."

"Oh."

"I happen to know she'd drop everything if he called. She was showing me around those new condos over in Seaside one day—John and I were thinking about one as an investment—and she got a call on her cell as we entered the upstairs balcony. She yanked me out of there so fast the door hit my butt."

"So how did you know who—"

"She called me the next week, thinking she might have missed a sale, which she did. Apologized and told me enough about this guy to raise my curiosity. But then she asked me not to tell anyone. She came right out and said he was married."

"And what did you say?" She felt like a schoolgirl swapping gossip.

"I said, 'Marty, you're telling me more than I want to know. And we've decided not to buy the condo.' She got a little huffy, but I didn't care. That was a couple of months back. We later made peace and became sorta friends. I guess my brother, the reverend, has taught me something about tolerance. Marty doesn't really have any friends, but I care if something has happened to her. So could you do me one more favor? Check by her house again, and if she's still not home, call Big Bob and tell him about the shrimp order."

"And the guy with the luxurious white boat?"

"Well…let's wait on that until we're more sure about what's going on. Your Uncle John thinks I'm overreacting. The other thing is, we're leaving for Key West as soon as I finish packing."

"Why Key West?"

"He likes deep-sea fishing there, I like wandering around Papa Hemingway's house and grounds, and we both love watching the sunsets from the balcony of the Riptide."

"Sounds great. Go have fun."

"You have my cell number, and so do the gals. Keep me updated."

"I will—"

Dianna had already hung up. Christy picked up her coffee mug, thinking more about Key West than her aunt's information concerning Marty. She stared at the rainbow on the mug and sighed.

Funny thing about loneliness. She supposed it was different with everyone. For her it wasn't the long evenings, for she could bury herself in work. It hit hardest at times like this, when she thought of something romantic like sharing a sunset over Key West, holding hands, snuggling if there was a cool breeze or a full moon. Or if there wasn't.

She and Allie did a lot together, but Allie definitely did not fit that role.

The phone rang again. If she had to repeat the story about the bottle and the note one more time, she'd be rattling it off in her sleep. The caller ID showed Roy's number at the newspaper, and she gasped. It continued to ring, and she let the answering machine pick up.

She heard his voice, ripping out a reminder. "Christy, I haven't gotten this week's Beach Buzz column from you. Now you *know*..." He ran on. If words could run, his could beat anyone on the track. Roy's entire world revolved around his little newspaper. She couldn't imagine how his wife lived with him. He was such a nervous workaholic that she got the jitters just looking at him.

She wasn't sure why she had committed herself to writing this column. It wasn't for Roy, and it certainly wasn't for the money. She'd been so caught up in her own mystery, and the mystery of the bottle and note, that she had completely forgotten her column. Actually, it had occurred to her to interview a few Snowbirds, but... She glanced at the clock. She had less than an hour to think of something and zing it to Roy as an e-mail attachment. She usually procrastinated on her Beach Buzz article, but this time she'd pushed her time frame to the eleventh hour. Everything went to print this afternoon, and she had to think of something fast.

Seated at the computer, she studied the swirling waves breaking at a shoreline on the screen saver. The view always calmed her. She hit the space bar, and suddenly an idea popped into her head: why not do a story about finding the bottle and the note? If readers wanted beach buzz, that was the latest buzz. She fidgeted in her chair, wondering if she should make a reference to a missing lady... No, of course not.

Christy opened a new file and stared at the blank screen for only a few seconds before her small fingers began to fly over the keyboard. A green antique bottle...a note tucked within the bottle...

She began the article with two provocative phrases and lost herself in time and space as the story zipped from her brain into her fingertips, filling the screen with words, sentences, paragraphs. She built up to the question of who left the bottle, omitting the contents of the note.

In the next hour she polished the article, saved a copy to her file, then flung it through cyberspace to Roy's computer. The story of the bottle and a mysterious note would be read by all the locals, plus subscribers in distant cities who either owned a vacation place or loved the area and wanted to keep up with the news. Quite likely the article would result in some idle speculation, a few snickers, but what if the lady who bought the bottle read the article and called? Then everyone could put the matter to rest, and Christy would consider her little mission completed.

Now if only Marty would get back from her secret trip… Did that really make sense? Another reminder jolted her: a promise to her aunt to check on Marty's house again.

Resigned to the task, she headed for the shower.

Later, snuggled into her sweatshirt, jeans, warm socks, and tennis shoes, she cruised through Marty's neighborhood, rubbernecking the yellow house and garage. She pulled into the driveway and got out, crossed the yard, and climbed the steps once more. More palm fronds lay on the front step. She rang the doorbell. Again, no answer.

The big dog started barking again, and she hurried down the driveway to peer through the fence. This time his bowls were empty.

Deep in thought, she was walking back to her car when a door slammed. She turned to see a man from the next house walking down his porch steps to the mailbox.

"Excuse me," she called to him.

He paused, glancing her way. He was a short plump man wearing an Auburn T-shirt and baggy gray shorts above a couple of knobby knees. He was bald, with a face as round as a dinner plate. Sleepy eyes peered through thick-lensed glasses.

"Hi, I'm Christy Castleman."

"Sam Benson," he answered, looking her over. "Are you the local mystery writer?"

"I am." She turned up the sidewalk to his front porch.

"Too bad Anne isn't home. She's a big fan of yours. Loved the last mystery, bought a couple for our grown daughters. She's looking forward to your next one."

"Then please thank her for me." She glanced toward Marty's house to the left of his. He had a clear view of the driveway and the back fence from his windows. "I'm looking for Mrs. McAllister," she said. "Have you seen her?"

"Not since Sunday. But I might have missed her if she came in at night. I go to bed right after the ten o'clock news. As for knowing when she's home, I have no idea. She wheels in and out of that driveway more times than I go to the kitchen for snacks. And that's a lot."

He glanced toward the silent house, a frown settling over his brow. "One thing puzzled us, though. Her dog was running around loose Monday morning. I put him back inside the fence, and Anne took him food and water. When I shut the gate, I noticed the latch was loose, which is probably how he got out. I took a hammer and nailed it tight."

"I'm sure Mrs. McAllister will be grateful."

"Is anything wrong?" he asked, glancing from Christy to Marty's house.

She hesitated. "I just need to speak with her. Concerning some real estate," she added. If he relayed her message to Marty, the words *real estate* would send her racing to the phone. "If you see her, would you please ask her to call?"

"Be glad to."

"Thanks, have a nice day."

"You too," he said, turning to his mailbox.

Christy drove home, troubled. Something was wrong, she was certain. A warning light above her gas gauge winked at her, and she breathed a sigh of relief at the sight of a gas station nearby. She turned in and angled her car down to the end pump.

In the next lane Valerie's fancy green car swooshed up. "Hey, lady," Valerie called, getting out.

"Hi, Valerie." Christy studied Valerie's cute vest and turtleneck sweater over dark pants and ankle boots. Somehow she seemed younger than the other women her age. Maybe it was because she was always laughing and cheerful.

Today, however, she looked troubled as she came around the pumps to Christy's side. "Did you know a homeless man was arrested this morning at the Quick Stop for trying to use Marty's gold credit card?"

"No! What happened?"

"Apparently the guy followed some tourists into the Quick Stop hoping he'd look like part of the crowd. It was eight in the morning, and everyone was wanting coffee and doughnuts. When he tried to use Marty's card for his purchases, Leslie, the cashier, saw Marty's name on the card and made an excuse to go to the back and get more coffee. She went to the office and called Big Bob, then took a bag of coffee out to the coffee station. She asked the guy to give her a minute since people were waiting for coffee. He agreed, and then Bob showed up and arrested him."

"Smart," Christy commented. "I hadn't heard."

"Well, it just happened an hour ago. You know, Christy, I've been bothered by this whole thing of Marty's disappearance. I have a bad feeling, and I trust my feelings. For one thing, she loves that big dog. I don't think Marty would have left him outside the fence."

Christy nodded, recalling her conversation with Sam Benson, the neighbor, but keeping that to herself for now.

"Another thing, although it probably isn't important. Sue Ann, my last customer yesterday, said the last time she saw Marty, she was arguing with Frank in the parking lot back of the restaurant. Said they both looked angry."

"Marty seems to anger a lot of people," Christy said.

"That's for sure. But I wish Big Bob would go search Marty's house."

"I just left there; her car's not in the garage."

"I know, but maybe someone stole her car. But then, that car would be easy to spot. It reminds me of the ones I used to see in those gangster movies."

Christy smiled at her description of the black PT Cruiser.

"I do her hair, and she's been telling me about some guy who owns a fancy boat," Valerie continued. "She's talked about men while she's in the chair—most women seem to feel they can say anything to a hairdresser. But I've kept a good clientele because I don't repeat what I hear. That's why I wouldn't say anything at the luncheon. But I'm going to call Big Bob."

"I'll tell him. I need to call him anyway." She had more than one thing to tell him.

A horn beeped behind her, and as Christy looked around, she realized all the pumps were taken and two cars were waiting in line while they stood talking.

"Guess we'd better fill our tanks," Valerie said. "In fact, mine can wait. I'm gonna be late for work." She lifted a split end from Christy's ponytail. "Stop by and I'll give you a trim."

"I will. Thanks." She hurriedly pumped gas, pulled into a parking space, and paid the cashier. Then she floorboarded to the Quick Stop. Apparently the excitement had died down, for there were only a couple of cars with out-of-state tags parked out front.

Inside, it was not Leslie, the middle-aged owner, who stood behind the cash register but a young guy she had never seen before.

"Hi, I'm Christy Castleman. Marty McAllister is a friend of mine, and I just heard about the homeless man."

"I'm Nick, Leslie's cousin. We're not supposed to say anything about the homeless man. The big guy made that clear."

If he didn't say Big Bob, he had to be new in town.

"Well, I'm the one who told Big Bob that I thought Marty was missing."

He frowned. "I didn't know she was missing."

"How did a homeless guy end up with her gold card? Or do you know?"

He glanced around to be sure he was out of earshot of the customers milling around. "Claimed he found a purse down in the weeds at Bayside Bridge. The purse was empty except for the credit card. His excuse for using the card? He was cold and hungry. He's been taken into custody, and that big deputy wanted Leslie to meet him at headquarters to make an official statement. She called me to come in."

"Thanks, Nick. See you later."

She hurried out the door, glad she had dressed warmly. The temperature had dropped during the night, and the palm trees swayed back and forth in a wind that promised to gain momentum.

She jumped in her car and drove toward Bayside Bridge. From Bayside Bridge to Shipwreck Island—a mile, maybe a mile and a half.

She opened her cell and punched in Big Bob's number. He

answered on the first ring. "Big Bob, I just heard about the homeless man being arrested. Do you think—"

"I don't know. Marty's nephew's on the way over from Pensacola. We'll go through her house, talk to her neighbors."

Christy flinched. He'd find out she had been snooping.

"Aunt Dianna is out of town but asked me to check on Marty. Could I…" She bit her lip.

"No, you cannot. I know you're trying to be helpful, but no one is allowed in that house or on the grounds now. So you and the Sassy Snowbirds need to leave the police business to us."

She knew she wasn't going to get any information from him about the homeless man, and he had forbidden her to tag along when Marty's house was searched. Then she remembered she still had some leverage with the bottle, note, and check. "What did the sheriff's department in Panama City think of the bottle and note I gave you?"

"Don't know yet."

She suspected he knew more than he was saying.

"One more thing. She was dating some guy who owned a fancy white boat."

"I'm checking on that."

"And she ordered ten pounds of shrimp from Hal for Sunday night. She didn't pick up the shrimp; she didn't call to cancel the order."

Aha! Big Bob was silent for a moment. She'd given him information he didn't have.

Christy knew he would have to double-check every tip—no hearsay for Big Bob. Then she thought of something else. "Dad told you about selling a bottle like that one to the woman with the little boys?" Despite all the concern about Marty, she felt it only fair to mention the budding pirate and spy.

"Yeah. But we need to find Marty."

Christy nodded. "I know. Well…good luck," she finished lamely, closing her phone.

When Marty left Frank's, she had been headed west toward Destin, not east toward Bayside Bridge. Had the purse been in those weeds for days? Weeks?

Christy's tires rumbled over the Bayside Bridge like a volley of drumbeats in the gray morning stillness. Just ahead, a gravel road angled to the boat launch ramp.

Her mind shot back to the boyfriend with the yacht. If Marty wrote the note, hurled the bottle from the mysterious boat into deep water…if the bottle floated to shore…she wouldn't use the term *someone*. She would name him.

She accelerated as she headed toward Shipwreck Island, thinking of the green bottle that held the note. Maybe the little sandpiper who had led her to the bottle would be waiting with another clue. Not likely.

She reached the turnoff to Shipwreck Island in minutes, and now she slowed the car, studying the woods. To the east, Lost Lagoon encircled the high ground; to the west, a hundred-acre marshland provided a wetland refuge for seabirds. In some ways this was a typical Gulf Coast swamp, and yet Shipwreck Island, due to its fabled history, was like no other place in northwest Florida.

She reached the shell-and-gravel parking area above the beach. Pushing her phone into her jeans pocket, she parked and got out. Her eyes scanned the deserted beach and moved on to the gray water, rolling and churning beneath a steady wind. No sandpipers today. Not even a sea gull.

As she walked along the beach, she glanced behind her at the only new house on this end of the island. A man stood twenty yards or so from the driveway. Her eyes darted around. He seemed to be alone.

She froze in motion, studying him for a moment. He stood beside a dark green SUV, parked in the sandy road that ran along the front of the house and on to Buster's digs.

She shoved her hands in her pockets, and one hand gripped the cell phone. Something told her not to hang around this deserted area with a stranger in sight. She ignored her inner warning and watched him. He seemed to be looking at the upper story of the house, or maybe the roof. She only had a side view of him, but he was tall and muscular and looked to be…late twenties, early thirties.

He turned toward her, and their eyes met across the space of forty-five or fifty yards. From that distance, he appeared to be an attractive guy with handsome features above the collar of a brown fleece pullover. She didn't think she'd ever seen him before, and the SUV was parked parallel to the house so she couldn't read the license plate.

He began to walk toward her, and she caught her breath. Her first impulse was to race to her car, but his long legs had crossed the side yard in a loose, easy stride. It was too late to run.

She pulled out her cell phone and opened it, ready to punch 911 if necessary.

"Hi," he called to her.

Beneath thick, dark brown hair, his deep blue eyes held a friendly expression. There was nothing sinister in the eyes or the smile. Then she remembered Ted Bundy and took a step back from him.

"Hello," she responded coolly.

He glanced at her feet, noting her backward step. He stopped walking. "Do you live here?" he asked.

"Do you?" She kept her tone polite yet formal.

"No, I live over at Bay Point. My name's Dan Brockman." He took a step forward, extending a broad hand with slim, tapered fingers and neatly rounded nails.

She hesitated, her hand poised above the numbers on the phone.

"Sorry for interrupting. I didn't realize you were making a call."

"I was about to," she said, still wary.

"Don't look so frightened. I'm not that kind of guy."

"What kind of guy?"

He lifted a hand, rubbing his cheek, and she noticed the dark brown stubble, as though he had forgotten to shave and was just now aware of it.

"I'll try again. I'm Dan Brockman, and I live over at Bay Point."

"Christy Castleman."

Suddenly a glimmer of recognition nudged her. There was something familiar about his face. As a writer accustomed to describing facial features, she made a quick study of his. Long forehead, brown brows, wide-set deep blue eyes, slim nose.

"Have we met?" she asked suddenly, as her eyes swept the brown pullover, pressed jeans, and sturdy hiking boots.

"No. I would have remembered."

She glanced toward the beach, ignoring the compliment. "A woman has disappeared." She looked back at him, studying his face. No change of expression.

"Disappeared from here?" He looked up and down the deserted beach.

"We're not sure."

Her gaze dropped to the edge of the shoreline, to the damp sand that held only the scalloped imprint of waves. The tide had swept clean the indentation of the bottle, but she saw it clearly in her mind. Pale green reflecting the glint of the sun. And she saw the folded square of paper with those chilling words...

Call the police. Someone is trying to kill me.

"Does the woman live here?"

"Excuse me?" She knew what he had asked. She needed a second to clear her mind and focus her thoughts.

"Does the woman who disappeared live around here?" he repeated. His voice was smooth, the words and their inflection hinting of a man who was well educated or who had learned to speak properly, without mushing vowels and swallowing consonants, as some Southerners were prone to do. As she often did among locals or whenever she got lazy.

"She lives across the bridge in Summer Breeze."

He nodded, as their gazes locked again. He cleared his throat. "When did she disappear? I didn't see anything in the morning paper."

"The information hasn't been publicized. Well, actually, I hinted at it in a column I write in Summer Breeze's weekly paper, but the *Courier* won't be on the stands until tomorrow."

Why was she standing here talking to him? Why didn't she make an excuse and sprint back to the car? Or dial someone?

Because she had a gut instinct that she was safe with him.

"So you write for the *Courier*?" he asked. This guy didn't seem to miss a word or a nuance; he had picked right up on her apprehension when he approached her.

"I write a column, Beach Buzz, which is just a word-around-town type of thing."

"I've read it. You're a good writer," he said, then he seemed to think of something else. "Christy Castleman. Do you write mysteries?"

She always experienced a moment of self-consciousness when someone asked her that. She had decided it stemmed from some basic insecurity that people wouldn't like her books.

"Just one. But I'm working on another."

"Well...again, it's a pleasure to meet you. I'm sorry to say, I haven't read your book. Now I will. Books have always been a passion of mine, but I've been...out of touch."

"What do you do?" The wind picked up, yanking at her ponytail.

"I finished my commitment to Uncle Sam last month and came here to spend some time with my parents."

"You were in the military?"

"For years. I've just returned from the battle lines, so to speak."

"So what are your plans now?"

"I've always been interested in architecture, even though I was a business major in college," he continued, unaware of her suspicions or choosing not to acknowledge them. "I have some free time, so I'm studying architecture at the community college."

That news sliced an edge off her suspicion. She made a mental note to ask Dr. Clayton about him. She closed the cell phone and thrust it into her pocket, but she kept her hand wrapped around it.

"I teach a class there," she said.

He nodded. "I remember reading your course description in the catalog. And I saw the article on the bulletin board."

A reporter from the *Atlanta Journal-Constitution* had interviewed her for their book page. The article had been picked up in newspapers around the Florida Panhandle; someone had even posted a copy on the bulletin board at school. She'd been intending to take it down.

"I thought by now that article had been removed," she said, relaxing a bit.

He smiled, and as he did, he seemed to be studying her more closely. "Nope, it's still there."

So she had probably seen him at night school. But…that didn't quite fit the puzzle nagging her.

"I'm working on a class project and looking for an unusual structure. I'd been exploring this island recently and noticed that house."

She followed his gaze back to the two-story white house built on eight-foot pilings to protect it from high water. Underneath the house was an enclosed basement and two-car garage.

"I think the windows designed like portholes really give it the look of a ship," he said.

"Yeah, in fact it's called the ship house by locals."

She had seen the house so many times that she'd taken for granted how unique it was. The windows reminded her of the round glass in the door of her clothes dryer, only smaller. A concrete patio ran the length of the rear, but the patio furniture had been removed.

"The house was built last year by a retired sea captain," Christy said. "Unfortunately, soon after he and his wife moved in, he died.

I guess she didn't want to stay in the house alone, so she moved back to Maine. The house is unoccupied now. I'm not sure if she's planning to sell it or not. Is there a Realtor's sign in the yard?"

"No, but I don't need to see the interior; it's the exterior that interests me."

The wind bit through her sweatshirt, and she shivered. "I'd better be going. Maybe I'll see you at school."

"I hope so." He smiled down at her. "I enjoyed talking with you."

"You too." She turned and walked quickly to her car.

Dan Brockman. She intended to check him out. If he was looking for an unusual structure, the ship house fit that requirement. Or…maybe she was getting paranoid, but who wouldn't with all that was happening?

First an unsolved murder over in Panama City, and now a woman in Summer Breeze had disappeared.

She reached her car and settled into the front seat, then sneaked a glance toward the ship house. Dan Brockman was still standing there, his back to her, his attention focused on the house.

4

Christy took the phone out of her pocket with a notion to dial Dr. Clayton, who taught some of the evening classes and knew most of the students. They were take-a-break buddies. Instead of dialing, however, she laid the phone on the passenger's seat. She was overreacting. She'd see Dr. Clayton on Thursday evening.

She started the engine, backed out, and took off, tires spitting gravel. In the distance she could see the woods, the site for her fictional pirate's grave. The wind had yanked Spanish moss from the trees, and now it drifted through the air like the mystic ghosts of gothic novels. Oddly, goose bumps puckered her skin. Maybe she'd bring someone with her and have a look around.

But what was the point? She had tromped all over that area yesterday morning. Had found the bottle and note. If Marty McAllister had disappeared, she wasn't up there or anywhere else on Shipwreck Island. Big Bob had already checked. But finding

Marty safe was beginning to seem an unlikely ending to the mystery of her disappearance.

A horn blasted her out of her thoughts. She hit her brakes a microsecond before she would have bashed a car crossing the opposite street under a green light. Everything in the seats ended up on the floorboard.

She had better pay attention; she couldn't afford another fender bender. Or another rise in car-insurance rates. She stared straight ahead until she reached her driveway.

The dull throb of a headache that had begun at Bayside Bridge now accelerated to bongo beats. She roared into her driveway, hopped out, and dashed to the back door. She unlocked it and hurried inside. Her little house settled around her like a warm bathrobe, comforting and familiar. This was her safe haven in a shaky, unpredictable world. She locked the back door.

Hurrying to the cabinet, she reached for the coffee. Her mother tended to get migraines and vowed that caffeine opened up the blood vessels. She took a few deep breaths, trying to calm herself. What a morning.

Outside her window, the wind moaned against the house, and she busied herself with spooning coffee into the filter, pouring water into the container, and turning on the coffee maker.

Why couldn't Aunt Dianna run her own errands? And why did Christy feel compelled to return to Shipwreck Island? Because she'd found the bottle and note. Or maybe she was just plain nosy.

While the coffee gurgled, she grabbed the sassy woman mug,

studying the lady with the provocative wink. Christy felt neither sassy nor provocative, but just holding the mug boosted her confidence. Dan Brockman had thrown her off balance.

The kitchen phone rang, and she turned and read her mother's number.

"Hi, Mom."

"Christy, why haven't you called? Dad told me all about the bottle and the note. And he said Seth had called you! Why didn't you tell me?"

Christy winced at all the questions, then assembled her answers. "I asked Dad to relate everything to you. Sorry, Mom. I've been running in circles. And Seth will be calling you soon…maybe tonight."

"That's good to hear. Did he sound okay?"

"Sure."

"I worry about him. And I worry about you. You need to slow down."

Christy knew her mom would really worry if she found out her daughter had been over to Shipwreck Island, looking for a body, meeting a stranger, talking to him. And Mom would set a record on her migraines if she knew Christy's suspicions about Seth.

"I don't intend to leave the house, Mom. I'll be typing until my fingers fall off."

Her mother laughed. "Let's hope not. Okay, stay in touch."

They said their good-byes and hung up, and Christy paced the floor. Either she must get back to running or buy a treadmill.

Exercise did wonders for her when she was wound tight. In order to finish her novel, she'd given up exercising, socializing, everything except eating and sleeping, and now even those basics were getting sacrificed.

She turned to the fruit bowl, grabbed a banana, and began making a peanut butter and banana sandwich. With the sandwich resting on a paper plate and coffee mug in hand, she retreated to her living room, separated from the kitchen by the eating bar.

A sofa and matching love seat upholstered in blue chenille dominated the small room; glass end tables and a coffee table completed the grouping. She sat down, munching on her sandwich. She dug the remote from under a cushion and aimed it at the television screen in the middle of her entertainment center.

A corny advertisement she hated popped onto the screen, and she diverted her attention to the books, CDs, and videos. A separate stack contained reruns of *Murder, She Wrote, Cold Case, CSI,* and *Profiler.*

The familiar voice of the news anchor filled the room. He was detailing another trouble spot brewing in Afghanistan. She switched to the weather channel. Snow was blanketing the southeast, stretching as far south as Atlanta, which surprised her. The coast was a soggy mess. So she shouldn't complain about a rainy day in the neighborhood.

She finished her sandwich and had just picked up her coffee mug when she heard a *tap-tap* at her back door. She pulled herself up, peering down the hall. Through the glass pane, a round, dark face, wide smile, and friendly brown eyes greeted her. Bonnie Taylor.

She hurried to open the back door. "Hey, Bonnie."

"Hey, girlfriend." Bonnie closed her gray umbrella and propped it outside the door. She was wearing a red pantsuit which helped offset the gloom of the day.

Christy tried to smile. "My, but you're perky on this dreary morning. Did you get your hair cut?" She studied the short black curls.

"Styled, baby. But this style goes on and off whenever I want. It's a wig. My hair's still thin a year after the chemo, so this is how I remedy the problem. Wallace sneaked into the dressing room and counted my wigs this morning—the old coot. Let me know he knew I have eight."

"That's why your hair always looks nice. And do I dare hope that covered dish in your hand contains my favorite pie?"

"It does. Got hungry for a pie myself after you mentioned it yesterday. Made two last night. One for us, one for you."

"A whole pie? Bonnie, you're an angel." Christy reached for her purse on the counter, but Bonnie's large hand stopped her.

"Don't insult a good deed."

Christy frowned. "But this is how you make a living. I don't give away copies of my book."

"Well, you gave one to me." She set the dish so firmly on the counter that Christy dared not argue.

"Want a cup of coffee?" Christy offered meekly.

"I need one bad."

"Coming right up." She filled a mug and motioned Bonnie to the living room. "I'll share the pie with Dad. At every church supper, he circles the tables until he spots your pies."

"Well, I bet that little bitty mom of yours doesn't search for pie or anything else loaded with calories," Bonnie chuckled. "Praise the Lord for fresh coffee."

"How about a sandwich?"

"No, honey, don't have time. Just wanted to talk."

Christy watched as the big woman stopped at the love seat and, in a single fluid motion, settled onto the cushions.

"Listen, I've got some information about Marty," Bonnie announced. "Big Bob searched Marty's house and found nothing out of order. And no hint as to where she'd gone. The nephew's worried now."

"Really?"

"Big Bob has an APB out on her, and they're combing Destin. Also, they're taking that note you found seriously. Seriously enough to check it out for fingerprints. They got a special system. But when it comes to absolutely identifying the handwriting, they'll have to send the note to the Florida Department of Law Enforcement in Tallahassee. They're getting handwriting samples from Marty's real-estate office, her house, too."

Christy stared at Bonnie, stunned. "You didn't learn all that from Big Bob. Or did you?"

Bonnie leaned back on the cushions and grinned. "I cannot tell a lie. My daughter Sherrie has moved back from Tallahassee, and she's working downtown in an office full of detectives." Downtown meant Panama City. "She's my source, as they say."

"Sherrie's moved back?" While Sherrie had been gone for years and was younger than Christy, she remembered her from high school. "I know you're glad, Bonnie."

"Glad she's back, sorry she got divorced. But at least there were no children involved. I tried to talk her into moving in with us, but she got an apartment near her work. She had a clerical job at FDLE, so when she heard about an opening in the Panama City office, she applied and got it. God works things out."

Christy nodded, thinking about how Bonnie applied her faith in every situation. She could take a lesson from Bonnie on that.

"Did you hear anything about the man who was killed a week ago?" Christy asked.

"Just that he was a tourist. A doctor from New York with a pocket full of money."

Christy stared, her mind working. "Any suspects?"

"I didn't ask."

It occurred to Christy that Sherrie could be a valuable source in keeping up with the investigation. "Do you think Sherrie can keep us informed without getting into trouble?" Christy asked. "I wouldn't want to take advantage of her."

Bonnie studied the diamond and sapphire rings on her fingers, then looked up with a little grin. "Nobody takes advantage of

Sherrie. But I already told her if it weren't for us, those folks wouldn't be getting anywhere in this so-called investigation."

Both women sipped their coffee, deep in thought, as Christy silently absorbed what Bonnie had told her.

"Bonnie, have you heard anything about Marty having a boyfriend with a big fancy boat?"

Bonnie shook her head. "No, but you might ask some of the girls who know her better."

Christy nodded, absently touching her ponytail and remembering her conversation with Valerie. "I need a trim. I'll ask Valerie."

"Well, I gotta get this big body moving," Bonnie said, placing her empty mug on the coffee table. "I'm overdue at those sales at the mall. I just love helping Wallace spend his paychecks. You wanna come with me? I've never known you to miss a sale."

"Can't. Gotta work."

"That reminds me, I tried to call you on your cell phone after I drove by and your car was gone. Is your battery down?"

Christy frowned. "No. I used my cell earlier, but…" She shoved her hands into her empty pockets, then got up and went to the kitchen, where her purse sat on the counter. It was not in the side pocket where she usually carried it. She looked around the kitchen.

Bonnie stood in the door, chuckling. "Let's do this the easy way." She pulled her phone out of her purse and dialed. "It's ringing."

Christy looked around, listening for a ring. She turned and walked down the hall, into the bedroom, bath, back to the office. If she had lost another phone…

Then she remembered her near fender bender earlier. "Let me check the car." She ran out to the car, staring at the empty passenger seat.

"Got your voice mail." Bonnie stood inside the screened porch. "I'll dial again."

A distant jingle sounded from within the car. She followed the sound to the floorboard. No phone. She stretched across the front seat and peered at the floorboard on the passenger's side. The ringing grew louder. She was practically standing on her head when she dug it out from under the passenger's seat.

"Thanks, Bonnie." She got out of the car and slammed the door. "I hit the brakes, and my purse slid to the floorboard. My cell phone went farther."

A big grin spread over Bonnie's face. "Glad you found it." She picked up her umbrella beside the door. "Looks like the rain's stopped. I'm just hoping the big-lady store hasn't sold out of tent size."

"Stop that," Christy laughed. "Thanks for the pie."

"You have a good day, honey," she called over her shoulder as she swung down to her baby blue Cadillac. Then she hesitated as she opened the door. "I'm thinking about Marty again. You know, it's funny how you don't like a person that much till you think something has happened to them. Reckon we're all feeling a little guilty about her. Most of us had a run-in with her at one time or another, but when you're dealing with a woman who knows it all and is never wrong—at least that's what Marty thought."

"I know."

Bonnie settled behind the wheel of her Cadillac, and soon the engine was purring.

Christy waved and returned to the kitchen, gripping her cell phone tightly. This habit of losing stuff had to stop. Every year she got worse. She shoved the phone into her jeans pocket and hurried to her office.

Pirates and trunks filled with gold provided a wonderful escape. Even though she wrote about theft and murder on the high seas, she got the shakes when real danger hit her community.

She decided to light a candle, one that promised to soothe and calm. Sometimes she preferred her fictional world to her real world. She didn't want to examine the psychological ramifications of that, so she homed in on her own version of Blackbeard and his pirates.

Her first novel had dealt with the 1622 Spanish treasure-fleet disaster and the theft of a valuable chest of gold coins. Murder and mayhem followed, but the chest was never found. The second novel moved to the mid-eighteen hundreds, and told the story of Johnny B and his daring escape from Havana up the Florida coastline, where he hid out in the woods of Shipwreck Island and buried the gold.

Christy lost herself in the feel of the island, the mist and fog, the triumphant location of the mysterious grave…but then her neck and shoulders screamed exhaustion. She sat back in her chair and blinked wearily at the clock. Ten minutes till seven! She had exactly ten minutes to get to the prayer service.

During the month of February, the prayer service was held on Tuesday nights. Her dad was leading a religious-beliefs workshop at the college on Wednesday evenings, and the congregation had agreed to switch to Tuesdays.

She hurried to the bathroom to freshen up. She had already missed dinner. She knew from past experience that Joan, the efficient kitchen supervisor, would have shooed everyone out and closed the church kitchen by a quarter till seven. She changed from her sweatshirt to a white turtleneck sweater over her comfortable jeans. After a quick touch-up, she dashed out to her car and drove toward the church.

In minutes she was turning into the parking lot, her eyes peeled for stray kids. None in sight. She nosed her car into the last parking space. Hurrying to the side door, she entered the long hall and came face to face with her petite mom. Cold-natured even in summer, her mother wore a thick navy sweater and navy and red tweed slacks with thick navy socks and leather loafers.

"Hey, Mom." Christy looked down into the small face and smiled.

"Good news, honey. Seth called just before I left the house. He has a job busing tables at a restaurant in Alice Springs. I think this will make him more conscious of saving his money," her mother continued cheerfully. "Oh, and he's met a nice girl from Sweden who's working at the same restaurant."

Christy stared at her mom while thinking of Seth. An IQ of 140, a straight-A student in marine biology at Florida State until he dropped out. Now he was busing tables halfway around the world. Yet Beth Castleman, as usual, was determined to see the bright spot in her son's latest adventure.

"Great," Christy replied listlessly as they entered the door to the right of the pulpit.

Polished oak pews formed straight rows on the red carpet, and half a dozen windows on each side overlooked the water. The raised pulpit was large enough to accommodate the podium and two chairs. Behind the dividing rail, two dozen chairs held the choir on Sunday mornings.

It was their custom at the weekly prayer service to light a candle for someone if a family had lost a loved one or had a critical illness. Sometimes an unspoken request warranted a candle. Valerie stood at the altar, lighting a candle. For Marty, no doubt.

Christy took a seat in the "family" pew and glanced around, smiling at the people she knew. She looked toward the door, wondering what was keeping her mother. Beth stood in the doorway, talking to Will Birdsong, an eight-year-old in the Sunday school class she taught.

Christy studied his impish face. A budding Seth! She didn't want to think about Seth and his problems, and yet she couldn't escape him. Stress affected everyone differently. Each move to a new town, a new church, had made Seth physically ill. When her parents had announced that the family would be moving to Summer Breeze, Seth ran away from home. On a cold winter night, half-frozen and embarrassed, he had returned with his father's arm wrapped lovingly around him. A tip from Scooter, Seth's best friend, had sent her dad to the school's football stadium, where he found Seth under the bleachers, huddled up, sobbing. His dream of being a star player for the Cougars would be demolished by their move to another school.

"Christy," someone whispered behind her.

She turned to face Valerie, who leaned forward to whisper to her. "Big Bob has alerted the Coast Guard to check boats up and down the coast, and he's organizing a search of the area around the bridge all the way to Shipwreck Island."

"What do you think about the homeless man who's been arrested?" Christy whispered.

"Let's open with a prayer." Her father's voice cut off further conversation, and Christy turned around.

She could hardly keep her mind on the prayer requests that followed. All around her, people were going to the altar to light candles. Christy looked up at the cross. Only this time instead of seeing the cross, she was seeing the green bottle wedged in the sand. She felt its cold dampness on her fingers, saw the crumpled note, read those desperate words.

Call the police. Someone is trying to kill me.

Wednesday, February 18

"Good morning, Dad. Got a minute?" Christy wound the phone cord around her fingers while she paced.

"For you, I always have a minute. Or an hour or a lifetime. What's up, hon? You worried about Mrs. McAllister?"

"Well, like everyone else, I guess. Have you heard anything?"

"Nothing. But then I try not to listen to rumors."

"Rumors? Come on, Dad. What did you hear?"

A deep sigh filled the wires. "Ran into Big Bob at the market last night. He seems to have some doubts about the homeless guy harming Marty. Said he's a Vietnam vet who never got over the trauma. He didn't say it, but I gathered he thought that if the man had harmed Marty, he wouldn't be hanging around to buy coffee and a sandwich. They're getting records for her home and cell phones, which should be a big help."

"Hmm, interesting." She took a deep breath, staring at the calendar with today's date circled in black. "Actually, the reason I called…today is… Well, I need to go out to see Jack."

A moment of silence preceded her dad's words. "Honey, I wish you were here so I could give you a big hug. But I'll be sending prayers your way instead."

"Thanks. Dad, why does life have to be so difficult? Not just for me or you or our family but for everyone?"

He paused again. "Honey, life may not seem fair, but God gave us freedom of choice. Sometimes we make choices that have difficult consequences."

She knew he was referring to Chad.

"And those choices break hearts," she said and sighed.

"And then we ask questions of ourselves and of others. What we have to do is trust God, Christy. That's all any of us can do, and in doing that, we find a strength, a peace that really does pass all understanding."

"When will I find that peace? That strength?" she asked.

"You've been finding it one day at a time. Maybe you don't always see it or feel it, but I've watched it growing in you."

"Thanks, Dad. As always, you've said just the right thing. I see why everyone in the state of Florida adores you."

"Spoken like a truly prejudiced daughter."

They said their good-byes, and Christy hurried to her bedroom. She tossed a fresh pair of jeans and a Florida State sweatshirt onto the bed and headed for the shower.

Driving out to Rainbow Bay, she passed the familiar piny woods thick with palmetto and gallberry bushes. At the service station–convenience store, she turned onto the narrow sand road leading out to Jack's place.

She gazed at the towering live oaks and the secluded ten acres where she had planned to live happily ever after. But her plans had been drastically changed.

The small frame bungalow came into view, the home that had been weathered by time and disrepair to a pale gray. She turned into the narrow driveway and parked behind Jack's green truck. He sat in a deck chair surrounded by fishing net. A country music station blared from a radio in the toolshed, telling a story of love gone wrong. Seeing her, he got up and went inside the toolshed. The music died.

He emerged with a chair, unfolded it, and pushed aside the green fishing net he had been mending. She got out of the car, lugging the ice chest and a plastic container of fudge brownies.

"Hey, girl. Give me that thing," he called, reaching out to take the ice chest from her.

"Hello, Jack." She smiled into the sad blue eyes. He didn't look surprised to see her; he had known she would come.

"Thanks for the grouper fillets." She was careful to keep the lilt in her voice and the smile on her face. "I brought some of those brownies you like."

He set the ice chest inside the toolshed, grinned at the container of brownies, and placed it on top of the ice chest. Then he spread his arms wide.

She stepped into his embrace, feeling the jutting bones of his shoulder blades. He'd lost more weight.

"Glad to see you, gal."

"Could I talk you into going to town for a barbecue?"

He attempted a grin but failed. "Nah. You know me. I'd rather stay home and eat a can of sardines."

She started to ask about his and J. T.'s wild night on the town, but neither of them was in the mood for humor.

"Well," she said, brushing a piece of fishing net from his shirt, "I had hoped I could drag you in for lunch, sneak a healthy salad onto your plate."

He made a face. "I don't eat rabbit food."

Christy laughed and sat down in the lawn chair beside him. There was a moment of awkward silence. She reached over and touched his hand. Even in the sunshine, his hand was cold as he grasped hers and squeezed it gently. The skin of his palm was callused and rough, yet the grip was as strong as ever.

He turned his eyes toward the blue gray water of the bay, looking far out to the horizon. She knew he was seeing nothing, seeing everything. Mostly seeing Chad.

Christy cleared her throat. "I know it's hard…" Her voice trailed off as he turned to face her, his eyes locking with hers.

For a moment the thing they would try not to talk about hung between them like smoke from a fire, a fire that had almost destroyed both of them. It was hard to be here today, but she knew he needed her.

"Why'd he have to do it, Christy?" he asked hoarsely. His eyes were bleak and tortured before he lowered them, not wanting her to see the tears.

She sighed. "I don't know. He just did. And nothing you or I said or did could stop him."

Automatically she turned and looked toward the back room of the house, where the curtains were open and the light was on in Chad's bedroom. Jack had been in there this morning, torturing himself on this hideous anniversary. And now she was torturing herself, too, as her eyes locked on the shelves of trophies, Chad's pride and joy.

"Racing was in his blood from the time he was a kid winning those stupid go-cart races." Jack's words plunged her back to the past. "Then he set his sights on dirt racing and won every race up and down the Panhandle." He took a deep breath. "He thought he was ready for Birmingham International, but he wasn't. I knew it, tried to tell him that. He wouldn't listen."

Suddenly a sob tore through Christy's throat, and her carefully erected defenses crumbled. She put a hand to her mouth, trying to shut off the sobs, and clamped her eyes together so hard it hurt, but the gesture was useless. The tears broke through.

"I watched him get more and more daring...until I just couldn't go to the races anymore," she said. Her throat held an ache the size of Texas, but she forced herself to keep talking. "I begged him to get serious about college, to focus on what he wanted to do."

"I know you did, honey." Jack's tobacco-edged voice had turned as gentle as the light morning breeze drifting up from the water and settling over their faces. "I tried to talk to him about what he wanted to be. I wanted a better life for him than being an old weather-beaten fisherman like me. But…you know Chad. If it was possible, he was more stubborn than me. And that's saying a lot."

Christy wiped the tears. "I begged…pleaded. Didn't work. The night he left for Birmingham…my fear turned to anger." The words were torn from her throat, as tears spilled from her eyes onto Jack's hand, which gently cupped her cheek. "The last thing…I said to him…was I never…want to…see you again. And…I… never…did."

Jack's arms circled her heaving shoulders as he cradled her against his thin chest. "Sweetie, we've been over this. What you said had nothing to do with what happened." He paused, mumbling an expletive. "I ranted at him too. But we gotta let it go. He knew we loved him. He always knew that."

"But somehow that doesn't help," she said.

In the years since the night Chad's car had smashed into the wall and exploded in flames, she had never been able to forgive herself. Or to forgive him for cheating them out of a lifetime together with the three kids they had already named and the house Chad and Jack would build for them on Rainbow Bay.

"Jack, I did love him. So very much. And even before like turned to love, he was the greatest guy I had ever known. He still is." She sniffed, lifting the sleeve of her sweatshirt to wipe her damp cheeks. Blinking through her tears, she looked over at Jack and with the cuff of her sweatshirt wiped his tear-stained cheeks.

He nodded, and for several seconds neither spoke. There was nothing left to say.

Suddenly she recalled a conversation with her dad about prayer. At the dinner table he had mentioned that another call had come that day, asking him to explain why prayers were not answered.

"And what did you say?" Beth had asked.

Grant had studied the bread he was buttering. "As humans we don't see the big picture. I just encourage people not to give up."

Christy had kept on praying for the pain to ease, for her and for Jack, over the loss of Chad. And she had prayed for relief from the guilt she harbored over her spiteful words at their last good-bye. Sometimes she felt she was fighting a losing battle, but she knew she must keep on until the battle was won, no matter how long it took.

A horn began to beep, intruding on their reflection. Both turned to see J. T.'s old, black truck hiccuping to a stop.

Jack muttered something uncomplimentary about the way the truck backfired, and Christy smiled, feeling a huge relief that J. T. had showed up this morning. J. T. would provide a good respite for Jack; nothing cheered either of them more than a good shouting match, which, from the looks of J. T., was about to begin.

"Waited down at the station for thirty minutes. You could let a fella know."

"I'm sick and tired of their leftover coffee," Jack shouted. "I think they throw their dip sticks and grease rags in the same box with the coffee filters."

"You coulda let me know," J. T. shouted back. He turned and squinted through his thick lenses at Christy. "Mornin', Miss Christy."

"Hey, J. T. How're you doing?"

J. T. shuffled, studying a tear in the toe of his right tennis shoe. "I'm okay, I reckon." He looked up at her. "Thanks for askin'." He looked at Jack. "She's the only woman in town who'll even speak to us."

"I just want to be sure you two guys keep up your fishing and bring me grouper and shrimp," she teased.

"What's this about that rich lady going missing?" J. T. inquired as he reached them.

"What rich lady?" Jack wanted to know.

"It appears Marty McAllister is missing."

Jack waved a hand. "That one. She's out on a boat with some unsuspecting nitwit who's got more money than sense."

Christy looked at him curiously. "Have you seen her out in a boat with someone?"

Jack shrugged. "Looked like her."

"When?" Christy stared at him, wondering if he might know something.

"A few weeks ago."

"I didn't know you knew her, Jack," Christy said.

"Everyone knows *her*," J. T. put in. "She came snooping around here one day, wantin' to know if anything could be developed. Jack gave her the what-for and sent her off in a huff."

Christy arched an eyebrow. "Did you really?"

Jack slapped the left breast pocket of his shirt, where his cigarettes had once lived. Even though he had quit months ago, he still slapped the empty pocket whenever he got nervous. "That was a while back."

"Well, are we gonna get that coffee, Jack? You wanna go with us, Miss Christy?"

"I wish I could." She smiled at J. T., whose nose had turned red, a sign that his blood pressure was soaring. "I have an appointment. Jack, go in and make coffee for you and J. T., and open up the brownies. But mark your calendar for barbecue with me on March 16."

"I'm not having any more birthdays," Jack growled.

Christy looked at J. T. "Did I say birthday? I thought I said barbecue."

"Aw, he's half-deaf," J. T. hollered.

Christy laughed and stepped over to give Jack a quick hug. She could feel his arms pressing hard around her. Then she stepped back. "You two try to stay out of trouble."

Jack smiled tenderly at her, and before she choked up again, she waved and hurried across the backyard.

As she got into her car and backed out of the driveway, she wished she could stay and spend more time with them. They were so funny together, and it would be a good way for her and Jack to push the sad memories of today's anniversary aside.

Choices. She thought about the words her dad had spoken earlier. Chad had made a choice to race cars, despite her pleas, despite his dad's warnings. And she had made a choice to keep loving him, even when his reckless nature surfaced and frightened her. Still, Chad had a heart of gold. There was nothing he wouldn't do to help someone in need. It had been one of the reasons everyone loved him.

But now...she and Jack could wallow in sorrow and regret, or they could find new purpose for their lives and move forward rather than backward.

Her parents had offered guidance while encouraging their children to make their own choices. The irony of it was that God had done the same thing. And in testing their wings and learning to fly, both she and Seth had floundered. But Chad had crashed.

She turned down the road that ran past the beach, trying to divert her thoughts. A man and a little boy, probably father and son, flew colorful kites. They were running up and down the beach, hanging on as their kites rose higher, dipped lower, rose again. Her hopes and dreams were like those kites, drifting higher and higher, then spiraling downward. She needed balance in her life to make choices, just as those kites needed the right current of air to keep them going.

Her faith and her family had given her balance, when she remembered to turn in that direction. She also knew she had been blessed, and she owed it to herself and those who believed in her to move forward with her life. To give herself a fair chance at happiness again. Maybe Seth had spoken the truth after all.

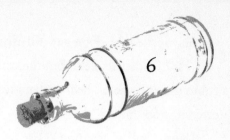

6

Facing her decision to move forward with her life, Christy decided to take Valerie's advice about getting her hair trimmed. She was only a couple of blocks from the lovely retirement complex where Valerie ran her salon. Since she was the best hairstylist in the area, her other customers didn't mind making the trip over to the retirement center.

She turned into the circular parking area, trying to find a space. The van was loaded, ready to pull out for a shopping excursion. Curious faces framed the window; people waved. She waved back.

She hurried through the spacious lobby and down the stairs to the lower level, where a small group sat in the game room, playing bingo.

Through the glass door of the salon, she could see Valerie, busy as always. Her strawberry blond hair was a good advertisement for her work, because she always seemed to have just the right cut and color.

She opened the door, and Valerie turned. "Hey, lady."

"Hi." Christy looked from the man in the chair getting a haircut to the sofa where Thelma what's-her-name sat waiting. "Valerie, can you work me in?"

"Sure. Grab a magazine."

In the cheerful shop, there were always stacks of magazines and treats to entertain those who waited.

"You don't look like you need a thing done to you," Thelma said, staring at Christy. "What kind of makeup do you use?"

Christy blinked. "No certain brand. I usually pick up something at the drugstore."

"No kidding?" Thelma was a tall, sturdy woman who ruled the Pancake House with a firm hand. No lazy cooks for her.

"What's going on with you, Thelma?" Christy took a seat beside her.

"Why don't you stop in and find out?" she challenged.

"I will."

"Everybody's talking about that McAllister woman who's missing. I'll put in my two cents worth," Thelma said stoutly.

"And what's that?" Christy asked, while flipping through a magazine.

"I already told Big Bob. I saw Mrs. McAllister in her car that Sunday afternoon. She almost hit the car in front of her trying to stop at that red light. Can't believe she didn't ram a fender, I said to Wally, who delivers our pop. He stared at her too. She roared off when the light changed."

"Which way was she going?" Christy put down the magazine and stared at Thelma.

"Toward Bayside Bridge."

Christy and Valerie exchanged puzzled glances. "Do you know what time that was on Sunday?"

"Sure I do. It was sometime between one and one thirty. Wally was due around one fifteen, and he was running a few minutes late. I took a smoke break to watch for him. Didn't they arrest that homeless guy?"

"Yeah, but…" Christy's sentence trailed off. She had better keep her opinions to herself.

Valerie chose not to. "You know what? Marty would never toss one of her designer purses out in the weeds. Or if she sold it at a garage sale, she'd never leave a gold credit card in it."

"You said you told Big Bob about seeing her heading east at that specific time?" Christy asked.

"I did."

"What did he say?" Valerie asked.

"What does he ever say?" Thelma drawled. "Nothing. He just wrote it down and said he would check it out."

Valerie laid down the scissors; the man in the chair stared at Thelma.

"Wait a minute," Valerie said. "Your Pancake House is several blocks east of Frank's restaurant. If she was going to Destin, she would have been headed west."

Christy pursed her lips, thinking. Why wasn't she headed to

Destin? And if she was headed east, that was the area where the homeless guy hung out. Maybe there was something to his having her credit card after all. He could have jumped in the car if she had failed to lock the door. Marty was pretty scatterbrained.

Christy looked at Valerie, who was staring hard at her. "You know what, Valerie? I'll come back later. I need to run an errand."

"I'm getting this stuff chopped off." Thelma indicated her shoulder-length blond hair. "It may take her awhile."

"That's okay. See you two later."

Valerie was still staring at her, questions blazing in her hazel eyes. They couldn't talk now, Christy realized. It would have to wait until later.

She hurried back to the car, not sure how to interpret what Thelma had told her. What did Big Bob think of this? The homeless guy was beginning to look more guilty than anyone else. Even traumatized by the war, he could still yank a car door open and jump inside.

She was just driving out of the parking lot when her cell phone rang.

"Hey, Christy." It was Aunt Dianna. "What's going on? Nobody's called me."

Christy winced. She had completely forgotten. "I intended to call you in the next few minutes. Marty hasn't returned, and some strange things are happening. A homeless man was arrested for using Marty's gold card at the Quick Stop."

"*What?*"

"And Big Bob is taking this seriously now. As a matter of fact, I just left Valerie's shop, and Thelma from the Pancake House was there. She said Marty almost hit a car at the red light Sunday afternoon. This was around one fifteen. Thelma seemed pretty certain."

There was a moment of silence while her aunt digested this information. "But she was supposed to be driving to Destin. Why was she headed in the opposite direction? I'll bet she went home to feed her dog and, being in a hurry, didn't close the gate tight."

Christy pulled into the street and was caught behind a car with Michigan license plates. "Yeah. And that homeless guy hangs out on the beach near there. But I don't think Big Bob believes he's sharp enough to have…done anything to Marty. Claims he found her purse in the weeds at Bayside Bridge."

"She probably dropped it when she jumped in the boat with her mysterious boyfriend," Dianna put in.

"But there was nothing in the purse except the credit card. Or so the man claims."

"I don't believe that."

"Well, he's been arrested, so I'm sure the authorities will get to the bottom of it. Listen, you're on vacation. Try to relax and enjoy yourself."

"I know, but still…"

"Are you having fun in Key West?"

"So much fun that my hubby wants to stay another week."

"What about you?" Christy asked.

"It's okay with me. We've met a really nice couple from Birmingham. We're going to dinner with them tonight. She's a nurse at a medical center up there, and we have a lot in common."

Dianna had been a nurse for years but was taking a break so that she and Uncle John could do some traveling, since he had just retired.

"Sweetie, John's yelling to go eat, but don't forget to call me."

"I will. Tell Uncle John hi. You two have fun." She had reached her driveway, wheeled in, and cut the engine.

It had been a long morning and a challenging one. Just when she had decided to work on improving herself, beginning with her hair, another Marty question rerouted her plans.

Hurrying into the kitchen, she opened the freezer and popped a frozen lasagna into the microwave. While it was cooking, she wandered into the office to check her messages.

As though on cue, the phone pealed out, and she checked the caller ID. It was a name she didn't recognize, and out of curiosity she answered.

"I'd like to speak to Christy Castleman, please."

"This is Christy," she replied, staring at the notations on her calendar.

"My name is Earl Woodley, and I just read your article in the *Courier*. I don't know if this is important, but I had an odd experience in the location you described on Shipwreck Island."

She suppressed a sigh, wondering if half of Summer Breeze would be calling to relate a curious experience there. "What is it, Mr. Woodley?"

"Well." He paused, clearing his throat. Then he continued, louder than before. "In your article you mentioned finding a note in a green bottle on Shipwreck Island Monday morning. Am I understanding correctly that the area where you found the bottle is near that house that's built like a ship?"

"Yes, it is. Do you know something about the bottle, sir?"

"It may just be one of those crazy coincidences, but I was out there on Sunday afternoon around two o'clock. I'm retired and do metal detecting on the beach as a hobby. Matter of fact, it's earned me the nickname of Sandpiper. But to tell the story, I hadn't been over to Shipwreck Island, so I decided to go. Once I got to that strip of beach near the ship house, I saw a small Private Property sign. About that time I heard a woman yelling. She was leaning out one of those round windows on the upper story of the house. She looked upset. I wear a hearing aid, and the wind was beating the surf, so I couldn't hear what she was saying. But she was gesturing at me, which I took to mean 'Get off my property.' "

Christy was listening carefully, her interest piqued. She had thought the house was unoccupied.

"So I picked up my backpack to leave, but as I glanced over my shoulder one last time, I saw her throw something green out the window. At the time I thought she was a kook throwing something to run me off. She had a strong arm, because whatever she threw barely missed my head. I got out of there in a hurry, never looked back again. But when you mentioned a green bottle and a note, I thought I should give you a call."

Christy considered his words, wondering if what he was telling her could possibly have a link to the green bottle she had found. It was certainly in the right location. "I'm glad you called, Mr. Woodley. Let me ask you something about the woman who threw the bottle out the window. Do you recall what she looked like?"

"Didn't get a good look. Like I said, I got busy grabbing my stuff to get off the property. All I remember was the expression on her face, like she was real upset. Oh, and she had red hair."

Christy's stomach did a somersault as she grabbed the daisy pad and scrambled for a pen.

"Where do you live, Mr. Woodley?"

"In Summer Breeze, over on Fifth."

"Thank you. Are you free to talk with me?"

"I guess so. Marjorie took the car to the grocery, but—"

"You don't need to drive anyplace. I'll come there if it's okay. Fifth Street, you said. What's the number of your house? And may I have your telephone number in case I need it?" She jotted down the information. "I'll be there in five minutes."

"You sound awfully excited. Please understand, I don't want any publicity over this."

"I understand, sir. Good-bye."

Address in hand, she grabbed her purse, checking to be sure

the cell phone was in her pocket. She raced out the back door and jumped into her car.

She would call Big Bob if necessary, but first she needed to check out Earl Woodley. Sandpiper. Was he the kind of guy who chased fire engines and made crank calls? No. Her instincts told her he was for real. Everything he said made sense. And the red hair…

She careened around the curve and slammed on her brakes as the traffic light turned red. Second Street. Three blocks to go. She took a deep breath and tried to calm herself.

"It could be a fluke," she said aloud, meeting her reflection in the mirror.

Some of her hair had slid out of her ponytail and hung in gold and brown wisps around her face. It didn't matter; nothing mattered except checking this guy out.

Marty McAllister. Red hair. Christy had spotted her at the Quick Stop last week. The designer suit Marty was wearing would merit a second glance, but it was her short, bright red hair that always seemed to distinguish her from other people.

Another interminable red light stopped her at Fourth before she finally pulled into the driveway of a neat white cottage with green shutters. The grass in the small yard looked pampered, along with the lush ferns in hanging baskets on the front porch.

She tried to calm down, getting out of the car in a normal fashion, glancing at the house. The screen door opened, and a small man stepped out. She thought of his nickname, Sandpiper, and understood the reason, particularly if he hung out at the beach. He was a small man with a long nose, a rounded chest, and thin legs beneath Bermuda shorts. She guessed him to be in his sixties. She saw as she hurried up the sidewalk that the keen dark eyes looked alert and intelligent beneath brown hair shot with gray.

"Mr. Woodley?" she called to him as she reached the front steps. From a hook and chain on the front post, a life-size black silhouette of a sandpiper dangled.

"That's me. Just call me Sandpiper. Everyone else does. And you'd be Christy Castleman?"

"I am." She extended her hand to him, and he gripped it firmly, surprising her with a strength that belied his frail appearance.

"Marjorie's not back yet. Want to have a seat here on the porch?"

"Sure." She dropped into a cushioned wicker chair. "Mr. Woodley, er, Sandpiper, would you happen to know the Realtor Marty McAllister?"

"No. We just relocated from Sarasota in November to be near our son and his family."

Christy nodded, her hands clasped tightly in her lap. "Marty McAllister disappeared this past Sunday. That's the day you were out at Shipwreck Island. No one has had any contact with her. Yesterday her purse was found in the weeds at Bayside Bridge. What I'm getting at is this: Mrs. McAllister has short red hair, is in her fifties, and had some real-estate interests on Shipwreck Island."

Sandpiper had taken a seat and cocked his head to the right, where Christy could see the hearing aid. She could tell he was paying close attention to everything she said, and now as he processed the information, she wondered if he was about to tell her the woman he had seen was much younger.

He shook his head. "I'm no good at guessing age, but she was no spring chicken. Like I told you, the lady had red hair and looked upset. I figured she was angry with me for trespassing on her property."

Christy held her breath, hoping for more, but he was silent for a moment, staring at one of the ferns. Then he looked back at her.

"I suppose all you can do is go out to that house and be sure everything's all right," he concluded.

"Right. The odd thing is," she said, more to herself than to him, "I was there yesterday, and…" Her voice trailed off at the memory of Dan Brockman standing half a block from the ship house.

She focused on the man before her. "I need to phone Deputy Arnold and have you repeat what you've just told me. I'm afraid we're both obligated to do that, even if what you saw turns out to be a strange coincidence."

"I don't know. My son won't like me getting involved in something like this. Fact is, he's scolded me about going off by myself with a weak heart. But at my age, there isn't a lot left to enjoy. I like looking for treasures."

"So do I." She reached over and touched his hand. "And we can talk about treasure hunting later. Listen, I don't think your son will be upset if you help out in an important investigation." She pulled out her cell phone and began punching Big Bob's number.

"Maybe we should wait until Marjorie—"

"Hello," Big Bob shouted.

"Bob, are you in Summer Breeze? It's really important…"

An hour later Big Bob and Tommy, his assistant, were preparing to enter the front door of the ship house. Christy had refused to be left out, following them to the island after Big Bob decided Sandpiper's story had merit.

Christy parked her car in front of the house, rolled her windows down to hear what was being said, and waited.

Bob had surprised her by going over to a piece of decorative driftwood, lifting it up, and extracting a key.

"Got permission from Mrs. Thomason in Maine," he said to Tommy. "Key's gone from the real-estate office."

Christy watched Big Bob charging toward the garage first, while Tommy rang the doorbell. Then a loud *crreeaakkk* broke the stillness as Big Bob lifted the garage door.

A dark shadow…something black.

The garage door shot up, and the black car huddled like a giant cockroach. A PT Cruiser, Touring Edition, with dark tinted windows. *Marty's car!*

Fear crawled over her, cold and icy, bringing an involuntary shiver. Big Bob began to yell for Tommy, nosing around the side of the house.

Tommy ran to the front. When he saw the car, he touched the holster that held his pistol.

Bob ran to the front door, inserting another key.

Christy put a hand to her chest, pressing hard. It felt as if her heart were doing flips from her stomach to her throat and back. She sat frozen in her seat, staring at the front door. Big Bob pushed the door open and called out. Tommy hovered behind.

She held her breath, her ears straining for the sound of Marty's voice answering Bob. The only sound was the distant hum of a boat somewhere out in the water.

Then…the car moved, or did she? She felt the crisp breeze on her warm face…as the front yard surrounded her. She was halfway up the walk before her mind processed her actions. Moving on her own…toward the front door. She had promised to stay in the car, but something stronger had taken hold.

She could hear their footsteps clattering up the stairs as she paused at the front porch and inched toward the open door. Some inbred mystery-writer instinct caused her to check the lock on the door. Equipped with a split lock that was half-spring and half-deadbolt, the door locked automatically when closed. It took a key to turn the lock, or someone to turn the thumb knob inside, for the door to be opened. And yet it was possible that a professional had gotten inside, or maybe Marty had unlocked the door after she entered from the garage.

The alarm panel mounted by the door indicated the alarm had

been turned off. Had Big Bob done that? Then suddenly an odd odor began to fill her senses, seconds before Tommy lunged down the steps, heading for the car. She saw him pick up a cell phone.

She stepped into the foyer. A stairwell captured her attention first, because a jumble of books littered the stairs from top to bottom. A bookcase had been slammed between the wall and the wooden stair rail near the top step. It would have taken effort, but someone had managed to shove it sideways, splintering one of the rails. The stairs were no longer blocked if you walked sideways past the bookcase.

To her left, a great room with cathedral ceilings was partially furnished. To her right, a spacious dining room led to a huge kitchen. On the eating bar, clearly visible, she could see a Realtor's book and a silver key ring containing two keys. Keys to the house, she suspected.

But then as she turned back to the foyer, Big Bob's deep voice ricocheted off the walls and bounced down the stairwell. "Need the medical examiner and crime-scene people ASAP. I want every inch of the house and grounds covered. Yeah, we'll need pictures of the body and the house, inside and out. Looks like a sharp object sliced her jugular. I'd say robbery. She wore a lot of rings; they've been removed from her hands. No purse anywhere."

A pause. Then…

"Yeah. Could be the same MO as that doctor in Panama City last week. I don't know. But we may have a bloody footprint on a sheet of tablet paper here on the carpet."

Christy gasped into her palm, scarcely able to believe what she was hearing. Then Big Bob was rattling off directions to the house.

She grabbed the thick white frame of the door to steady herself as the sickening truth washed over her. She knew she should get out of the house, and yet a morbid curiosity pulled her up the stairs.

She sidled past the strewn books and upended bookcase. At the top of the stairs, she could see from the imprint on the carpet where the bookcase had stood. She passed two rooms, empty of furniture, as she moved toward the room at the end of the hall.

Three feet from the door, splinters of white wood littered the carpet...and then she saw the gaping hole in a two-inch-thick door. She took another step, saw the left side of the room. A small overturned desk lay on the floor just inside the door. And beyond the desk, she could see this was a child's bedroom. A double bed was covered with a Snoopy bedspread. In the center of the rumpled spread, a large white pillow lay at a careless angle. She spotted a Monopoly Junior set against the wall, and then...a tablet and pens scattered across the carpet.

Suddenly Big Bob loomed before her, looking slightly pale and glaring down at her.

"Christy Castleman, you defied my orders." He grabbed her arm and pulled her down the hall. "Watch your step," he said as they maneuvered into the narrow space between the bookcase and the wall. Then they stepped over the books scattered down the steps.

Soon they were out in the front yard, where she threw her head back and gasped for fresh air. Was it Big Bob's gruff voice or the reality of Marty's murder that started the tears flowing down her cheeks? Whatever the reason, she couldn't hold back a sob.

"If I had gone into the house the day I found the bottle and note," she said, her voice breaking, "maybe—"

"No. It was already too late."

Tears blurred her vision as she looked up at Big Bob. "I'm sorry."

"It's okay. I'm not mad at you." His voice was surprisingly gentle.

Tommy was wheezing. "It's a mess, isn't it?"

Big Bob nodded, then faced Christy. "Go home. Don't tell anyone what you've seen until the crime-scene people have finished. They'll have to vacuum, sweep, lift prints, run tests. The last thing we need is a crowd of gawkers."

"I won't say a word." Her voice was a mere whisper.

"I checked the back of the house," Tommy said. "If she'd jumped out that window, she'd have hit the concrete. With a pile of broken bones, she'd have been easy prey."

"The bolts on the window frame held threads from her green pantsuit. She may have tried to get out and couldn't. Or she changed her mind."

Christy walked slowly toward her car, ears peeled. Apparently Big Bob didn't know how far his voice carried.

"My guess is, when she entered the house, the killer either came in behind her or was already inside. He cut off her exit…so she ran up the stairs. Looks like she beat him up the steps, grabbed that bookcase, and upended it. With books flying at him and the top of the stairs blocked, it took him longer to shove a path to the second floor. She ran as far as she could go—to the end room. She closed and locked the door, but she was trapped. Didn't have her cell phone, and there was no phone in the room. She shoved that desk against the door and ran to the window, couldn't get through it."

"Then she spotted Sandpiper and started yelling to him." Tommy's voice took up the theory. "She saw him staring at her and knew she had his attention."

"He had a cell phone hooked to his belt." Big Bob was talking fast, detailing his theory in jackhammer sentences. "She saw his phone, grabbed a sheet of paper and a pencil, and wrote the note. But she couldn't throw a limp piece of paper. So she grabbed the bottle and shoved the note inside. Then threw it as hard as she could. That's why she worded the note 'Call the police. Someone is trying to kill me.' She must have hoped that between the up-ended bookcase and books and the thick door with the desk against it, she had bought enough time to get help. I imagine she was thinking the scream of a siren would run off the killer."

He sighed, slowing his pace. "Only he was faster and stronger than she realized."

"Must have been a sinking feeling when Sandpiper turned and walked off," Tommy said, standing before the open garage to stare at the car. "But it still doesn't make sense."

"Murder never makes sense to me. As for understanding what really happened, Marty can't tell us, and the killer won't."

Christy thought Bob's reasoning about what had happened sounded as logical as anything she could think of. With the bookcase upended, temporarily blocking the stairwell, and books flying, then the desk pushed against the door—a thick door— Marty hoped to stall the killer until she could think of what to do. And yet nothing had stopped him.

A siren screamed through the stillness just as she reached her car. By the time she turned the key in the ignition, a police car slid to the curb.

How, she wondered, did Big Bob expect to keep this quiet?

A few quick glances shot her way as doors flew open and police raced toward the house. Lucky for them, no other people lived here except for Buster down at the end of the island, and he wasn't likely to appear.

She stared through the window down the gravel road leading past the two open lots and on two hundred yards or so to Buster's place. Old, weather-beaten buildings loomed as an eyesore to the ship house and surrounding grounds. She could see a barn with a patched roof that probably hadn't been used in ten years, a couple of outbuildings, and through the low-hanging limbs, the outline of the small bungalow where Buster lived. In contrast, a new-looking white truck with extended cab was parked in the driveway, and a boathouse sat near the water. No sign of the boat.

Was it possible...

No, Buster wouldn't have done this. And if he had, Marty would have written "Buster" rather than "Someone."

She studied the oyster gravel, which wouldn't hold tire tracks. Even if a trail led straight to Buster's house, it would take CSI to find it. Breathing deeply, she steered the car into a wide U-turn and drove off.

She had been trembling and half-sick minutes before; now she felt completely numb as she drove home by rote. She crossed the bridge, trying not to think about the boat launch or the purse in the weeds. It was best not to think of anything other than getting home. She had promised Big Bob not to say anything or show emotion.

She pulled down the visor and glanced in the mirror. Her face looked as though it had been drained of blood. The blue eyes that always seemed too large for her face had widened to a scary stare. She snapped the visor back into place. Just ahead she saw the turnoff to her street, and a sigh of relief quivered through her. She slowed as she turned into her driveway, and her fingers trembled against the car keys as she cut the engine. If her knees shook like her hands, she'd be forced to crawl to her back door.

She thrust the door open and swung her legs around, testing her strength as she got out. Her legs held, and she hurried to the screened porch and opened the back door she hadn't bothered to lock. She stepped inside and twisted the thumb bolt. Then she came to life. Movement eased the tension, as her feet flew over the hardwood to her bedroom. She peeled off her clothes, opened the glass door to the shower, and turned on the faucets. With warm water pelting down, she stepped into the shower and reached for the soap.

After a thorough shower and shampoo, she felt better. If only she could cleanse her mind. With another towel, she enveloped her discarded pile of clothing and rolled the towel into a ball. She lifted the lid of the clothes hamper and deposited the bundle. As an afterthought, she reached under the sink for the Lysol and sprayed into the hamper.

She brushed her teeth, then gargled mouthwash. Her pink terry robe hung on the back of the door, and she pulled it on, huddling into its softness like a child enveloped in a blanket. *A Snoopy blanket...*

"Oh dear God..." It was a half-finished prayer.

With her hair turbaned, she flopped on the bed, pulling her knees to her chin. Her little community was no longer safe. A killer lurked.

She had promised Big Bob she wouldn't tell, but she simply had to speak to her dad. She grabbed the phone on the bedside table and dialed his private line.

His voice filled the wire, and immediately she felt better.

"Dad, something terrible has happened."

"I assume you mean Mrs. McAllister." When she acknowledged she did, he continued. "I just got a call from Bob. He's contacted her nephew, who wants a service as soon as the coroner releases her. How did you find out so fast?"

Christy hesitated. Obviously Big Bob hadn't mentioned that

she was at the crime scene, and her respect for him deepened. "I…saw Big Bob. Listen, Dad," she said, switching subjects, "I feel strange, and a little spooked, about finding the note."

"Thank God you did find it! If not for you, it might have been days. Christy, I want you to keep your house locked and be more aware of the people around you. I don't think anyone local did this, but we can't be sure."

"Right."

"Another thing. I just spoke to your grandmother. I'm helping with her taxes, and she needs to send some paperwork. Why don't you ride up there and spend the night with her? And you can bring back what I need."

Christy thought it was a good idea. Her phone was going to be ringing off the hook, and she didn't want to be put in the position of having to lie after her promise to Big Bob.

"Good idea. I don't think I can work on my manuscript."

"Go. You'll come back with your soul strengthened. Mom always does that for me. So have a safe trip. And bring back a jar of scuppernong jelly."

"Okay, I'll leave in half an hour. Will you call and tell her I'm on my way?"

"Gladly, and she'll be thrilled."

Christy hung up, slicked her damp hair back in a ponytail, and put on fresh clothes. After packing an overnight bag, she did a walk-through of the house, leaving on the night-lights. In her office she turned everything off, then disconnected the surge protector from the wall. She was taking no chances. While she had the latest and best devices to protect her computer, a sudden storm could wreak havoc.

She grabbed her purse, stuck her cell phone in her jeans, and remembered the charger just in time. She pulled the cord and tiny plug from the desk drawer and stuffed it in her other pocket. She had enough power now, and she could recharge the phone at Granny's. With keys in hand and the strap of her overnighter over her arm, she hurried out the back door, double-checking the lock for the first time since she'd bought the house.

Amazing what seventy-eight miles could do, Christy thought. She'd been transported into another world: a sleepy little town on the Florida-Alabama state line where citizens wound yellow ribbons around the big oaks and upheld the tradition of Decoration Day at cemeteries. She needed that world now.

Passing sand hills covered with scrub oak and stunted pines, she turned off the main highway to the 250-acre Castleman farm. Cotton fields filled her view on the right, and lush green pasture stretched to the left. She approached Cypress Lake, mirroring blue sky and white clouds. Huge cypress trees surrounded the lake; in the shallow edges, cypress knees reached up out of the water like the long necks of Loch Ness monsters. This was where her father and Aunt Dianna had grown up, and she'd heard lots of stories.

The road wound past peach and pear trees and the scuppernong arbor. Then the white frame farmhouse came into view. It was a typical farm where children and dogs had free range. The two-story house had been built tall, with a high roof to keep the rooms cool in summer. Christy glanced up at the dormer windows in the attic, recalling rainy days when she and her cousins, Beth and Angie, had played dress-up with the clothes in Granny's trunk.

She got out, dragging her possessions. The smell of frying chicken wafted through the screen door, and Christy's mouth watered. For the first time she remembered the lasagna in her microwave at home. Food had been the least of her worries, but now she had entered another world that calmed and soothed her. Here she would clear her mind and draw new strength to figure things out.

No matter how clever, a killer always left a trail. It wasn't easy to find; sometimes it seemed impossible. But she had spent years studying profiles of criminals and reading hundreds of mystery novels. There was always a clue, maybe only one, but the smart detective found it or figured it out.

From the side of the house, Lobo, Granny's brown and white German shepherd, bounded to meet her. Christy leaned down to scratch the lovable dog behind his ears. "Hey, Lobo. Are you taking care of Granny?"

He began to bark, making his best effort to communicate a yes.

Her grandmother appeared at the door, wiping her floured hands on the skirt of her apron. A huge smile creased her fair skin, bringing into play the deep wrinkles earned from seventy-one years beneath a Southern sun.

"Hi, Granny." She climbed the steps to the wide front porch with its scarred oak swing and two rockers.

"Christy, I'm so glad you came for a visit!" She was a tall woman with gray hair and sparkling blue eyes. Christy hugged her, breathing in the familiar scents of lavender sachet and good food. Unexpectedly, she felt the threat of tears.

"Do I smell fried chicken?" she asked.

"And I've made biscuits to go with the gravy. Lobo, you go on around back and check your dish."

Again, he seemed to understand. With an eager bark, he loped around the house.

"Come on, Granny. I don't want that chicken to burn."

When Christy stepped into the wide hall, she felt as though ten-pound weights had been lifted from her shoulders. She understood why her father had always seemed so solid, so unshakable as minister to his flock and guardian of his family. He had been given a rock-solid foundation here on this farm, by wonderful parents, who instilled a deep faith that stood strong and firm in the winds of circumstance.

"Supper's ready, or dinner as you call it in town. Is it too early?"

"It's never too early at your house." Christy set down her overnighter and entered the large wood-paneled kitchen. "Before I forget, Dad wants me to beg a jar of scuppernong jelly."

Granny was pouring sweet tea into tall glasses. "I have a few jars left. Here, sit down, honey." She indicated one of the ladder backs at the oak table.

Christy smiled as Granny took her seat. She did an amazing job of keeping her house and vegetable garden in order, without asking for help or appearing grumpy or melancholy about the life she spent alone.

Christy surveyed the bowls of food. "Where are the other dozen people?"

"Figured you could take some home." Her grandmother joined hands with her and lowered her head to say a blessing.

"There's nothing like coming to your house for a real meal," Christy said.

"Well, you can eat fancier in town, but if you want country cooking, you can get it here."

"And everything tastes better here."

An hour later both were seated in a wooden swing on the L-shaped back porch. Lobo nestled at their feet. It was a beautiful evening, warm for February. Christy had told Granny the entire story, beginning on the day she found the bottle and note and ending with their trip to the ship house.

Her grandmother had listened, wide-eyed, making an occasional comment. Christy chose not to elaborate on the crime scene.

"I didn't see…her. Just a corner of the room."

"Did you say that a man in Panama City was killed the same way?"

Christy hesitated. "Well, I'm not sure it was the same way. Big Bob is keeping quiet."

"Why? Looks like he'd be informing people. Maybe someone would come forward with information. Honey, it bothers me that you were inside that house. Does your dad know?"

"He'll find out eventually but not from me. You know, I think everyone who went in that house was surprised to find a child's bedroom. This was an older couple from Maine who lived alone, Granny."

As usual, her grandmother had a logical answer. "Sounds like a room designed for a grandchild."

Christy nodded. "Makes sense. Tell me what you think of this. I didn't see it, but I heard Big Bob say there was a bloody footprint on a sheet of tablet paper. He didn't mention another one, and I didn't see anything on the carpets. I'm sure the crime-analysis people will use luminol throughout the house to pick up anything that might go undetected otherwise."

"I know what luminol is. I watch *Court TV,*" Granny boasted. "I especially like the profiles and the crime-analysis part."

Christy grinned. "Then having watched units go over a crime

scene, why do you think there was only one bloody footprint? I mean, no other obvious ones."

Granny was quiet for a moment. "Tell me about that bed again."

Christy arched an eyebrow. "The bed?"

"Was it made up neat?"

Christy thought back to that moment she had approached the room. The bed had been the first thing she saw.

"No. The Snoopy bedspread was rumpled. And turned down at the head. The pillow…was tossed in the center of the bed. Are you wondering if there was a struggle, or if—"

"Did you see a sheet where the bedspread was turned down?"

Christy frowned, searching her memory. "Blue. I saw a strip of blue. A blue sheet."

"The pillow. Did it have a case on it?"

Christy's eyes widened. She could see where Granny was going now. "No, it didn't have a pillowcase."

Granny arched an eyebrow. "If nobody stripped the bed of sheets, then why take the pillowcase? Maybe the killer put his bloody shoe in that pillowcase." Granny shrugged. "It's just an idea."

"And a very good one."

"You see, having kept house for fifty years, I know something about making beds and washing sheets."

"You know something about everything."

"Except what's going on with your personal life. You got a boyfriend now?"

The abrupt change of subject took Christy by surprise. "Do I have to have a boyfriend to make me happy? No, and I'm not looking. Granny, a single gal can be happy without a male."

Granny studied Christy for a moment. "Well, I'm not current on you career gals. I guess because I married your grandfather at eighteen and spent my life as a wife and mother, I have trouble visualizing another lifestyle." She reached across and patted Christy's hand. "I just want you to be happy. That's all. And when the time is right, God will lead you to the right person."

She held her grandmother's hand and swallowed against the tightness in her throat. "Not everyone is as blessed as you. You found the right man at an early age, and the two of you lived a full, rich life. I know you had your struggles and hard times, but you certainly produced two wonderful people."

Granny smiled, although tears glistened in her blue eyes. "Not a day goes by that I don't miss your grandpa so bad I hurt all over. Why, I still turn around to tell him something. Sometimes I get so batty I put his plate on the table before I catch myself. I don't do that very often, and I sure don't tell anyone. But I keep busy. Tomorrow is my quilting day, and the next day is potluck at church."

Christy breathed a sigh of relief. Her grandmother kept busy.

She wiped her eyes. "Come on, let's cut that chocolate cake."

Later, despite the tranquillity of the house and the farm, sleep eluded her. She lay still, listening to a whippoorwill down by the lake, and she found its plaintive cry soothing rather than saddening. The soft feather bed cradled her body, and Gran's handmade quilt and duvet gave her the comfort and security she needed. But tonight her sleep was troubled by the knowledge that she had followed the sandpiper to the green bottle with no idea that Marty lay dead in the ship house.

7

Thursday, February 19

Christy had left Granny's house after an early breakfast, the backseat filled with food and a shoebox of tax receipts. The trip had worked its magic, recharging her emotional battery.

All the way back to Panama City, she thought about the murder and the crime scene. By the time she reached the building that housed the investigative unit where Sherrie worked, she had hatched a plan. She parked across the street, glancing at the clock on her dash. Exactly 12:00. Lunchtime.

For ten minutes she watched secretaries come out the front door and walk down the sidewalk. Just when she had given up on Sherrie, she popped out the door. She was tall—five feet ten—with glossy dark hair worn in a bob. A short floral skirt and a pink sweater set complemented her slim figure. Stepping quickly, she crossed the street toward the deli just three cars down from Christy.

Christy grabbed her car keys and purse and hopped out.

"Hey, Sherrie!"

"Christy! Good to see you." Sherrie waited as Christy caught up.

"I just stopped by to talk to the detective on the Summer Breeze murder."

"Sorry, the guys are out there today."

"That's okay. Listen, Sherrie, I haven't seen you in a while. Can I buy you lunch and catch up?"

"I'll have to take a rain check; I'm having lunch at my desk. Hey, are you writing another book now? Mom sent me your last mystery. Girl, you're really talented."

"Thanks." Christy fell in step with her as they entered the deli. "Speaking of your mom, she's been a great friend."

A smile lit Sherrie's face, and her dark eyes glowed, reminding Christy of Bonnie. "Yeah, Mom's great. I need to go see her and Dad."

They had reached the counter of the takeout section. Sherrie ordered a tuna sandwich with chips, while Christy asked for an iced tea to go.

"Gonna be a minute," the guy behind the counter informed them, grinning at Sherrie. "But here." He handed them paper cups. "Hit the drink machine over there while you wait."

"Thanks, Bill." Sherrie gave him the full impact of her hundred-watt smile before the two women filled their cups with ice and drinks and found a small table in the corner.

"So why do you need to talk to the detectives?" Sherrie asked.

"I just…thought of something I wanted to report concerning Marty McAllister."

Sherrie's eyes widened. "I forgot! You were out there when they found her, weren't you?" She reached over to touch her hand. "You poor girl. I'll bet you're having nightmares." Sherrie shoved a straw into the icy drink. "Mom sure is upset. Well, everyone's upset. As for this office, you can cut the tension with a butter knife after two robbery-homicides so close together."

Christy looked up from her tea. "Sherrie, you must really be overworked with all the phone calls and reports. Are they making any progress on the other robbery-homicide?"

"A little. We're pushing FDLE on some things. They've got a lot of sophisticated technology over there. And they've been real helpful already."

"But you guys have sophisticated technology here. It didn't take long to find out the fingerprints on that note belonged to Marty." She was testing her theory, and Sherrie's response proved her right.

"Yeah, but there has to be proof that Mrs. McAllister actually wrote the note. That's why we had to send it over to FDLE. They have an expert in handwriting analysis over there."

Christy nodded. "How did they find Marty's fingerprints so quickly?"

"Because Mr. Alexander is the suspicious type." Sherrie leaned in, lowering her voice. "You know him?"

"The broker at the real-estate office where she works?"

"Yeah, he requires all his employees to be fingerprinted, and their prints are kept on file. That way, when they're showing those swanky homes and condos around the Panhandle, no one from his office is likely to steal anything valuable. Isn't it tacky to even think like that?"

Christy stared at her, processing the information. "Well, he's just protecting himself and his employees in the long run, although that may sound a bit extreme. It's a good thing he had Marty's prints on file. That saved a lot of time and effort in getting a match. So has anything else come to light in the investigation?"

Sherrie hesitated. "Everything here is confidential. I can't seem to get that through Mom's head." Sherrie paused, staring at Christy. She leaned closer. "Did you see the footprint?" she whispered, glancing around the busy deli as the lunch crowd poured in.

"On the tablet paper." She remembered what she had heard from Bob as he called headquarters on his cell phone.

"From the tablet Mrs. McAllister used to write the note."

"The size of the shoe…" Christy let her voice trail off and grimaced, as though the memory was painful.

"Yeah. It was a big shoe. But the print was so smeared they can't match the sole to a type of shoe. And there weren't tracks anywhere else. Not even outside, because most of that area is gravel. But they're working on it."

As Christy listened, she realized Sherrie could be a gold mine of information if she could catch her alone. A twinge of conscience pricked her, but this was a murder that needed to be solved, and quickly.

Christy watched Sherrie carefully as she tried another approach. "It's too bad they can't get tire tracks." She stared at Sherrie, waiting to see if she was right.

"Yeah, but…" Her voice trailed as she looked toward the counter. "He's taking his time with my order," she said.

"Also, the way she was murdered." Christy whispered. "The type of weapon. That's really gruesome."

Sherrie whirled and stared at Christy. "Did you see her neck?"

Christy heaved a sigh. "I can't bear to think about it."

Sherrie put her hand to her throat, clasping it hard. "Makes me think of that awful Nicole Brown Simpson murder."

"Your takeout is ready." The guy behind the counter waved to Sherrie.

She jumped up. "I'd better get back before the detectives return."

Christy nodded. "Yeah, I should go too."

They walked to the counter and paid, then stepped into the warm sunshine.

"So"—Christy lowered her voice—"Marty's robbery and murder looks like the other one? The doctor's?"

"Same type cut, same—" Sherrie broke off. "I can't talk about this anymore."

Christy struggled not to press for details. "I know. Well, good luck, Sherrie. I'm sure you're overworked."

Sherrie smiled as though appreciating the fact that someone acknowledged her hard work.

Christy waved and hurried to her car.

On her way to Summer Breeze, thoughts buzzed in her brain like the bees around Granny's hives. Even though Granny had prepared a huge breakfast for her, Christy decided to head to Frank's restaurant. A cup of gumbo sounded good. More importantly, she had been thinking what Valerie's customer had said about a heated argument between Marty and Frank. In fact, Frank might have been one of the last people to see Marty alive.

She turned into the parking lot, grateful the lunch crowd had dispersed. Grabbing her purse, she hopped out and beeped the car locked. It was the first time she had been mindful of locking doors and casting glances over her shoulder.

As she entered the spacious driftwood lobby, she saw that Frank had added yet another decorative palm—this one a bit large for her taste, but Frank liked doing things in a big way. His taste in décor didn't matter to his customers; it was the taste of his food that brought people in from all over the Panhandle.

Only a few diners lingered in the main dining room. Hattie stood at the coffee station, pouring herself a cup while chatting quietly with a waitress Christy didn't recognize.

"Hey there, Mystery Writer!" Frank entered the dining room hoisting a platter of appetizers. "Take a seat. I'll send Jamie right over." He hurried toward a table where two businessmen were seated.

"Thanks, Frank." She found a small table in a quiet corner.

"Hi, there." A slim woman in her midtwenties with a thin face and brown ponytail handed Christy the lunch menu. "Would you like something to drink before you order?" she asked in a soft-spoken voice.

"Hi…Jamie." Christy read the name on the small brass name-plate attached to her yellow shirt. "I don't remember seeing you before."

"I'm new in town," she said, her eyes skipping over Christy's shoulder, then back to her face. "I just moved here three weeks ago."

"My name's Christy Castleman. Welcome to Summer Breeze, Jamie."

"Thanks." The tight smile began to relax.

"Grant Castleman, the pastor at Community Church, would be disappointed if I didn't invite you to church," Christy said.

The young woman stared at her, obviously puzzled.

Christy smiled. "He's also my father. But seriously, our congregation is a wonderful, caring group of people, and we'd love to have you visit."

Jamie's brown eyes lit up. "Is there a good children's program there? I have two boys, six and eight, and I'm a single mom."

Christy nodded. The single-mom population seemed to be expanding. "We have a great children's program. In fact, my mom teaches the eight-year-olds. And I've heard her say there are more boys than girls in that class, so I'm sure your older son would feel at ease."

"That sounds nice. But I'll have to wait for a paycheck so I can buy some clothes."

"You don't have to do that. The only time people our age get dressed up is Easter and Christmas. Everyone dresses casually, and the kids wear jeans."

"Really?" Jamie looked pleased for half a second, then glanced nervously toward the kitchen. "Well, I'll leave you to study the menu."

"No need. I already know I want a cup of gumbo."

"Good choice. And to drink?"

Christy was still floating from all the coffee and tea she had consumed at Gran's house. "Just bring me water with a slice of lemon, please."

"Coming up," Jamie said, hurrying off to the kitchen.

Frank appeared at Christy's table, an extra-large mug of coffee in his broad hand. "Christy, how's it going?" he asked, pulling back a chair and settling down.

"Okay, Frank. What about you?"

"Can't complain." He placed his mug on the table, then crossed muscular arms shadowed with dark hair. He wore a larger version of the canary yellow shirt his employees wore, and the color accented his olive skin and black hair.

"Heard about Marty." He shook his head, his dark eyes sad. "Awful thing. Marty was here on Sunday. Sat right over there." He pointed to an empty table. "Ate a seafood salad and Key lime pie. Coffee, as always."

"Did you talk with her, Frank?" Christy asked.

"Not for long. She was all fired up about selling a beach house in Destin."

Christy leaned forward. "Frank, I want to ask you something. Someone saw you having an argument with Marty out in the parking lot."

He looked surprised, then slowly he began to nod. "That's right. I went back to the kitchen to talk to the cook about the dinner menu. When I came out, Marty had paid her bill and headed out the door." He hesitated. "I'd heard some bad stuff about that Miami guy. In fact, she brought him in for lunch the last time he was in town."

He shook his head. "When she introduced him—name was Ridge Cohen—I had a bad feeling about him. Made a phone call to a guy who lives in Miami but owns a condo at Summer Breeze. He eats here whenever he's in town. I asked him about this Cohen, and he'd heard of him. Fact is, lotta people have heard of him. Rumor is, one of his ships was confiscated with cocaine on board. He was *real* popular at South Beach."

"Really?" She wondered why Big Bob had been so mum about that.

"I caught up with Marty. Told her what I'd heard and that she'd better be careful. You don't mess with people like that. She flew into a rage, told me to mind my own business and stay out of hers. Then she hopped into her PT Cruiser and tore out of the parking lot."

"Did you tell Big Bob?"

He nodded. "I'm sure the investigators are looking into it." He lowered his gaze to the thick black brew in his mug. He seemed to be thinking about something, and for a moment she wondered if there had been something romantic between Frank and Marty. They were both in their fifties, and Marty ate here often, even brought real-estate prospects.

"I didn't know her that well," Christy began cautiously. "Did you?"

Frank shrugged his large shoulders. "No better than most folks. I asked her if she'd like to take in one of the clubs in Panama City. But she was always busy."

"Frank, you heard about that doctor in Panama City who was killed last week?"

"Yeah, I heard." He looked at Christy with new curiosity. "You know anything about it?"

"Not really. Do you think whoever killed him also robbed and killed Marty?"

A deep frown settled over Frank's forehead as he thought it over. Then his face relaxed, and he shook his head. "Nah. That just seems too far-fetched to me."

"Yeah, it may be. Frank, I heard she was seeing a guy who owned a nice boat. Have you heard anything about that?"

Frank began to nod. "Don't know who it was. She just said that she was going out on a terrific boat with some guy. Anyway,

Marty reminded me of a hummingbird darting around, always lookin' for the red juice—or the green stuff, as in big bucks. That's why I never had a chance."

Christy looked around the spacious restaurant. "You've done all right for yourself, Frank."

He shrugged, glancing over his shoulder. "Yeah. I had to work hard to get here, though."

Christy nodded. "When she left here that day, do you remember what time it was or if she made a left or right turn?"

He stared into space for a moment, thinking. "Big Bob already asked me that. I can't say for sure. She musta left a little after one. And I didn't notice which way she turned. I went back through the kitchen door. Like I said, it was a Sunday, and we were busy."

Jamie returned with a steaming bowl of gumbo and a frosty glass of iced water with lemon. She smiled briefly at Christy, glanced at Frank, then disappeared.

"I can always depend on your gumbo to taste great." Christy's appetite had diminished at the mention of Marty's name. Still, with Frank sitting at the table, she tried to look enthusiastic. She picked up the soup spoon and dipped into the gumbo. "How do you always keep the quality of your food consistent?"

He leaned forward, peering into the gumbo. "I'm a perfectionist, Christy. You being an educated woman probably had psychology in college. You know about the Type A personality—that's me. Gotta be on top of everything. Comes from my upbringing."

Hoping to divert her thoughts from Marty, she began to eat, focusing her attention on Frank. "What was it like being raised in the Bronx, Frank?"

He leaned back in the chair, draining his mug of coffee. "It was rough!" Coffee breath wafted across the table. "Would you believe I was the runt of the neighborhood? Used to sell everything from shoeshines to Christmas trees down on the corner. Had to fight for my spot. And lost the fight more than once."

"You?" Christy arched a brow. "I can't picture you as the runt of the neighborhood, or ever losing a fight."

"Well, I did. But when I got to be about twelve years old, I had a growth spurt. Didn't stop growing till I was eighteen. Then I went back and whipped every one of those sleazebags who beat me up when I was kid."

She looked up from her soup, startled. "You didn't really."

"I did." He gave a nod of satisfaction. "I got even." He shook his head. "I hated that place, woulda done anything to get out. And I did."

"Which part do you mean? You got out, or you did something to get out?"

He leaned back in the chair and laughed. "Both. But there you go with that sharp brain of yours. I'm always afraid to say much, afraid you'll put it in a book." He glanced toward the kitchen. "I don't hear pots and pans rattling back there, so I'd better go check 'em out. You take care of yourself. And stay out of Big Bob's business."

Christy had to smile. "Why does everybody keep telling me that?"

"Because you're our famous mystery writer. And you gotta snoop around a little to get your scoops. Take care," he said. "That could get dangerous." The friendly wink was missing; he looked alarmingly serious.

Christy tried to resurrect her appetite, but it was useless. Marty's death kept nagging her.

"Do you need anything else?" Jamie had slipped up quietly and was looking intently at Christy.

"No, thank you. I can't even finish this. I'll take my ticket, though."

"Come back," she said, placing a ticket on the table.

"I will. I'm a regular. And I'll look for you at church," Christy said, reaching into her purse.

"Thanks." Jamie hurried off.

Watching her for a moment, Christy was pretty sure she wouldn't be seeing Jamie at church, but then you could never tell. People did things for their children that they wouldn't do for themselves.

She left a generous tip and paid the bill. She was walking out the door, her head lowered as she rummaged in her purse for car keys.

"Hi."

Dan Brockman caught her by surprise. He stood on the third step, she on the fourth, and yet he was still taller than she. He was wearing dark jeans and a blue denim, button-down shirt that complemented his tanned skin and deep blue eyes.

"Hi." She smiled, met his gaze for another second or two, and then started to move on.

"You must be in a big hurry," he called to her as she brushed past him down the steps.

"I am," she answered, reaching the walk. She felt a compelling urge to run each time she saw him, and yet she didn't want to appear rude.

"Then I won't keep you. Just wanted to say how much I enjoyed *The Secret of Blackbeard's Treasure*."

"Why, thank you." She hesitated, realizing he must have bought the book and read all three hundred pages in two days.

"I agree with the good reviews. I can hardly wait to read the next one."

As he spoke, she studied him carefully. There was an intenseness about him that led her to believe he listened and cared about everything.

"Thanks. Glad you enjoyed the book. Which reminds me, I'd better run. I'm fighting a deadline on this one."

"Well, don't let me keep you. However, I'd love to talk with you about your writing sometime. Too bad you're in a rush. Maybe we could meet for coffee before your class this evening."

She tried to remember if she had told him she taught a class tonight or if that's when he took his class. For a moment she entertained the idea, but then she knew she had to refuse. "Sorry. I just don't have an extra hour to spare until I finish this book."

He nodded. "I understand."

She knew he didn't, that he thought she was merely giving him the brush-off. He seemed like a nice guy, and he had bought and read her book. Even said he liked it. That scored big points with her. She felt compelled to explain further.

"I only have a few days to finish the manuscript, and I'm behind. I'll probably be typing until ten minutes before my class tonight."

He nodded and grinned, and immediately she felt better, although she wasn't sure why his believing her was that important. After all, he was still a stranger, even if he had read her book. And yet something about his eyes nagged at her again, making her think she had met him—no, not met him—had seen him somewhere before that day at Shipwreck Island. It had to be at night school.

"Tell you what," he said, "when you put that manuscript in the mail, maybe you'll let me treat you to dinner. You do have to eat," he said, glancing toward the restaurant door she had just exited.

"Yes, I do." She smiled, liking him in spite of herself. "So maybe I'll see you then. In the meantime, good luck on your project." The ship house was the focus of his project; in fact, she had seen him near the house right before Marty's body was found. "Hey, are you aware that the house you were using as a project is now a murder scene? The day I saw you, if you remember, I mentioned a woman was missing. She was found in that house."

He shoved his hands in his pockets and nodded. "Yeah. In fact, when I went out there this morning, the house was cordoned off with yellow tape marked Crime Scene. A big unfriendly guy let me know he didn't want anyone prowling around."

She suspected the big unfriendly guy was Bob.

"Did you know the lady?" he asked, concerned.

"Not well. Listen, I gotta run. Maybe we can talk later."

"Sure."

Hurrying to her car, she thought about his invitation to dinner. She had promised herself to move forward with her life, but that would have to be after she finished her manuscript. Right now she had enough going on to make her half-nuts. He was giving all the signs of someone who was interested. Did that interest have anything to do with the ship house and Marty? Or was he honestly interested in talking about writing? People were always wanting to write a story; everyone seemed to have one. This guy, she would guess, might have more than one.

8

Christy was in work mode: computer humming, file of the mystery novel opened to the ending she was about to write, and a cup of coffee half-full in her Mystery Lady mug.

But work mode wasn't working. She stared at the blank screen, her mind stalled. Her gaze kept sneaking to the icon for the Internet. Despite her intense battle to stay focused on her novel, her overactive curiosity surged forward and won the skirmish. She pointed the mouse to the icon, zipped to the Internet, and in seconds was pulling up back issues of the Panama City newspapers.

Scrolling back to Sunday's newspaper two weeks earlier, she tried to find an account of Dr. Peter Stewart's murder. A frown puckered her brow in concentration. Had the robbery-murder not even made the front page? Now she'd have to go back and—

Her eyes widened at a front-page story with a photo, and as she read the caption, she caught her breath. She was not looking at a strange face but rather a familiar one, the face of Dan Brockman wearing a military uniform. This was the picture she must have glimpsed at some point, which explained why he looked familiar. True, he looked quite different in military dress with a serious expression on his face, and yet there was no doubt about the intense eyes and the shape of the face.

The caption read: "Major Daniel Brockman, one of the officers in Red Dawn, the operation that captured Saddam Hussein, now making his home in the area."

She leaned forward, reading with fascination the brief account of how Major Brockman of Operation Red Dawn had been one of the soldiers who brought the infamous Saddam out of his obscure rathole on December 13, 2003.

> Major Brockman, after completing eight years with the U.S. Army, has chosen to become a civilian once again and is spending time with his parents, retired General Joseph H. Brockman and his wife, Ginny. We are honored to have this hero in our area, if only for a short while.

"Well, Major Dan Brockman, excuse me!" Christy said, studying the picture once again.

She recalled what he had said about being out of touch the past year. The short military haircut, the in-shape, athletic build, and the quick reflexes and keen observation should have tipped her off—if she had remembered the newspaper article. She glanced at the date of the newspaper.

She stared into space, thinking. She had gone up to celebrate Granny's birthday. She must have seen the front page of the paper through the glass window of the newspaper box at the service station when she filled up with gas.

She turned in her chair and gazed at her bookshelf. One of the small flags everyone was buying and displaying leaned out from a tiny vase. All her life she had been patriotic. She got goose bumps just hearing the national anthem, and she was, indeed, proud to be an American. She felt enormous respect for the men and women who served in the military, making great sacrifices to keep America free.

Pride swelled in her chest when she thought of how Dan had served his country. Then pride turned to embarrassment when she thought of how she had brushed aside his polite attempts to ask her out.

So…maybe after she finished her novel, she'd get back on that self-improvement kick she'd been thinking about. For starters, she would quit being so defensive—her mother was quick to point out that flaw. In retrospect, Seth did have a point about her fear of loss.

She turned back, focusing on the computer screen and the newspaper photo. She had been looking up an account of the Dr. Stewart robbery. It should be here somewhere, because he was killed on the previous Saturday night.

Her eyes drifted to the clock, and she gasped. She had to be at school in exactly one hour; actually, it was an hour and a half until the class began, but she had to make some copies in the main office, and she needed to stop by the library.

A nagging voice in her brain reminded her that another day had come and gone without progress on her novel. Well, she'd dig in tomorrow. She always worked better under pressure, didn't she? Hopping up from the computer, she dashed to the bathroom to take a shower.

She stepped out of the copy room, her arms loaded with handouts, and headed toward her classroom. As she turned a corner, she met Dr. Clayton.

"Christy! Here, let me help you. That top page is sliding off."

"Oh, thanks."

She smiled at the tall man, the proverbial beanpole with intelligent eyes and a helpful nature beneath his reserve. Unlike the other faculty members, who dressed casually, he usually wore a suit and tie. He was from Chicago but had spent some time in Colorado, just as she had. That gave them something to talk about in the break room as they sipped pop from the machine.

"By the way," she said, as he was about to leave her classroom, "I wanted to ask you about someone who's taking a night class in architecture."

He didn't seem surprised by her question. In fact, he was very open and easy in conversation. "Who is it?"

"Dan Brockman."

"Oh, sure. I know Dan. His mother plays bridge with my wife. What exactly did you want to know about him?"

She hesitated, then decided to be honest. "He asked me out."

"Go," he was quick to reply.

"I don't really know him."

He studied her thoughtfully. "Well, I don't know him that well. I know he's in that architecture class, and he seems like a gentleman."

Something occurred to her. "Are they working on some special project?"

"They're always working on a project. That's the object of the class. Find a structure that interests you, draw up a plan... I'm not sure about all of that, Christy. I could ask Jim."

"No!" She cleared her throat, trying not to sound so emphatic. "I wouldn't want you to do that."

He nodded. "I understand. Well, I believe people should make their own choices. Gotta run now." And he was out the door.

Choices. There was that word again, the word that kept tripping her up.

She shook herself out of an empty stare and headed for the library. She needed to be sure that *Writers' Market* was still in the reference section. She was going to advise her students—the ones who were serious about getting published—to study the various publishing houses to learn the type of material they published and their requirements for submission. Most would go to a bookstore and buy a copy, but those on a strict budget would need to review the book in the library.

Entering the library, she spotted Dan sitting alone at a table in the back. She hesitated, weighing her options. She could veer right toward the reference section, where a wall of bookcases blocked his view of her. There she could quickly scan for the reference book, then scoot back out the door.

Or…she could speak to him. After what Dr. Clayton had told her, she thought she should at least say hello. Or she thought she *wanted* to say hello.

She stood up straighter, taller, with the help of her three-inch navy sling-backs. She checked her outfit: soft red turtleneck, navy khakis. Both freshly dry-cleaned. She'd twisted her hair up in a little knot on the back of her head and brushed some golden wisps around her face. She had decided to pay more attention to her appearance in her new campaign to improve herself.

Thrusting her hands in her pants pockets, she sauntered over to his table. "Hi," she said.

He looked up, his eyes slightly glazed, like one who is completely absorbed in a book. He blinked, and then a slow grin began to form. "Hi."

"I…" She glanced around the library, where only a few people sat at tables, poring over books. "I've had my head buried in a computer. I didn't read the newspaper article about you until today when I was going back through the paper looking for something else. Thanks for being a good soldier."

He seemed to be thrown off balance for a moment. "There are a lot more around. I'm just an ordinary guy now."

I don't think so, she thought but didn't say.

"What time is your class over?" he asked.

"I usually finish around nine. What time is yours over?"

"About that time. Don't guess you'd want to have a cup of coffee afterward? Or tea?"

She remembered her promise to herself to get back on the horse that had thrown her. "There's a great little place on the edge of campus. Wonderful teas and coffees."

"Sounds good to me."

"Well," she glanced at the wall clock, "I have a class in five minutes."

"Want me to come by your room when I get out?" he asked.

"Sure," she replied, trying to look and sound casual as she turned and strolled over to the reference section.

This wasn't a date, she told herself. Peach tea and conversation. She'd allot herself fifteen minutes, maybe thirty, and then head home.

—

Paula, the friendly hostess, led them to a back booth and handed them menus. When Dan's head was lowered, Paula caught Christy's eye and quickly gave her a big thumbs-up.

Dan looked up from the menu. "Are you sure you only want something to drink? We could have a hamburger or something better."

"If you'd like a hamburger, go ahead. I happen to be a great fan of their ice-cream cakes. Particularly the Oreo cookie cake."

He grinned, closing his menu. "I've always been a sucker for Oreos, so why not?"

Her eyes lingered for a second as her mind registered the fact that this guy was witty, charming, and intelligent, and it would be easy to like him. Maybe like him a lot.

A smiling waitress took their order and hurried off.

"So you're a local hero," she said, a smile playing over her lips.

"Everyone who serves his country is a hero."

"Tell me about it. I mean, the part about going into that hole and bringing him out."

He leaned back in his chair, assessing her with a cool expression. "Are you going to use this in a novel?"

"No! I'm just patriotic, and I love patriotic stories."

He took a deep breath and stared out at the neon lights. "I was with the Fourth Infantry. We'd been working in extreme heat along the Tigris when we got our orders. Based on intelligence, we'd been covering his home area, then got a lead on the farmhouse. We searched it and found no one. Just a tumbled-up little place. But then…" He paused as the waitress delivered coffee. "We searched the area and found a rug lying out on the ground. When we lifted the rug, we found a piece of Styrofoam and under the Styrofoam the bunker."

"And?" She was totally mesmerized by the story, scarcely aware of the luscious ice-cream cake being placed before them.

"He was cowering down in his rathole. When he identified himself, I recalled what I had read and heard about him. Here was the man who had vowed to fight to the death." He shook his head, his disgust apparent. "I thought of all his followers who had died by that creed."

He sighed. "That was it. We took him prisoner."

Christy let out the breath she had been holding. "And there was dancing in the streets and praise for our soldiers. I saw it on television. So what made you decide to get out of the service?"

"My time was up, and I had to make a decision. I felt I had served my country as best I could for eight years, but I didn't want a military life. My father was military, and we moved all over the country. I'm not complaining," he added quickly, sipping his coffee. "It's just not what I want for myself or the family I hope to have someday."

"Do you think you'll stay in this area?"

The blue eyes deepened. He seemed to take every question seriously, which was, of course, what people should do. Some people tossed out easy answers; this guy took his time. "I like it here. In fact, I've been looking at property. I'd like to invest in something of my own."

"You'd had enough of the battle lines?"

He looked out toward the streetlights, then back at her, and the deep blue eyes lost their twinkle. "Yeah. I lost one of my closest friends over there," he said, his voice low.

He was no stranger to sorrow; they had that in common, in a different way, of course.

"I'm sorry about your friend," she said gently.

"Thanks. I'll move on to a more pleasant subject. When we crossed the border, it was like stepping back into the twenty-first century. I remember stopping in the middle of the sidewalk to stare at an American car, and then I saw an ice-cream store down the block, and I felt like a kid again. Ran down there and ordered a double scoop of chocolate chip."

They laughed together, and then he looked at their desserts, still untouched. "Do you realize we're ignoring this Oreo thing?"

She took a deep breath and smiled at him. "What a shame. No more questions from me."

"Then it's my turn. Tell me about yourself. I know that you're a writer, you teach a class, and that you are pleasant company. What about family?"

She sampled the ice-cream cake, enjoying the rich flavor. "Well," she began, "my father is a minister here, and my mother owns a gift shop—the Treasure Chest. I have one brother, Seth, who has gone to Australia in search of himself."

He grinned. "Is he having any luck with the search?"

"From our late-night conversations, I'd say no. He's met a Swedish gal named Ingrid, and they're busing tables."

He tilted his dark head to the side, studying her from a different angle. "Do I detect a note of cynicism?"

"You do." She sighed, fighting the usual exasperation when she thought of her younger brother. "Seth is…a work in progress. He's very bright, and I think he's wasting a good mind." A grin broke through her frustration when she thought of one of Seth's antics. "He's also funny, and I miss his wit. And he's shy and overly sensitive. I guess that almost sums him up. Of course, it's easy for me as the big sister to see his mistakes. I tend to forget I've made a few."

"Seth sounds like my kid brother, Max, except for the sensitive part. Max is about as subtle as an elephant and is well on his way to weighing as much. Obviously, I'm exaggerating, but he does like to eat. And he's your typical couch potato. Drives Dad crazy. Dad has never been one to sit still for long, but since retirement he's channeling his energy into jogging and playing golf."

He paused, taking another bite of ice cream. "I shouldn't be bashing Max. I've gained almost ten pounds. If Mom doesn't quit plying me with her good food, I'll be giving Max a run for his money."

"Then you must have been thin when you got home," Christy

answered too quickly, then concentrated on her cake. He looked great to her just as he was now. She moved to a different subject. "What type of job does Max have?"

"He's going back to school to get his master's at FSU–Panama City."

"Good for him."

"Well, it's his third go at it, but maybe this time…"

Christy got the picture, but Dan smiled as he spoke those words, and she smiled back.

For a moment, neither spoke as they looked at one another. Christy broke the eye contact and glanced at her watch.

"I should go," she said.

He didn't respond. He seemed to enjoy her company.

"Could I ask you something?" He leaned forward. "If I'm being too personal, you can say so. But I was wondering if you're seeing anyone now."

She shook her head. "No."

Although he was a hard one to read, she sensed that he relaxed just a bit.

"Then remember when you turn in that manuscript, I'm offering dinner at the best restaurant. You even get to choose the place."

"Thanks. I'll keep that in mind." She opened her purse, but he reached forward and stilled her hand. "I've got it."

Glancing at the check, he pulled several bills out of his wallet and dropped them on the table.

Servers must love him, she thought, as they walked out of the restaurant and headed for their cars. Across the parking lot, she saw Roy Thornberry, the forty-something owner of the *Courier.* The guy who drove her nuts. He was a small man with dark hair and narrow-set black eyes. He reminded her of the old cartoon with the Tasmanian devil. He was everywhere, like a chain saw out of control. Christy wondered if he ever slept or, when he did, how he managed to shut down his active mind.

"Christy!" he called, then reached into the backseat and grabbed a file. He flung a few words at Andrea, his wife, who waited in the car. Then, file in hand, he trotted across the parking lot.

"I just heard…" He paused, his eyes sweeping Dan Brockman. "Major Brockman," he shifted the file to his left hand and extended his right. "It's an honor to meet you. I'm Roy Thornberry. Sorry to say, I never served my country, so I thank you for representing us."

Dan's eyes seemed to measure and categorize Roy in the space of a few seconds as he shook his hand. "Thank you, Roy. It's a pleasure to meet you."

Roy's eyes shot from Dan to Christy, obviously putting together that he might be intruding on a date. But Roy was never one to follow etiquette when something as important as a breaking story filled his world. He obviously had something important on his mind from the way he was nervously shifting from one foot to the other, as though he had an itch he couldn't scratch.

Roy leaned in, speaking low. "Christy, I'm putting an article together for the paper on Marty's murder. Think you could stop by first thing in the morning and look it over? Oh, and here's the picture I'm using."

He opened the file and moved under the nearest streetlight. Christy and Dan followed. She turned to Dan, intending to roll her eyes in apology for Roy's intrusion. But she saw that Dan's eyes had widened at the picture, and a frown creased his forehead. She wondered what he was thinking.

Turning back to the picture, she saw it was a black-and-white of Marty that seemed to be an enlargement of the composite of her on her business cards.

"That's the right one to use," she said. A vivid memory flashed through her mind: the day she had entered the ship house, fearing that Marty's body would be inside. And it was. She felt weak, and Dan, standing beside her, seemed to sense it. His hand slipped around her waist, steadying her, and she could feel his eyes on her face. She was sure he had noticed the change in her.

"Good!" Roy was all business. "See you in the morning, then? Around eight?"

Christy tried not to show her irritation. Of course she wanted to help, but why did he have to start so early?

"Are you running an early issue? I mean, this is only Thursday."

"And the paper doesn't come out until next week, I know. But I'm thinking of doing a special edition. This is the first time we've had this sort of thing in our community. Well, in the years that I know about," he added, glancing at Dan. "Sorry if I'm coming off as an insensitive news hound, but frankly, that's what I am."

Christy had to laugh. "He's right," she said, looking at Dan.

Everything about Dan's expression remained pleasant, unchanged to anyone who didn't know him. And she didn't know him that well. But the time she had spent with him had earned her one bit of insight: he had changed inwardly. While he was pleasant to Roy as they said good-bye, there was a firm set to his facial expression, a tenseness not present before. Character study was a part of her work, and she had been gifted with good instincts about people. She decided to test her suspicion.

As Roy's quick steps faded over the pavement, she looked up into Dan's face. "What's wrong?" she asked.

He didn't seem surprised that she had read him.

"I had a little disagreement with that woman who was killed." He was staring at Roy and Andrea as they disappeared through the door of the restaurant.

"You did? But you never said—"

"I didn't know her name. The first time I went over to Shipwreck Island, I spotted the ship house and parked my car in front of it. As I was getting out to study the house, a black PT Cruiser whipped into the parking space in front of me. This little redhead jumped out and asked if I'd like to see the house. Told me she had just listed it but hadn't yet put up her sign. She was about to introduce herself when I shook my head and said 'No, thanks.' I wasn't in the mood for an aggressive Realtor, and that's what I judged her to be."

He took a deep breath and released it slowly. "She seemed to take offense and told me that I obviously hadn't read the No Trespassing sign on the property. Which I hadn't. I apologized, but she came back with something sarcastic." He shrugged. "I don't remember how I answered her, but it's accurate to say we parted on unfriendly terms."

Christy stared at him, troubled by this information. Had she told him Marty was a Realtor or described her? She didn't think so, and yet it seemed odd that he was just now putting it together.

"Christy, I noticed that you seemed a little upset when you looked at the picture."

"Yeah," she said, lowering her eyes to the pavement as they headed toward their cars. "I…" She bit her lip and sighed.

"Want to talk about it?"

She reached into her purse and pulled out her key ring, hitting the button that automatically unlocked her car. No, she didn't want to talk about it.

"It's just a troubling thing," she said. "As Roy told you, we've never had anything like this in our community."

He nodded slowly, studying her face. "I'm sorry," he said softly.

"Well." She paused. "Thanks for the dessert. And the conversation. I'm sorry we ran into Roy." She was hoping for a lighter mood, but it wasn't working for her or for him.

"Me, too," he said, watching her carefully as she slid in behind the wheel, then closing the door for her. "See you soon, I hope."

She smiled again as she started her car and pulled out, waving to him. In her rearview mirror, she could see him standing in the parking lot, watching her drive out of sight. Leaning back against the seat, she stared at the car lights along the beach highway that ran past high-rise hotels and condos. This was one of those times when she would drive home on autopilot, not really seeing anything along the way as her mind lapsed deep in thought.

Why was she troubled about Dan's running into Marty? From what he had described of their meeting, Marty's behavior was typical. She never wasted her time on anyone who didn't spell SALE when it came to her listings. And yet…it seemed odd that he had gone back near the house again after being warned that he was trespassing. But, she reminded herself, he had parked half a block away. Still, he had seemed so calm about being there, as though he had no fear of the little tyrant of a Realtor showing up to chase him away. Maybe if she showed up again, he was going to pretend an interest in buying the house. Or maybe he did have an interest in the house. He certainly seemed fascinated with it. There was no other house like it.

The night breeze rolled in off the Gulf, crisp and clean, working its magic on her nerves. A few more deep breaths and the knot in her stomach began to dissolve.

She decided to push aside her writer's obsession with clues and puzzle pieces that didn't fit. She had taken a step toward a goal she had set for herself: be open to dating again. The Canadian Snowbirds were always referring to spring breakup, when the ice melted and the streams began to flow. That's the way she was feeling tonight: Something frozen inside her was thawing out; numbed feelings were coming back to life. Once again, she felt the promise of spring.

She wasn't sure if it was because she had been with Dan Brockman or if it was knowing she could be with someone who really interested her and have a good time. She had laughed with Dan about their brothers and felt her eyes lock into his as their mood ranged from humorous to serious, depending upon the conversation. A strong chemistry simmered between them, and this surprised her. Dan Brockman was different. He challenged her intelligence and her wit, and she liked that; in fact, she'd have to stay on her toes just to keep up with him.

Even though it was after eleven, she was still too wired to sleep when she got home. It occurred to her that she had gotten sidetracked by locating Dan among the past issues of the newspapers on the Internet. She had never found the account of the doctor who had been robbed and killed shortly before Marty's murder.

Kicking off her heels, she hurried down the hall to her office and flipped the light switch. The computer was in sleep mode, but she quickly brought it to life and resumed her search through the

Panama City newspapers. She found the story of Dr. Peter Stewart's murder on the second page following Dan's story.

Carefully she read the article. His murder had happened late Saturday night in the parking lot of a popular restaurant known for good seafood. It was a large restaurant, and of course the parking lot was huge. His rental car had been parked in a far corner, away from the light. An interview with his server indicated that Stewart was wearing a gold Rolex and a gold ring with diamonds arranged in a star. Both were missing along with his wallet when he was found dead around midnight. He had ordered the most expensive dish on the menu and left a very generous tip, according to his server.

> Since Dr. Stewart's jewelry and wallet were missing,
> investigators believe that robbery was the motive for
> the murder.

The article went on to say the restaurant staff as well as the patrons that evening were being questioned, and all leads were being investigated.

The account of the murder told her nothing more than she had already heard. Strange, she thought, that the type of weapon was not mentioned, but she knew it was a sharp instrument. A knife, Sherrie had hinted. That made sense. No one would use a gun in such a public place. What about someone in the kitchen who would have access to all sorts of knives? What if the server mentioned the Rolex and diamond ring to his co-workers? It would be simple for that person to slip out the back door during a smoke break when Dr. Stewart headed for his car.

But could the investigators tie that person to Marty?

She picked up the phone and called Valerie, who was a night owl. She'd start by apologizing for not getting back to the salon, then move on to the question she had concerning Marty.

Valerie answered on the second ring. Her voice sounded funny.

"I'm sorry. Did I wake you?"

"No, I was lying on the sofa watching a movie. Trying to get my mind off Marty."

Since Valerie had gotten to the heart of the matter, Christy asked her question. "Do you know if Marty ate at the restaurant where Dr. Stewart was killed?"

"I don't know if she ate there that particular night, but I know it's one of her favorite places. She told me their seafood was better than Frank's, because they used mesquite for their grilled fish. You know Marty; she had to have the best. Do you think there's a connection?"

"I just read the account of Dr. Stewart's murder behind the restaurant. Don't really have any news or inside information."

"I haven't heard anything other than what I told you before: one of my customers had eaten there earlier. I'll try to find out more when she comes back in next week."

"Thanks, Valerie. Good night."

Neither had mentioned that Christy hadn't returned to Valerie's shop, but when news of Marty's murder broke, everything else was forgotten.

Leaning back in the chair, she stretched her arms over her head and tried to dredge up a yawn. No use. She wasn't sleepy. Pressing her head against the back of her tall desk chair, her mind rolled through the events of her day: her conversation with Sherrie, her conversation with Frank, her class, and the hour she had spent with Dan. Then she recalled Roy's untimely intrusion.

He wanted her at the newspaper office at eight o'clock.

She grimaced and began to shut down the computer, but her mind jumped back to the conversation with Sherrie. What had she taken away from that conversation? A knife was the weapon. A shoe print, which she already knew about. A large shoe size… Who wore a large shoe and knew Marty? And if Marty knew that person, had opened the door to him, why hadn't she identified him in the note? What if the homeless man had forced his way into her car and made her drive out to the island? After all, he claimed to have found the purse at the bridge. It wasn't that far…

Marty had been alone in the car when she passed the Pancake House. But then…she had almost wrecked at the red light. Was she trying to attract attention? Was the homeless man cowering on the floorboard, forcing her to drive back to the house? Did he hold a knife on her? Even so, couldn't she have done something to save herself? Why had she driven into the garage and gotten out with him? Of course, the part of the puzzle that fit was that she had written "someone" on the note. She wouldn't have known the man's name.

And if this was not the scenario, why had she gone back to the house when she had an appointment in Destin?

She had gone back to show the house. Why else would she delay her trip to Destin? Or… She stopped in the hallway, her eyes wide. She remembered what Frank had told her about the guy from Miami. He sounded dangerous. Had she spoken with this Ridge Cohen and persuaded him to drive over to Shipwreck Island to see the ship house? That would explain why she was headed east when Thelma saw her in front of the Pancake House.

"That's it," she shouted, snapping her fingers. She whirled, looking at the clock. She needed to talk to Big Bob, but if the phone roused him from a deep sleep or started one of those five kids yelling, he would never listen to her theories about the pillowcase and the guy from Miami who had driven up to this area to buy a house.

Then another thought struck her, and she shook her head, sighed, and headed to her bedroom. She seemed to be playing this entire scenario on the assumption that the detectives were not pursuing the obvious leads. Of course they were. She would sound like an idiot telling them things they had already considered.

She reached her bedroom and flopped onto the bed. Her dad was right. She'd better leave the detective work to the authorities, who knew what they were doing. Bone-tired weariness began to creep through her as she set the alarm for seven so she'd have time to shower and dress before meeting Roy at the newspaper office at eight.

She squinted at the clock. That would be in exactly seven hours. She undressed and slipped on her T-shirt nightie. Turning out the light on the nightstand, she snuggled under her covers and sighed.

She was almost asleep when Dan Brockman's face appeared in the twilight of her mind. She sighed with contentment. If only he didn't seem too good to be true.

9

Friday, February 20

She was not in the best of moods when she spun gravel in the parking lot of the small modern building that housed the *Courier*. She saw Roy's sports car parked out front, along with Big Bob's SUV. Her eyes snapped open wide as she stared at the SUV.

She peered into her rearview mirror, glad now for her freshly scrubbed face and shiny hair. The shower and shampoo had been routine, and she had penciled her brows and applied lip gloss at the last minute.

Once again she was trying to take more pride in her looks, having acknowledged some truth in Seth's words. Maybe she wasn't being fair. To herself or anyone else. With that in mind, she was wearing a blue denim shirt, tan khakis, and navy boots. She'd forgotten to set the coffee maker and hadn't had time to make it. A no-caffeine headache was threatening.

As she climbed the steps to the square building that housed the *Courier,* she recalled the ideas she'd had at midnight and the urge to call Big Bob. Now here he was at Roy's office. She smiled, grateful for the first time that Roy had asked her to come in at this early hour.

"And I don't want that in the paper!" Big Bob's stern voice echoed across the reception area as she stepped inside.

The two men were deep in conversation back in Roy's office, but through the open door she could hear them clearly. Obviously they hadn't heard her enter. She closed the door softly and lingered.

"I wouldn't put anything in the paper that would hinder your search, Bob. You know that," Roy whined.

Although Bob's big frame seemed to consume half of Roy's tiny office, she could see enough to recognize that Roy's face was red and mottled. Embarrassment or fear? If he had seemed fidgety the night before, he was absolutely in a quiver now.

"It isn't just *my* search," Big Bob snapped. "That's what I want you to understand. The investigators have taken over, so I'm merely assisting them. You go putting down in your paper the size of the wound on her neck or the fact that the homeless man isn't our only suspect, and I'll...wring *your* scrawny little neck."

Christy gasped before she could stop herself, and both men turned toward the reception area. Bob groaned aloud.

"You don't need to make the same speech to me, Bob," she said, trying to keep her voice pleasant yet firm. "I haven't talked to anyone in Summer Breeze and—"

"You talked to Sherrie yesterday," he said, glaring at her. "Christy, I'm telling you right now. Stay out of this!"

She sighed, knowing she had been caught. Still, she was determined to defend herself. "I went up to Granny's to spend the night and stopped at that deli to pick up food on my way home."

"Headquarters is not *on your way home,* little gal, so don't try to pull that dumb blonde act with me."

"I'm not blond," she replied blandly.

"And you're not dumb, not by a long shot. For you, siphoning information from some unsuspecting soul is like me going out in my boat to fish with my fish finder." He was tugging nervously at the end of his nose.

Christy sighed, thinking she'd better try another method with Bob. "I don't suppose you'd care to hear my theory of why you found only one bloody shoe print."

Big Bob stared at her. "Who says there's only one?"

"I bet those guys won't find another one, and I know why."

He narrowed his hazel eyes suspiciously at her. Glancing at Roy, who was all but climbing over the desk, he motioned Christy toward the front door. Then he turned back.

"Remember what I told you, Thornberry. Only the facts: Marty's name, age, address, and the location where she was found."

"Can I mention that man's name who saw her throw the bottle?"

"No, you cannot," Bob shouted. "You could endanger the poor old guy's life. The killer was obviously still in the house when she threw the bottle out. He could suspect that the man saw him.

You are *not* to mention the name. Just say that a tip led us to that location. You can mention that robbery appears to be the motive and that the Criminal Investigation Division has taken over the case and is pursuing all leads. That's it. I repeat, *that's it.*"

"Hardly worth a special edition then," Roy mumbled as Big Bob strode to the door and opened it for Christy. When they were standing in the parking lot beside his SUV, Christy folded her arms over her chest and waited.

"All right, Christy. Tell me your theory."

"Snoopy's pillowcase."

Big Bob's head shot back a half inch, as though she had just spit on his polished boots. "Have you lost it completely?"

"The bed was made, the comforter turned back, the blue sheet visible. But the pillow was not in place and had no slipcover on it. I think the killer chased her up to the room. And in those desperate last seconds she ripped a page out of the tablet…" She faltered. "Was that a room belonging to a grandchild?"

"It was. And you were right about your mother selling the bottle to the mother of the two boys. They live in Atlanta and come down here two or three times a year. Mrs. Thomason left some furnishings there in case the daughter and her little boys wanted to come back a couple more times."

Christy nodded. It all made sense now.

Christy thought of something that had been bothering her.

"Did you turn off that alarm, Bob?"

He shook his head. "No, it was already off."

"I looked at the door. She had to have opened it to…whomever. And this Ridge Cohen. You know about his bad reputation? Maybe he has a hair-trigger temper. Maybe he was disguised."

"You aren't coming up with anything we haven't already thought of. And, unfortunately, his alibi has been backed up by three different people who are too frightened to lie."

"A hit man, then? Thus the 'someone' written on the note."

"Cohen didn't have a strong enough motive to go that far."

"I disagree. Maybe she knew something about his shady activities. Maybe she was blackmailing him."

"Christy, you're wasting my time."

She couldn't resist the challenge. "Bet you hadn't figured out about the shoes though."

"You're back to that again. What are you talking about with this Snoopy nonsense?"

"Okay, because everyone was studying the door and the footprint on the tablet…"

He shoved his hand through his steel-gray hair in obvious frustration. "I reckon you got that from Sherrie too."

"Bob, I was there, remember?"

He shook his head and turned to study a passing car. "I wish you hadn't been. That was a bad scene." He looked back at her. "So you think he saw the footprint on the tablet, sat down and removed his shoes and put them in the pillowcase."

She nodded, holding to her conviction. Or rather Granny's.

"Okay, Christy. Obviously, you've kept your word about not

telling anything. The community is hounding me to death. And they wouldn't be asking some of their questions if they knew what you know."

"Do you want to hear my other theory?"

"Do I have a choice?" he asked, cracking the first grin of the morning.

"You know that Thelma at the Pancake House saw Marty heading east between one and one thirty, when she should have been going west. I believe she got a call from Ridge Cohen as she was leaving Frank's place. Or maybe she called him. Either way, they agreed for him to drive over and look at the ship house first."

"The man was at the Silver Sands Hotel with his girlfriend, waiting for Marty to call. Said she never called, never showed up."

Christy frowned. "You're taking the girlfriend's word as a solid alibi?"

"And the word of the cleaning lady who knocked on their door to deliver towels and the word of the guy who delivered lunch to their room at one fifteen. The coroner judges Marty's death to have occurred somewhere between one thirty and two thirty Sunday afternoon. That corresponds to Sandpiper's claim that he saw her throw the bottle out around two o'clock. His wife said he didn't leave the house until nearly one thirty, which could have easily put him out there around that time."

Christy listened, her mind working the facts. "So you think it was a robbery after all?"

He hesitated, saying nothing more.

"What? Bob, you owe me."

"Nope, Christy, I don't owe you anything. But I will mention your suggestion about the pillowcase."

"Tell me if they found blood anywhere else in the house or on the property."

"Don't know," he replied nonchalantly as he turned toward his SUV. "Now you take care of yourself. I've come to feel kind of protective toward you, and, of course, you're the darling of Summer Breeze. If anything happens to you, these folks will have my head on a platter."

"So that's why you feel protective toward me?" she teased, as he hauled his big frame into the SUV.

The engine roared to life, and he never looked back at her. She heard a hoarse choking sound and saw Roy standing in the open door, having a coughing fit.

"Roy," she said, hurrying up the steps, "you should know better than to push Big Bob."

"What did you say to him?" he croaked.

"Nothing he didn't already know."

"And what was that?"

"Come on, Roy. I can't talk to you about this. I mean," she corrected herself quickly when she saw the quick flash of anger in his dark eyes, "I don't know anything they haven't already figured out. After all, they're professionals."

"What was that about a pillowcase?"

She sighed. There didn't seem to be any harm in sharing her

theory; after all, it was only a theory. "If they don't find any other bloody prints, maybe the killer put his shoes in the pillowcase from the bed."

Roy groaned. "I'll bet Big Bob hooted at that silly idea if that's all you had to tell him."

"Thanks for the vote of confidence." She could hardly keep her temper in line with Roy. He was poking into police business just for the sake of selling papers.

"Well, that's a silly theory," he snapped. Then suddenly as he looked at her, a different expression crossed his face. "What were you doing out with Major Brockman last night?"

She resisted the urge to say, "None of your business." "I was having dessert. He's taking a night class at the community college, and I teach one. We started talking and decided to get a cup of coffee."

"Well, he'd be quite the catch, Christy."

Now she was really angry. "You make him sound like a prize blue marlin, and I'm the amateur fisherman. Fisherwoman," she added, feeling the headache accelerate.

"Come inside," he said, with an abrupt change of subject, "and take a look at my article about Marty. You saw the picture. Now I've got to edit out the part about Mr. Woodley and the name of the guy who was expecting her to meet him in Destin."

"How did you know his name?" Christy asked, following him into the office.

"I called the real-estate office, and Carl Alexander told me. Ridge Cohen. A blue blood if ever there was one."

She decided not to share the information she'd learned from Frank. "I'll bet Big Bob also told you not to mention that name and risk Carl losing a sale."

"He's already lost the sale. Cohen told him he wouldn't be dealing with them again, so Carl Alexander doesn't care what I put in the paper."

"Well, Big Bob certainly cares."

Roy bounded to his desk and yanked up two sheets of computer paper. "Who could blame Cohen for not dealing with that office again? He's had nothing but bad luck where Marty was concerned."

"What do you mean, bad luck?" Christy asked, taking the printout from him.

"The last time Cohen dealt with Marty, she took another cash offer on a house, knowing he was on his way from Miami. She let him drive all the way up here without calling to tell him the house was sold."

She stared at Roy. "Bet that made Cohen pretty mad."

"But see, Marty figured she'd find another house for him before he got here. So happened, that didn't set well with the guy. He didn't want *another* house. He wanted the one he and his girlfriend had seen in the MLS book and called about. In fact, I'm surprised he dealt with her again after that. Carl said Marty promised him this time she had an even better house, maybe two, and she would cut her commission in half because of the last foul-up. So he relented and came back."

"Hmm. Would you do that?"

"Do what?"

"Drive back up from Miami after a Realtor messed with you before."

Roy thought about it. "Probably not. She's not the only agent here."

Christy nodded, then glanced down at the printout and looked back at Roy. "Okay, Roy, since you are so wise, why do you think Marty went to the ship house when she was supposed to be going to Destin? Why would she risk angering Cohen a second time? And she would have, for sure."

Roy had popped a stick of gum into his mouth and was chewing furiously. "I don't believe the guy's alibi. I think he must have spoken to her on her cell phone—only nobody can find the cell phone. Down at headquarters, I'll guarantee you they have phone records on her home phone and cell by now. I think that for some reason he changed his mind and agreed to come up here. That, to me, is the only explanation for her not heading straight to Destin."

Christy listened to his theory, watching as he chewed the gum and popped it a couple of times.

"So you think that homeless guy is innocent?"

"I hear he's too dumb to have pulled off two murders. I believe he found the purse that the killer tossed out when he crossed the bridge. The credit card would have been hard to spot if it was in a zipped lining of the purse."

"What about the death of that doctor last week in Panama City?"

He shook his head and sat down behind his cluttered desk. "Coincidence. Maybe the killer staged it to look like a robbery just like the one in Panama City."

Christy took a seat, staring at Roy. What he said made sense. Most people knew about the doctor's death—robbery, a knife blade to the throat. If someone wanted it to look like there was a robber or serial killer on the loose, that's exactly what he would do.

"So are you gonna read what I wrote?" he prompted, his dark eyes darting from her to the printout.

She lifted the paper to her line of vision and began to read. He had given an accurate account of Marty's death, had freshly inked out Sandpiper's assistance in the matter. He had ended with a paragraph about Marty, how she had been named Realtor of the Year and how almost single-handedly she had been responsible for several developments in the area.

Christy stared at that sentence. Some locals resented her greed and still thought of her as an outsider who had moved in for the sole purpose of development.

She thought of something. "How do you suppose she managed to convince the city council to go along with the development on Shipwreck Island?"

He stared at her for a moment. "She almost didn't. The ongoing fight between her and Stan Browne is old news."

Stan Browne. He was a highly respected citizen, an elderly gentleman who had lived in the area all his life. "That must have happened before I moved back. I don't remember hearing anything about it."

Roy shrugged. "Well, Stan's a gentleman, but his son, Stanley Jr., is a wild card. Wouldn't put it past him…" His eyes met Christy's for a silent moment. Then he shook his head vigorously, his hastily combed hair flying in all directions. "The council decision took place several years ago. Junior's over it by now."

For some reason Christy found herself thinking about the conversation between J. T. and Jack, how J. T. had mentioned that Marty had come to Rainbow Bay with visions of development dancing in her head. Jack had, as J. T. said, given her the what-for, which Christy felt certain was a watered-down version of what Jack had really said to her. She knew Jack had a temper, even though he had mellowed with age, and yet she could imagine that he would throw a fit if Marty started messing with his land or any of the land around him.

"Well, quit staring into space, and tell me what you think," Roy snapped.

Christy looked at him, wondering if she should call him on his rude manner; in fact, rudeness seemed to be a habit with him. She didn't have the energy for any more debating this early in the day, so she let it pass.

"I think your article looks good, Roy. I didn't know Mrs.

McAllister was from Kentucky. I knew she was a widow but didn't know she had no children."

"That's all most people know. Maybe that's the way she wanted it."

She laid the paper on Roy's desk and looked back at him. "Why do you say that?"

"Do you know anyone who knew her very well? Bet she didn't have one close friend in this town."

She thought it over. "You may be right." She stood. "Listen, if you don't need anything else, I should go. When are you publishing this edition?"

"Sunday. First Sunday edition since I've owned the paper. But I'm including a couple of interviews about her, one from Valerie and one from Bonnie. Always helps to show this paper's not prejudiced."

She stared at him. He had just made a revealing statement about himself concerning Bonnie, but he lacked the perception to realize it.

"I don't have those interviews ready yet. The ladies are coming in around ten. Then I'll finish writing and polishing. Tomorrow we'll print it. Andrea is gonna help—unless you want to pitch in?" His attempt at humor fell flat as she turned for the door.

"Good luck," she called over her shoulder.

The wind had picked up, tossing particles of sand in her face. She could feel grit in her teeth as she hurried to the car. February and March were so unpredictable; one day would be sunny and beautiful, the next cloudy and cold.

As she got into her car, she realized her early morning trip had not been in vain. Meeting up with Big Bob had been an unexpected bonus. She began to replay their conversation in her mind as she drove out of the parking lot and headed toward the Treasure Chest. It was almost nine o'clock, and her mother would be getting ready to open the shop.

When she turned into the parking lot, the only car she spotted was her mother's white station wagon. Even though it was Friday, it was likely to be a slow day because of the weather. Tourist season had not yet begun, and few people, after checking the weather report, would be driving down from the cities for the weekend.

Reaching across the seat, she gathered up the sack that contained half a dozen pint jars of scuppernong jelly, along with two large Mason jars of green beans. She tucked the shoebox of tax receipts under her other arm and got out of the car. Hugging her load, she climbed the steps to the Treasure Chest.

The door was unlocked, and as the bell rang out, her mother turned from the gold-framed mirror she was polishing.

"Hey, Mom. Granny sent goodies." She put her load on the counter.

"Hello, darling." Her mother looked her over. "You're a pleasant sight on this blustery morning. What brings you out so early?"

"The thorn in my side. Specifically, Roy Thornberry. I would never be out this early on a Friday if not for the Thorn."

"What do you mean?"

"He's putting out a special edition just because of Marty."

"Maybe it's his way of paying tribute to one of our leading citizens."

"Mom, please. I know you try to see the good in everyone and often believe it. But Roy is simply trying to sell papers; that's the name of his game."

Beth merely sighed. Christy realized her tone had turned defensive again, so she tried a different approach.

"Have you heard any details on Mrs. McAllister's funeral?"

"It's scheduled for two on Sunday. Graveside services, as she requested. Your father will officiate."

Christy wondered if the request had come from Marty or her nephew. Christy hadn't seen her in church since moving back home.

"How do you know she wanted graveside? And Dad?" she added as gently as possible.

"Her nephew made the decision. Said she had expressed that wish several months ago when they were having a discussion about cremation. Her husband wanted to be cremated, and she scattered his ashes in a lake in Kentucky. But Marty wanted a traditional burial; in fact, she'd recently bought a plot here at Memorial Cemetery."

Christy thought about that for a moment. "I'm a little surprised she wanted to be buried here. Maybe she felt no ties to Kentucky. Do you know anything about the nephew from Pensacola?"

"His name is Bruce McAllister, and he's actually her husband's nephew. Marty and her husband had planned to move here when he retired, but he died a few years back. I suppose Marty liked the area well enough to move here on her own; apparently, the nephew has been helpful."

"You said the funeral is at two?"

"Yes, are you going? I didn't think you knew her that well. I know you bought your house from her, but aside from that…"

"You taught me to show respect, Mom. That's what I'm trying to do."

"That's nice, honey."

She felt a twinge of guilt at the glow of admiration in her mother's eyes.

To be honest, she wanted to see who would be attending the funeral. She was still curious about the boyfriend. But then, to be fair to herself, she admitted to feeling sorry for Marty, who seemed to have few real friends. She could almost hear Bonnie saying, "Honey, you can't take it with you when you go."

"Incidentally," her mother said, breaking into her thoughts, "how's it going with your writing? Are you going to meet your deadline?"

Christy flinched. "Mom, could you please leave *deadline* out of your vocabulary? But I do need to go."

"Will I see you on Sunday?"

The temptation to work straight through the weekend lay heavy on Christy's mind. It wasn't easy to get in the zone, but if she could, she hated to break the mood. Then, looking into her little mom's expectant face, she smiled and nodded. "See you Sunday."

When she got into her car, she fully intended to drive home.

Instead, the car seemed to move of its own accord toward the street where Marty had lived.

She drove slowly past Marty's house, noting the black wreath that someone had placed on her front door. A car with Pensacola tags was parked in the driveway, and she thought of the nephew. She wished she had a reason to go to the door to speak with him, but she didn't. She certainly wasn't delivering food.

Suddenly another car caught her eye. It was a red Lincoln Continental, the latest model, parked just down the street from Marty's house. The windows were darkened, but the driver had lowered his window halfway.

As she drew even with the car, she saw the face of a middle-aged man. He was looking toward Marty's house, and in the brief moment their eyes met, she read a terrible sadness in his face. Her car had passed his before she could put on the brakes, but from the side window, she read the Florida license plate and repeated it three times, committing it to memory.

Who was he, and why had there been such sadness in his eyes? *The boyfriend.* It had to be the boyfriend who owned the yacht. She turned down the next street and drove back toward Marty's, planning to approach the car from the rear, hoping for a better look at the man. But as soon as she turned the corner, she saw that she was too late. The car was gone. When she passed Marty's house, she accelerated, hoping to catch up with him. A quick glance down each side street proved fruitless. He had obviously driven away in a hurry after he caught her staring.

Since he had stopped to stare at Marty's house on a Friday morning, she had a hunch he would stay through the weekend for the funeral services. And if that was true, she would see him there. If not, she could still get his identity through the license.

She pulled to the curb, removed the pen and pad she kept attached to her visor, and wrote down the license number, along with the color of the car. She opened her cell and dialed Bob's number.

As soon as he answered, she jumped right in. "I have a prime suspect for you."

"Who?"

"I just saw a red Lincoln Continental parked down from Marty's house. Pensacola license plate."

"The nephew and his wife are from Pensacola. Maybe this is a relative."

"Don't try to throw me off. This is the boyfriend; I saw his face. If you don't tell me what you know, Bob, I'll track down the owner of that license."

He heaved a sigh. "Don't be asking questions around here or Pensacola. Do you understand me?"

"I do. But the Snowbirds and I have helped out with this investigation. I wrote the column that brought Sandpiper to *me,* and I called you. Otherwise, you wouldn't—"

"All right, blackmail me if it makes you feel better. I know who he is, and the detectives already checked out his alibi. It's solid."

Her mouth fell open. "Then you shouldn't mind telling me."

"Hold on." She could hear his heavy footsteps resounding over an uncarpeted floor. Then a door slammed. "Archie Cynaubaum. But like I told you, he has a solid alibi."

She scribbled the name quickly on her pad, guessing at the spelling. "With his money, no doubt he could buy several alibis. Like the guy from Miami."

"He was sitting out at his pool reading the newspaper. A neighbor saw him, and the guy cleaning his pool verified it. At two thirty he and his wife met with someone."

Christy pressed her lips together hard. She didn't believe that, but what could she say? "Okay, Bob," she tried to sound casual, "I'll forget about it."

"No, you won't. But what you'd better do is keep quiet."

"Whatever you say," she replied, her fingers crossed. "Bye." Another little white lie. Where had crossing the fingers when you told a lie originated? A lie was still a lie.

She closed her cell and thrust it in her pocket. She still believed he could buy those two alibis. Pulling away from the curb, she headed home to do the thing that bought her groceries and fuel and the clothes and shoes she loved. She'd work on her manuscript.

Later, sitting at her desk, she swiveled in her chair, staring at the bulletin board beside her. While writing her mystery, she tacked up a poster board that listed all her suspects and their motives in a red felt-tipped pen. An adjoining poster, which to the uninitiated appeared to be a graph of mountains and valleys, actually showed plot points, the highs and lows her characters faced. While she was looking at the poster, an idea struck. Why not approach the town's unsolved mystery the way she would construct a mystery novel?

She grabbed a sheet of computer paper and began to write down the people she believed were suspects in Marty's murder.

At that precise moment the phone rang, and she jumped, sending a jagged red line across the paper with her pen. She reached for the handset. "Hello," she snapped. She hated being interrupted when she was deep in thought.

"Hello. And I apologize."

She bolted upright in her chair and laid the pen down. It was Dan Brockman's voice.

"Hello again. And why are you apologizing?"

"From the tone of that 'hello,' I'm obviously interrupting you."

"Did I sound that bad?"

"I would never say you sounded *bad,* at least not to me. *Distracted* is a better word."

She glanced at the list of suspects she was putting together and sighed. "Well, you aren't distracting me from my manuscript, that's for sure. Which is probably the true source of my irritation."

"Sounds like you need a good meal. I'm told nutrition does wonders for the brain."

Leaning back in her chair, she found herself thinking about how much fun she'd had with him the night before. And yet...it still nagged her that he hadn't mentioned Marty sooner. She was determined to learn more about him.

"You could be right," she admitted after a moment of silence while her thoughts churned. "I'll accept that offer for dinner."

"We could make it someplace close to your home so you won't lose time. To further persuade you, I'm going to be out of town for the next few days, so that's the reason I called. And then we'll have a real celebration when you complete the manuscript. Where would you like to go?"

She hesitated. Dan Brockman—*Major* Dan Brockman didn't fool around. When he had a mission, he didn't alter his course. For some reason, she seemed to be one of his missions. Or maybe he was just lonely.

Her eyes drifted to the list of suspects, and suddenly she had an idea. "Actually I think a drive would do me good. Why don't we meet at the Seafood House? It's not far from you, and I do like their food." What had Marty liked about that place? "Particularly the way they mesquite grill their fish."

"Great idea. In fact, my parents treated me to dinner there on the second night after I arrived on their doorstep."

No point in mentioning this was the parking lot of the restaurant where Dr. Stewart was killed, for then he would think she was only using him. Was she?

"I'll be glad to drive over and pick you up if you'll tell me where you live."

"Thanks, but I have an errand between here and there. I'll just meet you." The errand was a stop-off at the Panama City Beach Marina.

"Okay, what time would you like to meet?" he asked.

She quickly calculated. A shower and shampoo were involved, and maybe she'd need to press something. On the other hand, she liked watching the sun set there, which meant—she glanced at the clock—she'd have to hurry.

"Around five o'clock?" she asked. "If we go at that time, we can watch the sun set over the bay. The view is great from there."

"Good idea. I remember they don't take reservations. I'll go a few minutes early and get our name on the list."

She smiled. He seemed like such a nice guy. "Okay. And, Dan, …thanks for calling."

She turned off her computer, satisfied she wasn't going to accomplish anything on her novel today. Too many other thoughts were chasing around in her head.

Looking at her list of suspects, she picked up the pen again, studying the three suspects she had written down.

1. Archie Cynaubaum. Boyfriend.

2. Ridge Cohen. Miami businessman.

Bob claimed Cohen had an alibi, but a suspicion nagged her that he might have called to change the appointment. It made more sense than anything else she had heard.

3. Homeless man.

Everyone seemed to think he was incapable of pulling off two robberies and murders, or even one. And she personally believed that if by some miracle he had, he would have been long gone in Marty's car.

4. The killer of the doctor—and Marty. Big Foot.

Perhaps he was really the one, but so far there had been little to go on. Or so it seemed, but she knew the authorities were keeping their leads private.

Her gaze shot to the bookcase, roaming the books on mystery writing. She knew there were always the red herrings—the person or persons the writer braided into the story with false clues or tricky motives to distract attention from the real killer. And she also used the "long shot" character—the one who seemed unlikely but who sometimes turned out to be the killer.

Who had the strongest motive? Who was the least likely to be suspected?

Rage? Had this been an act of rage, a quick murder by someone who wanted to get the terrible deed done quickly and quietly?

An odd chill ran over her. Dan knew weapons, all sorts of weapons. Knives. After all, soldiers were trained to protect themselves. But what would his motive be?

The note in the bottle jumped back to the center of her mind, bringing up the most obvious clue of all. She slapped the palm of her hand against her head. What was wrong with all of them? Why did they keep forgetting the obvious truth? If Marty knew who the killer was, she would have written the name on the note in the bottle. A name rather than "someone."

On the other hand, she wouldn't have opened the door to a stranger—or would she?

A stranger who pretended an interest in buying the house.

But Christy had seen Dan there the day after the murder. If, by some remote chance, he had killed Marty, he wouldn't be hanging around the scene of the crime. But then she wouldn't have stood up Ridge Cohen again while trying to sell a house to a stranger. And— to dispute the theory of her not knowing his name—she would never meet with a potential buyer without a name.

She tossed the pen down and shook her head. It was too bewildering without more information. Looking back at the computer, she poked out her tongue at the bad sentence on the screen of white space. She knew from experience the words wouldn't come if she was distracted. And today she was totally distracted.

Pressing a button, she put the computer in sleep mode and went to take a shower.

10

Shortly after four, she crossed the parking lot to the marina, wearing a long gored skirt painted with spring flowers and a blue sweater set. And her new Prada heels. Looking out on the water, she could see the tourist pirate ship heading back into dock.

She stepped from the concrete down to the wooden boards. She studied the pleasure boats bobbing lazily on the gentle water. There were fishing and charter boats as well, although not all were serviced and ready to go since tourist season was not yet under way. When that time came, numerous vessels would be spanking clean, their captains eagerly waiting as tourists gathered for deep-sea fishing or pleasure rides.

She paused, looking around. Just then the pirate ship blasted a cannon, and she lunged forward, catching a spike heel in a crack between the boards. Her eyes zipped from the ship down to the crack where her spike heel was lodged. What was wrong with her? She knew about the firing of the cannon. Why was she so jumpy?

Glancing around self-consciously, she removed her foot from

the stuck shoe and bent down, determined to gently wedge the heel loose. In the process she had a fleeting vision of herself limping in for her dinner date on half a heel or no heel at all.

At that precise moment, she heard a wolf whistle, and her spine stiffened. She dared not look around.

"Hey, Cinderella! Did you lose your slipper?"

The familiar voice brought a sigh of relief, and she whirled and glanced over her shoulder. Jack walked up to her, a grin sliding over his face.

"You old wolf," she laughed, delighted to see him.

"Here, let me get that thing. You'll ruin your skirt bending down on these dirty boards. If you're looking for a good boat, try looking around Rainbow Bay."

"Thanks," she said, glancing around nervously.

No one seemed to notice Jack or her or the expensive heel stuck in a crack. Everyone had gathered at the far end to watch deck hands toss the catch of the day from a fishing boat onto the docks.

Jack bent down and gently wedged the heel from between the boards. "Now put your pretty foot in," he said, extending it to her.

She slid her foot into the shoe, then turned to give him a hug.

"Don't get too close." He thrust out his palm in warning. "As pretty as you look and smell, you don't need to come in contact with a fisherman. Just unloaded a barrel at Hal's and drove down here to check out the boats. Then I saw you prissing across the parking lot. I hope that fancy outfit means some decent guy is buying you dinner."

"Well…yes. But it doesn't mean anything else."

He thrust his hands on hips and frowned at her. "Christy, stop feeling like you have to apologize to me whenever you want to go out with a guy. I expect you to have a social life. I also expect you to bring him out to pass my inspection if one happens along that you get serious about."

"I'll do that. But don't hold your breath. Listen, Jack, have you ever heard of…" She reached in the pocket where she had put that little slip of paper. Her pocket was empty. The other pocket was empty. She had lost that piece of paper. Her memory rolled. "I've forgotten the first name, but the last one is Cynabomb or something like that."

"*Who?* He doesn't sound like anybody I'd know or even sell fish to. Why?"

"A friend of Marty's, I think."

"Aha! You're following a lead, as they say."

"Jack, of all these fancy boats, do you recognize the one in which you saw Marty McAllister?"

He walked past her, looking over the dozens of boats anchored in the marina.

Christy watched him, and as she did, her gaze moved from his baseball cap, down the faded green Windbreaker and worn jeans, to his scuffed work boots as they clambered over the wood. Jack was such a great guy. Too bad people judged him harshly without really understanding him. A heart of gold rested beneath that faded jacket.

Pulling the cap lower to shade his eyes against the late afternoon sun, he took at least five minutes walking back and forth, studying in particular the largest boat docked there. A big white one.

Then slowly he shook his head and lumbered back to her. "Don't remember it that well, but none of these is big enough."

Her spirits sank.

"Before you pull that long face," he teased, "remember it could be in dry dock somewhere being worked on."

"Hmm. I forgot about that." She shook her head and sighed. "Another dead end."

He chuckled as he studied her. "You're just not gonna stay out of this Marty McAllister investigation, are you? What's Big Bob have to say about you snooping around?"

"Big Bob better be *glad* I'm snooping around. Between the Sassy Snowbirds and me—"

"Oh no." He made a face. "Don't tell me that red-feathered crew is quizzing Big Bob. Why, he'll resign and head for the hills. Christy, you gotta put a stop to this. He's the best deputy in the area. Better'n anybody they've got downtown."

"Big Bob is not going to resign. And, Jack, don't be bad-mouthing my friends."

The firmness in her tone began to melt beneath the hearty chuckle that rumbled up from his chest and eased into the deep lines of his face.

"All right. Sorry." He lifted his wrist and studied his watch.

"Gotta go. Me and J. T.'ve got a poker game cooked up with some buddies. I don't wanna be late. They may stack the deck against me."

"They wouldn't dare," she said. "Everybody knows better than to mess with you. They might end up as alligator bait."

He nodded emphatically. "You're right, little lady. That goes for the dude who's taking you to dinner." He looked back over his shoulder at the Seafood House in the distance. "You're eating in style, I take it?"

"I plan to. So I'll let you get on to that hot card game and—"

"Don't you dare say you'll get on with your hot date!"

She thrust her hands on her hips, and this time she did glare at him. "I don't go on *hot* dates, as you put it. That's your department, when you aren't so closemouthed!"

He threw his head back and laughed, a rich deep laugh that seemed to roll up from his toes. "That's a good one."

She was laughing too. It was such a relief to be with Jack in a different setting and be able to tease and taunt as they always had over the years.

"So go enjoy your meal. And wish me luck in my poker game!"

"Good luck, Jack. And don't *you* be stacking the deck on poor ol' J. T."

Jack had turned and headed toward his truck, parked next to her convertible. "J. T.'s not as dumb as he lets on," he called over his shoulder.

He had reached the truck, fired up the engine, and roared off by the time Christy got back in her car. As she turned the key in the ignition, she cast one last glance out at the marina, washed in gold by the setting sun. All big white boats looked alike to her, but she trusted Jack's judgment, and no doubt the mysterious boyfriend kept his boat somewhere around Pensacola.

She pulled out of the parking lot and drove across the street to the Seafood House. The clock on the dash told her she was fifteen minutes early, but the crowd was already gathering. While circling the parking lot looking for an empty space, she spotted Dan's SUV.

She found a place and parked. In front of her, a pretty blond woman dressed in the black-and-white attire of the restaurant's servers hurried along. Christy jumped out of the car and fell in step with her.

"Hi," Christy called. "I'm dining here tonight. Could I ask you a quick question?"

The blonde was young, early twenties. She looked at Christy and smiled. "Sure."

"I just need to verify something." She glanced toward the rear of the restaurant. "I'm assisting in the investigation of Dr. Peter Stewart's murder. That back area there—"

"We're not supposed to talk about that." The girl picked up her pace. "And we have a security guard who patrols now."

"I know; that's a big positive. We need security guards in parking lots of restaurants, I mean—ones as large as this one. I'll pass the word along."

The server appeared to relax a bit.

Christy reached into her purse and opened a tiny notebook. She flipped to a page scribbled with items about Shipwreck Island. She pretended to glance over the writing. "Wasn't it back there, away from the pole lights?" she asked, looking from her notebook to the woman.

The server glanced toward the farthest corner of the parking lot. "With his car and his money, he shouldn't have picked a dark spot. Most people like that know to park under the light."

"Well, that was his mistake. Why do you think he parked back there?" Christy asked, trying to keep up as her spike heels bit the concrete.

"He was from out of town. Probably didn't know folks get here when the place opens. He came in later, so he was forced to grab the only spot he could find. Look, I'm almost late."

"You go on, in these heels I can't walk fast," she joked.

She breathed a sigh of relief and studied the parking area. The kitchen was closest to the spot where she assumed Dr. Stewart had parked. She remembered the article she had read about his murder. All the kitchen help, the servers, even the patrons had been questioned.

A knife. Could someone working in the kitchen, perhaps even a server, have followed him out to the car after the meal and put a knife to his throat?

No, that wouldn't make sense. Why would someone call attention to his or her place of employment?

She tried to put herself in Dr. Stewart's place. He came out of the restaurant, happy and relaxed after a nice dinner. Maybe he'd had a drink or two. That might explain his dulled senses. With no thought of anyone watching him, he walked back and unlocked the car and then…

She shivered. Time to put these thoughts out of her mind. After all, she had a dinner date, and she shouldn't keep him waiting.

Pleasant conversations flowed around her as people climbed the steps to the front door. She followed and stepped inside.

The muted lights in the lobby softened the outside glare, and she blinked, trying to adjust her vision.

"Hi there." Dan stood beside her.

"Hi." She smiled at him.

Good instincts coupled with years of study had honed her observation skills. While she prided herself on lasering through the exterior to the real person, she suddenly found herself off balance when it came to Dan. The blue eyes welcomed her but revealed nothing. Reading Dan Brockman would be something of an art.

He wore a navy blazer, a conservative tie that shouted expensive through its simplicity, a white shirt, and tan pants. His dark hair was neatly combed, his face clean-shaven.

She turned and looked toward the hostess station. "Do we have a wait?"

"Only a few minutes. I asked for a table with a view of the sunset." He lifted his wrist, glanced at his gold watch. A light yet wonderful cologne reached out to her. "We won't have long."

"That's good." She smoothed down a strand of hair that brushed her cheek. She had tried a new shampoo and conditioner and hoped she didn't smell like an orange.

The hostess called his name and led them along the aisle, skirting one dining room and entering another. She stopped at a cozy table for two beside a glass wall overlooking the water.

Servers scurried about. Christy cast a nervous glance toward them, hoping the gal she'd questioned didn't turn out to be their server. To her relief, a young man who introduced himself as Mallon appeared.

"Hi, Mallon." Dan turned to Christy. "What do you think about getting an appetizer and something to drink while we watch the sun set?"

"Good idea. I'll have iced tea with lemon," she said. "I like all of their appetizers. Why don't you choose?"

"Okay. Iced tea for me, too, and bring us the seafood sampler, please." He looked at Christy. "Okay?"

"Absolutely."

As Mallon hurried off, Dan folded his hands on the table, glanced out at the glorious view beyond the window, then looked at Christy. He seemed to be holding back.

"Is something wrong?" she asked.

"No. I just feel tempted to say something that might sound corny."

"I like corny. I was raised with corny."

"Seth?"

"And I'm a little bit corny too." She leaned closer. "What are you tempted to say?"

"Like no sunset could match your beauty tonight."

She turned to the window. It looked as though an artist had swirled hot raspberry and sparkling gold from the horizon into the Gulf.

"And now I have sounded corny and embarrassed you."

She turned back to him. "No, I was checking out the magnitude of your compliment. Thanks."

His gaze swung toward the view that had cast a spell on diners around them. "I've been out of the loop too long," he said. "I was once more adept in the social graces than I am now. But then"—he looked back at her—"you're not just another pretty woman. I sense a greater depth to you than most of the women I've known. And they weren't shallow," he added.

Mallon was placing tall glasses of iced tea before them, and she used that pause to consider his compliment. She decided to be forthright; after all, she needed to know more about this guy.

"Have you ever been married?" she asked.

He didn't seem surprised by the question. "No. I've been engaged. A rather long engagement, in fact."

"What happened? Or should I not ask?"

He took a sip of tea and hesitated. "The wrong time and place. The wrong circumstances. And…the wrong people. We were slow coming to that conclusion. We realized that if we had the real thing, these other obstacles wouldn't end the relationship."

She listened, more questions popping into her mind. Where was the woman now? What had there been about her that had prompted Dan Brockman to consider marriage?

"That was almost five years ago," he continued. "I was still gung-ho with the military. She didn't want to be a military wife. I tried to understand that. Now I don't want a military career."

"At the time you thought you did?"

"I wasn't completely sure either way, and I wouldn't make a promise I couldn't keep. Also, our backgrounds and ideas about life were different. Anna Maria was from Italy," he explained, "and had come to Texas with her parents when she was young. I met her while I was stationed there."

He said nothing more, even though Christy sat listening, trying to visualize this woman. "Italian women are very beautiful," she said, breaking the silence.

"Yes, she was beautiful. But we weren't right for each other. If we had been, she wouldn't have married someone else six months later."

"Oh." She wanted to ask, "And since then?" but kept the question to herself.

They had started to nibble on the seafood in silence, glancing intermittently through the window as darkness began to swallow up the display of color, while farther out, the night-lights of fishing boats sparkled.

"Now it's my turn to ask a question or two," he said, watching her thoughtfully. "Why am I the lucky guy sitting here tonight?"

She touched the linen napkin to her lips, stalling for time. He had opened up to her, telling her something personal. Still, she wasn't ready to talk about Chad, not yet. She gave him an honest yet general answer.

"My story is similar to yours. Wrong time, wrong place." She picked up the fork and speared a crab cake.

"You didn't say wrong guy."

She chewed a bite slowly and looked at him. "No, I didn't."

"And since then, there hasn't been a *right* guy?" Dan asked. His voice was casual, but like the previous evening, she sensed a quiet tension within him.

"No, but that's the way of young love, isn't it? The first time you fall, it seems so intense. I suppose that feeling is hard to match again."

A full minute of silence followed, and then Dan leaned back in the chair and smiled at her. "And that's all I'm going to get from you for now. Right?"

She turned to face him, only half returning his smile. "Right."

"O-kay. Just wanted to be sure I wasn't interfering."

"You're not," she said, reaching for a shrimp. "I'm ravenous. Thanks for ordering this appetizer. It's the perfect dish—so perfect, in fact, that if I'm not careful, I may ruin the main course."

"We'll take our time," he said.

Something about the way he spoke those words brought her gaze back to him. She had a distinct impression that he wasn't referring to *just* the meal.

"You said you're going out of town?" she asked.

"I'm going to drive Mom up to Franklin, Tennessee, to visit relatives."

"Franklin? Isn't that just outside Nashville?"

He nodded. "Have you been there?"

"Several years ago I visited the home of a friend from Florida State. She lived in Nashville. I loved the area, even thought about moving there. Instead, I went to Colorado."

She reached for her tea glass, telling herself to shut up. Next he'd be asking why she left Florida. And, of course, he did.

"You wanted a drastic change?" He had already guessed the reason.

She shrugged. "Being in a preacher's family, we moved around some during my early years but mostly in Florida. When Dad accepted the job here at Community Church, my parents decided not to move again. Unless he's asked," she added, laughing at the idea, which for now seemed out of the question. Everyone loved Grant Castleman. And he loved everyone in return. "In any case, they'd like to retire and grow old here."

The server had returned, carefully removing the empty tray of appetizers and refilling their glasses. "Are you ready to order, or do you need more time?" he asked.

They shared a blank look before grabbing their menus again.

"Let me make a recommendation: our fresh catch of the day is mahimahi, and we serve it grilled with fresh vegetables."

"You just made up my mind," Christy said, closing the menu. "And I'll have the same."

They proceeded to give their choices of salad dressing and potato, and then Christy looked at Dan. "Are you always so easy to please?" she asked.

"No, but tonight I'm in a very good mood."

She grinned, appreciating his honesty.

"I hesitate to ask," he said, "but I'm concerned. Are there any developments in Mrs. McAllister's case?"

Christy crossed her arms, wondering what made him think she would know. "Not really. The motive appears to be robbery."

"Appears? Do you believe that?"

She hesitated. "I'm not sure. A robbery might indicate she opened the door to a stranger. That's hard for me to accept."

"You think she opened the door to someone she knew?"

She shrugged, wishing she could divert the subject. But how could she do that without acting secretive? She turned in her chair, thinking about the server she had so boldly questioned in the parking lot. She was nowhere in sight. She turned back to face Dan.

"There was an intricate alarm system, so the door was secured. It doesn't make sense to me," she said.

"Do you want to tell me the whole story? I've heard bits and pieces, but I don't really know what happened."

She looked at him, wondering how much to tell. Her instincts told her this man could not possibly have been involved in the murder. Roy's special Sunday edition of the *Courier* would give the basic facts, and Dan already knew about her finding the bottle and the note. He had read it in Beach Buzz, just as Sandpiper had done.

So she recapped the story, starting with the bottle and note, and carried him through to the end. She was careful to omit any confidential matters that she and Big Bob had shared. Lost in the story, they had finished their meal and become so engrossed in conversation, they'd had little time to talk or think of anything else. Yet, they had obviously enjoyed the meal, judging by the two empty plates before them.

He was silent for a moment, as though thinking about what she had told him. "Don't you think that the person could have been disguised?"

"But then she certainly wouldn't have opened the door," Christy replied.

"I mean, what if he somehow got inside before she arrived?"

Christy thought about what Big Bob had said and what she believed to be true. Now Dan seemed to be figuring everything out, even though he hadn't been inside the house or been privy to what the investigators privately knew and believed. If, in fact, Dan had been that person, he wouldn't be giving out suggestions. Now she felt guilty for being suspicious of him.

"That makes sense," she replied. "So do you believe that the same person who killed the doctor killed Mrs. McAllister?" Christy's eyes drifted toward a side window, recalling the five minutes she had been in the parking lot, sizing up the area.

"Maybe it's meant to look that way."

She stared at him for a moment. "You're pretty sophisticated with this stuff. Big Bob and the detectives could use you."

He pushed back from the table a bit and chuckled good-naturedly. Watching him, Christy liked the sound of his laughter and the way it lit his eyes and softened the lines in his face. In fact, she liked everything about him, and knowing that, she tried to dredge up a few suspicions.

"Well," he said with a grin, "I don't think Big Bob, as you call him, wants my help. He certainly didn't want me loitering anywhere near the crime scene." The amusement in his eyes faded, and suddenly his hand was on hers. "If you led them there, and you went in the house, that must have been horrible for you."

She took a deep breath. "It was. And now it's time to talk about something else."

He studied her face for another second and then glanced at their empty plates. "Dessert?"

Christy shook her head. "I couldn't."

"Glad you said that. I would have at least offered to share something, but I couldn't handle it either. How about a walk on the beach to get some exercise?"

"Great idea."

Dan paid the tab, tipping Mallon generously. As they crossed the lobby, the blond server she had questioned in the parking lot blocked her path.

Christy tried to keep her expression calm. She didn't want Dan to know why she had chosen this restaurant. He seemed to be well informed, so she suspected he knew this was where Dr. Stewart had taken his last meal. Since he didn't mention it, nor had she in relating the story, why bring it up now?

"Hi," the young woman called, looking from Christy to Dan. "Did you enjoy your meal?"

"We certainly did," Christy replied, tucking her hand inside his elbow and quickening her steps.

"Who did you say you work for?" she asked Christy, curiosity outweighing good manners. Or maybe she'd been told to ask.

Christy hesitated. Dan's hand closed over hers as she gripped his arm a bit tighter.

"She's modest," he said, glancing from Christy back to the server. "She's Christy Castleman, the mystery writer."

All pretense of friendliness vanished from the girl's face. A frown bunched the smooth skin between her brown eyebrows.

"I also write a column for the *Courier*," Christy added quickly. "I'm working on something concerning security guards."

The girl's expression ranged from suspicion to confusion. "Oh."

"See you later." Christy flashed her best smile.

Dan's steps seemed to lag as they moved toward the door. She looked up at him, flashing the same bright smile. Was he teasing her, gauging her reaction to see if she knew he knew what she was doing? Well, of course she knew. That he knew.

"Now you'll have to write that type of article," Dan said once they were outside, headed toward the parking area.

"Oh, I intend to. My car's over there." She pointed. "Still want to take that walk?" She tried to slow down her rapid speech or at least distract him from it, as she shivered lightly. "Glad I wore a sweater."

He watched her carefully and then he began to chuckle again. "I definitely think we should take that walk."

"Okay, I'll follow you."

"You saw my car when you came in?" he asked, a twinkle in his blue eyes.

"I did." *And thank you for not saying, "When you questioned the server."* She wondered how he seemed to figure everything out so quickly. She'd meant it when she said Big Bob and the detectives could use his help.

"I'll be glad to walk you to your car," Dan offered. "I don't see the security guard."

"No, I'm fine. I'll just pull in behind you."

She hurried toward her car, pressing the Unlock button on her key chain. She opened the door, sat down in the front seat, and glanced back.

He was getting into his green SUV, his head still turned in her direction. She shifted in her seat, inserting the key in the ignition.

She had never met anyone so sharp, so quick. At the same

time, she'd never met such a gentleman. He had known exactly what she was doing, from the moment the girl stopped them to pointedly ask questions. In her experience, most guys wouldn't be able to resist teasing her or at least letting her know they had figured things out. But Dan had a self-confidence about him that let her know he didn't need to prove anything. He was secure within himself—and perhaps she admired that trait as much as any of his others.

She backed her car out and pulled behind him as he smoothly steered around the row of cars jammed tightly into every space. She hit the button that lowered her window and breathed the balmy night. Slowly she began to relax as she followed him.

Traffic along Front Beach Road had picked up, but this was a ghost town compared to tourist season, when cars rode bumper to bumper past towering condos, restaurants, and amusement centers. She much preferred Summer Breeze, despite the limited dining choices.

Dan's left blinker began to flash, and she hit her turn signal and followed him into the parking lot at the pier. He pulled in beside a vacant space, leaving her room to park, then cut his lights. He had left his blazer on the seat, and now he tugged his tie loose from the white shirt that looked almost iridescent in the light from the pier.

She unlocked the door and accepted his hand as she got out.

"We've picked the perfect night," he said.

"Yes, we have." She beeped the car locked, then tucked her

keys in her purse. "Here, let me do something." She tiptoed up and reached to the back of his head, where a thick strand of hair stuck straight out. She smoothed it down, feeling its silky texture.

"Thanks." He smiled at her.

"You're welcome."

The breeze from the Gulf rushed to greet them, a soft caress on her skin.

He tucked her hand into his arm as they began to walk. "I like your shoes, but I guess they're not the best for walking."

For one heart-stopping second, she wondered if the guy who seemed to see and sense everything had watched her writhe around at the marina, her spike heel lodged in a crack. And had he seen Jack huddled down, freeing her shoe?

"I'm fine." She glanced toward the restaurant nearest the pier.

She could smell food and hear blues music drifting out. It took her back to a hundred other nights when she had walked the pier or the beach with others, especially Chad.

But tonight was different. She and Dan were both mature adults, and first love was long past for both of them. Despite the hectic evening, her nerves had begun to settle. A sense of peace flowed over her as she glanced at the dark waves whitecapping at the shoreline.

Yes…peace. That was the right word. With Chad, always unpredictable, she never knew what to expect. But she didn't want to think about Chad; he didn't belong here tonight.

With Dan there was enough suspense to keep her challenged

and entertained; at the same time, she felt that he was safe, solid. *But you're just getting to know him,* a voice in her head warned.

They had reached the pier, which was neither crowded nor deserted. They walked past an elderly couple standing together surveying the stars, then a guy hanging over the rail dropping bread crumbs into the water, watching the fish come up for a sample. Farther on, two young lovers meshed together in a passionate kiss.

They walked to the end of the pier and placed their elbows on the wooden rail to enjoy the view.

"Stardust and moonlight," Dan said. "It describes the night perfectly, don't you think?"

"You're very poetic."

"I read it somewhere."

They exchanged grins, and she looked up at the sky. A thousand stars winked at them while a full moon cast a silver river before them. It was a night for being poetic.

"This is nice," he said, as they leaned against the rail and drank in the beauty of the night. "It feels good to be home."

In his voice she could hear tenderness and nostalgia. Glancing at him, she thought about how he had dutifully served his country for the past eight years. That had been his choice, she thought, feeling her respect deepen. How many times during those years had he longed for home?

"It's nice to have you home, Major Brockman."

"Thanks. I'm glad we met, Christy Castleman."

"So am I."

The couple who had been locked in an embrace earlier had now broken apart and launched into a squabble. Christy tried to ignore their voices, distant at first, but growing louder with each comment.

"Funny," she said, talking louder. "I skipped the general questions and went straight to the personal ones tonight. So I'll go back to the generalities. Where were you raised? You don't have a Southern accent, but then you don't have a distinct one from… anywhere."

"That's because I've lived all over the country with Dad being military. While he was in the Far East, we lived on my grandparents' farm in Tennessee. I liked it there, but then Dad came back to the States, and we moved to Nebraska. So my Southern accent got compromised. I went to high school in Nebraska and on to college at the University of Montana."

The argument behind them had turned into a shouting match, distracting them from their conversation. Dan stopped talking, looking over her head with concern, then irritation.

"It isn't serious," he said, shaking his head. "But they've already run the older couple off."

"It's okay. I really should go home now."

She could see he was reluctant. "Okay. If you insist."

The teenagers hardly noticed when Christy and Dan walked by. Christy suspected they would soon patch up the argument and be smooching again.

"This time I really will leave you alone so you can finish your manuscript," he said to her as they reached her car. "Mom and I are leaving for Tennessee first thing in the morning."

"Have a safe trip," she said as she unlocked the car. "And thanks for a nice evening."

He nodded, opening the door for her. "My pleasure."

"While you're in Tennessee, I'll be hard at work. Don't you feel sorry for me?"

"Not really." His eyes teased her as a grin lifted his lips. "You enjoy your writing. That's pretty obvious to me."

She laughed. "You're right; I do."

He looked down at her, as though trying to read her expression. "I'll call you when I get back. If you want me to, that is."

She nodded, looking back at him through the open window. "I do."

He leaned in the window and touched his lips lightly to hers.

"Good night, Christy."

"Good night."

She forced herself to pull her gaze from his and turn the key in the ignition. As she drove off, she glanced in the rearview mirror. He stood watching her, the ends of his tie rippling out in the light breeze.

11

Saturday, February 21

C hristy had decided to ride the wave of adrenaline from her evening with Dan. Upon arriving home, she had gone straight to her computer and worked until after two o'clock. She had felt focused and sharp, which was a huge relief. With all the drama around her, she had begun to wonder if she would ever get back on track.

Today, as she reread the pages she had written last night and this morning, she was pleased with her work.

Stretching back in her desk chair, she opened the curtains and looked outside. It was a beautiful morning with a light breeze stirring the palm trees. She pushed back from the desk and stood, thinking about vanilla almond tea, just as the phone rang.

"Hey, Christy. It's Dianna. We're back. Grant called and told me about Marty. We left right away. I'm shocked to hear what happened to her."

"I know. It's terrible."

"What does Big Bob think?"

"Big Bob isn't talking." Much.

"Well, the reason I'm calling is that I want to invite you to have lunch with the Sassy Snowbirds today. A couple of ladies from Pensacola are visiting our get-together. Valerie thought you might want to talk to them. Maybe if you describe the boyfriend—well, it can't hurt."

"His name is Archie Cynaubaum," she replied.

"Oh? I should have known that you, being the little detective, would have found out. Great. Hey, I've got another call. See you at noon at Frank's?"

"I'll be there."

Christy crossed the hall to the bedroom and opened the closet door to study her choices. An hour later she was entering the restaurant. As she crossed the lobby, she spotted two ladies emerging from the rest room dressed in fancy red hats and nice purple outfits.

Christy stepped forward. "Excuse me. Are you the ladies from Pensacola?"

They turned to smile at her. "Yes, we are," the older of the two replied. "I'm Sylvia, and this is Carol Jane."

"I'm Christy Castleman."

"The mystery writer?" Sylvia asked.

"Afraid so. May I sit with you?"

"Please do."

Apparently someone had already clued them in that she would

be asking questions, but they didn't seem to mind. They motioned her over to a table where a beautiful arrangement of red roses was centered on the main table with a card that had "Frank" written in a bold scrawl. Frank, the perfect host, always pampered his customers. She'd heard someone say he'd gone to Mobile for the weekend to check out a location for another restaurant.

Christy took note of who was here: Maryann, Valerie, Dianna, and a couple of others she didn't know. Bonnie was noticeably absent. Maryann was addressing the group, saying something about how the attendance in their disorganization, as they called it, would dip at the end of February, when some of their Snowbird members would be returning to their homes to spend spring and summer.

"We're hosting a going-away party for our winter Snowbirds on Friday evening at my house," Maryann was saying. "And while you're away, we'll try to keep our chapter growing and strong." She turned to several ladies seated nearby. "And thank you again for teaching us locals something about fun and friendship after fifty."

Christy knew the only rule for their disorganization was to have reached fifty years of age and desire a sisterhood with other women from fifty to ninety-six. Miss Amelia, as she was affectionately called, was a retired schoolteacher who had never married. She lived in a nursing home but wanted to be a part of their group. If she was feeling up to it, someone went by to drive her over to the luncheon get-togethers. During the winter, she had been unable to attend, so the ladies took turns visiting and usually dropped off a red hat or a gift. The Sassy Snowbirds had become her family.

Maryann had stopped talking, and Christy saw that her expression had changed. "On a sadder note, we are all horrified by the brutal death of Marty McAllister. As a tribute, let's bow our heads in a moment of silent prayer."

All heads dipped, and each woman said her own prayer. Christy closed her eyes and prayed that the person who killed Marty would be discovered.

"Now," Maryann's voice lifted, "we have decided to discuss business after pleasure—pleasure being the wonderful buffet. So, gals, go for it!"

As the others flocked to the table, Sylvia and Carol Jane remained seated, turning in their chairs to look at Christy. "Maybe this would be the best time for us to try to help you," Carol Jane said.

"I want to know about Archie Cynaubaum." Christy came right to the point.

The ladies exchanged glances, and when they looked back at Christy, their expressions were troubled.

"He and his wife recently moved to the area; my husband said Mr. Cynaubaum owns a shipping business"

"What's his wife like?" Christy asked.

"If the stories circulating around town are true, she's a very jealous, possessive woman," Sylvia added. "We could tell you some rumors to back that up, but I can't prove any of it. Particularly if a lady here has been murdered."

Christy nodded, considering this new information. She told them about seeing him parked across the street from Marty's house the previous day.

Carol Jane nodded. "He probably cared for her as much as he's capable of caring for anyone."

"He's a very complicated person with few friends," Sylvia put in. "His main interest seems to be making money."

"Well," Christy sighed, "I'm afraid he and Marty had a lot in common. Perhaps that was part of the attraction."

"We really don't know much about him or his wife," Carol Jane said. "They moved to Pensacola from Mobile. They've only been there a year or so."

"They bought a doctor's place out from town," Sylvia added. "A friend lives in the area and says they're never outside, even with a nice pool in the backyard and a beautiful patio." She shook her head. "I'm sorry. That's all we know. It's probably all most other people know. They keep to themselves."

Christy thought about this. "I saw Mr. Cynaubaum, but what does his wife look like?"

They hesitated, but then Carol Jane spoke up. "She's a tall woman with black hair and sad eyes. I only saw her one time. She and Archie came into a restaurant where my husband and I were having dinner. My husband pointed them out to me and said he'd met the man on the golf course. Mrs. Cynaubaum was wearing a tan raincoat, but even with the coat on, I could tell she was quite thin, almost emaciated."

"Aren't you ladies going to get something to eat?" Dianna stopped beside them, her plate loaded. Her glance shot to Christy. "Don't keep them from all this wonderful food, hon."

Christy stood. "I won't detain you. Thanks so much for your help."

"Aren't you going to join us?"

Christy nodded. "In a minute. You two go on."

When they left the table, she sat back down and stared at the lush red roses in the center of the table, processing what they had told her about Mrs. Cynaubaum. Just then someone tapped her shoulder. She turned to face Valerie, who looked very serious.

"Christy, I just got a call from Bonnie. Her husband had a massive heart attack and died an hour ago."

"Oh no! Where was Bonnie when she called?"

"She'd just returned home from the hospital. Sherrie's with her. I'm about to make the announcement."

"I'm going over there now," Christy said, grabbing her purse. "Explain to Aunt Dianna."

Valerie nodded. "Tell her we're all thinking about her and want to do whatever we can to help."

Christy slipped out and hurried to the car, then drove to the market to pick up some items from the deli, along with ice cream and cookies.

After she paid the cashier and returned to the parking lot, she carefully wedged her load into the backseat of her car and drove toward Bonnie's house. She hoped she wasn't intruding on a family's need for privacy, but she couldn't resist the opportunity to help if possible. Bonnie always came to the rescue whenever there was a need. It was time someone returned the favor.

She pulled into the driveway and glanced at the modest gray stucco house. The garage door at the end of the drive was closed, and a small red Mazda was parked in the driveway. Sherrie's, she assumed.

Christy got out and reached into the backseat for two sacks of groceries. Carefully she made her way up to the front door and rang the bell. In seconds the door opened, and she faced Sherrie.

"Hi, Sherrie. I'm so sorry about your dad."

"Thanks, Christy." The half smile on her lips barely deflected the sadness in her dark eyes. "Here, let me help you with that."

The house was dim and cool as she stepped into the small living room and then followed Sherrie past the dining room, where a lone coffee mug sat on the table. The abundance of food so typical of Bonnie's kitchen was missing.

"Had your dad had heart problems recently?"

Sherrie shook her head as a tear rolled down her cheek. "No, or if he ever had pain, he never told us."

Christy asked nothing more as she helped Sherrie put away the food.

"I see you've brought chocolate chip cookies; that's what I call comfort food." She wiped her cheeks with a Kleenex and tried to smile. "Comfort food is what got me in trouble in Tallahassee. I gained twenty pounds after I realized Eddie and I were headed for divorce court."

"Well, those twenty pounds are gone now. You look terrific," Christy replied, her eyes sweeping Sherrie's tall, slim figure in white cargoes and a T-shirt. Her glossy black hair swirled around her pretty face, but her eyes were swollen from crying.

"Christy, you're so sweet to bring all this food. Mom thinks the world of you."

"And I adore her." Christy glanced around the house. "Where is she?"

Sherrie sighed. "She's gone to bed with a migraine and pain medication. I think she's asleep. Let's go out back where we can talk."

Christy followed Sherrie out to the small grassy yard, where a fat tabby cat chased something in the hedges. Rosebushes had been planted along the natural-wood fence, and a flower garden near the back door held a variety of pinks, purples, and reds that added beauty to the otherwise plain yard. Even though it was still February and cold snaps threatened blooming flowers, she suspected Bonnie covered them and protected them, just as she had so carefully tended her flock of children.

"Are your brother and sisters on the way?"

She nodded. "They're scattered all over the country, but they're catching planes and loading cars." Sherrie clasped her hands in her lap and stared at them for a moment, saying nothing.

The tears she had tried to hide now trickled down her smooth cheeks. Christy cast about for something to comfort Sherrie. "Valerie wanted me to send word that their group will be bringing food and doing whatever they can to help out."

"That's nice." Sherrie was silent at that, studying her white sandals. "I peeked at the coroner's report on Mrs. McAllister."

Christy fidgeted. She didn't want to use this tragic time to garner information from Sherrie.

"It said there was a… How was it worded? I think it said a small sharp-force injury to her neck from some type of knife or blade. They never found her cell phone, but now they've got the records from her cell, as well as her home phone."

Christy sat on the edge of her seat, waiting to hear more. "And?"

"The last call Marty got, which was at one ten, was made from a pay phone near Shipwreck Island. Whoever called her must have asked her to meet them at the ship house. The call before that is definitely traceable." She let the sentence hang in the air for a moment. "It's a cell phone that belongs to Stephanie Cynaubaum, the wife of Marty's boyfriend who owned the yacht. That call came in around one o'clock. Now why do you suppose she was calling Marty?"

"Good question."

Christy thought the woman might have pretended an interest in the ship house. She had already learned from the Pensacola ladies that Mrs. Cynaubaum was a very jealous woman.

"Look, I don't want you to think I came to get information.

I'm sure you have things to do to get ready for your family. Can I pick up anyone at the airport?"

Sherrie nodded. "That would help. I'll let you know when I get their schedules." Sherrie reached over to hug her. "Thanks for stopping by."

Sunday, February 22

When the music (not so soft this morning) pierced her deep sleep, Christy fought a strong temptation to throw her clock radio out the window. Instead she forced herself out of bed and blinked at the sunlit morning. Her eyes burned as though someone had thrown sand in them, but it was the sleepless night that had left her eyes gritty and her mind and body tired and listless. She kept thinking about Bonnie and Sherrie and feeling sad for them. She got up and headed for the shower.

After a shower and shampoo, she wound her hair around and clipped it up on her head with a pearl clasp. Then she stepped into a pair of black linen slacks and chose a white silk blouse. To offset the black and white, she wore a pair of burgundy pumps. Then she hurried out into the bright sunshine. It was a beautiful Sunday morning—just what everyone needed after dreary days and dreary news.

She had missed Sunday school, but as she headed across the parking lot, she met Jamie, the server from Frank's place, along with her two young sons.

"Oh hi," Jamie called to Christy, then stopped, saying something to her sons, who turned to stare.

"Jamie, how nice to see you," Christy said. She turned to study the little boys, who lowered their gazes. They looked scrubbed and polished in their shirts and jeans, with every crease pressed neatly in place.

"This is Jacob, and this is Will," Jamie said. "Boys, say hello to Christy."

"Hello," they said in unison, then went back to studying their tennis shoes.

"Hey, Jacob and Will." She looked back at Jamie and silently mouthed *adorable*.

"Jacob and Will went to your mother's class," Jamie said, looking pleased. "I couldn't seem to separate them, but Mrs. Castleman said it was fine for Will, who is seven, to stay with Jacob in the eight-year-olds' class. I think they enjoyed it," she said, glancing back at them.

Christy could see the strawberry suckers peeking from their shirt pockets, and she suspected some folded artwork nestled in their jeans. "I'm sorry I didn't get here in time to show you to the classrooms," she said, still surprised that Jamie had actually come and brought her boys. Generally, it took more than one invitation for most single moms.

"It's okay. A lady greeted us at the door and was real helpful," Jamie replied. She was wearing a navy pantsuit that looked as though it had been around for a while, but there was not a spot or a wrinkle anywhere. A red silk bow held her ponytail in place.

"Did you go to the singles class?" Christy asked. "That's the one I'm in."

Jamie hesitated. "Well, I felt a little funny about that, being divorced and all. I just went to the general session in the sanctuary, the one your father teaches."

Christy grinned. "Sometimes Dad gets a little long-winded."

Jamie shook her head. "No, I really enjoyed it. But the boys are a little antsy, so maybe we won't go for the full two hours today."

"I understand. Listen, where do you live?" She was already thinking about visitation, wondering if Jamie had filled out a card.

There were no bad neighborhoods in Summer Breeze. There was, however, one street with small rental houses, and that was the area in which Jamie lived. Christy knew the houses were tiny but well maintained, and the rent was reasonable. Still, it might be a stretch for a single mom with two little boys.

"I hope you'll come back," Christy said. "We do lots of fun things."

"That's what your mother said. In fact, she mentioned a spring picnic at the park."

"And there's a huge Easter egg hunt next month." Christy looked down at the boys. "We go all out for Easter here, guys. You may even win the prize egg."

"What's in it?" Will asked, wide-eyed.

While the boys were almost the same size, it was obvious that Jacob was the older of the two.

"A five-dollar bill," Christy replied. She looked at Jamie. "We get together the day before the hunt and dye a hundred eggs. We also have some plastic eggs with prizes inside and plastic-wrapped candy. The kids love it."

"Sounds like fun to me," Jamie agreed. "Well, we'd better go. Thanks for inviting us," she called over her shoulder as she herded the boys toward the parking lot.

"And I'm glad you invited them." Her mother's voice came from behind her, and Christy whirled.

"Mom, you're like a ghost—everywhere at once and always sneaking up on people."

"I beg to differ," she said, reaching up to smooth a strand of Christy's hair. "Anyway, Will and Jacob are good little boys, and they were very curious about which animals Noah took on the ark. I hope they'll come back. How did you happen to meet them?"

"Jamie works at Frank's. I invited her when I had lunch there this week."

"Good for you."

The choir had already started singing, capturing their attention as they turned to enter the church.

At Marty's graveside service a crowd of fifty or so were seated in the metal folding chairs. Christy slipped into an end chair beside an older lady who attended their church. She smiled at the lady, then glanced around the sparse crowd. She spotted Aunt Dianna and

Valerie in the second row, and in the third row sat Big Bob and Judy beside Carl Alexander, the broker from Marty's real-estate company. She recognized other familiar faces from around Summer Breeze, mostly businesspeople.

A blanket of spring flowers covered the casket, which Christy guessed had come from the nephew. Other floral arrangements flanked the sides and end of the grave. Christy couldn't help thinking that she had seen more flowers at other funerals, but then Marty had not been the most popular citizen of Summer Breeze.

Christy tried to peer around heads to the front row.

There, in the center, a man sat tall in his seat: Bruce McAllister, the nephew, no doubt. Beside him sat a woman with professionally styled blond hair and a designer suit. His wife.

She turned to the lady beside her. "Is the couple in the front row the nephew and wife?" she whispered.

The woman nodded. "Bruce and Melissa. I hadn't met them until this morning, when I spoke with them about the insurance claim."

Christy's eyebrow hiked before she could conceal her dismay, but the woman had turned to face the front. Christy remembered this lady was an insurance agent.

Aha!

Her eyes sneaked to the back of tall Bruce. He would wear a big shoe. He had motive: a large insurance settlement was involved. No doubt he was the beneficiary of the insurance and her estate, if she had no family. Perhaps he even knew how to get in the house.

Margaret Thomason had kept the key hidden under a piece of driftwood. Had Marty mentioned that to her nephew over the past year?

There were many theories about who killed Marty and why. Christy's mind wandered back to the only theory she believed. Someone entered in a disguise. That theory presented all sorts of possibilities. And people.

Christy's eyes quickly scanned the rest of the group, searching for Archie. She hadn't seen the red car with the Pensacola license tags out in the parking area, nor had she seen the man who had sat in his car staring at Marty's house. He wasn't here.

Her dad, still wearing his dark suit, came to the podium and began to read the Twenty-third Psalm. Soon the brief service ended, and the funeral director was suggesting that everyone might wish to leave before the burial.

Chairs moved, and people stood, preparing to leave. All were casting last glances at the white coffin. She noticed there were tears in the eyes of Aunt Dianna and Valerie. Truly, these women were Marty's only real friends after all.

Slowly Bruce and his wife led the procession toward the row of parked cars.

Acting on an impulse that she couldn't curb, she sidled up to Big Bob. "Her boyfriend isn't here," she whispered and watched as he grew wide-eyed.

"How can you think of that now—"

"Because I saw him parked in front of her house Friday."

Bob glanced around the crowd, his big face holding an expression that Christy could only guess was embarrassment. Okay, so she was being bold and insensitive, but every passing hour counted in solving a murder. And with each lost hour, investigators believed the killer was less likely to be caught. She knew that was true; she had read it and heard it too many times.

"Bob, I need to talk to you," she whispered. "When can I do that?"

His hazel eyes darted over the crowd, then shot down to her for an instant. "You have something?" His lips barely moved as he asked the question.

"I do," she said, thinking she had several somethings but unsure that he would consider them solid leads. Still, it was an excuse.

"I'll be at home all afternoon if you want to stop by. I try to spend Sundays with the family, but this investigation is turning into a twenty-four–seven ordeal."

"Around four?" she pressed. "I promise not to stay long." That would give Bob an hour or so with his family before she barged in.

Bruce McAllister was making his way toward Bob, and Christy lingered just long enough to hear him ask if there had been any developments in the case. *Are you hoping not?* she wondered.

Christy turned to Judy, Bob's wife. "How are the kids?"

Judy had nice blue eyes in a round face and, like her husband, enjoyed the food she prepared for their large family.

"The kids are up to their necks in homework," she answered.

"Of course, Tara, our sweet surprise, is still toddling around the house."

"I'm going to stop by your house in a little while to speak to Bob for about fifteen minutes. I'll do my best not to interfere with your family time."

Judy sighed. "How can you interfere when the phone never stops ringing, and we're all shouting at once? In fact, Robert Jr. and Ned have baseball practice this afternoon, so we'll have two less voices in the mix. The baby-sitter's there now; she may already have Tara down for her nap."

"Judy, you're the perfect wife for Big Bob."

"He might not agree with that," she replied, repressing a grin.

"I'm sure he does. See you later."

Christy wound around the crowd to give her aunt a hug.

"Hey, sweetie. How you doing?"

"Good. Have you talked to Bonnie?"

Dianna nodded. "I talked to her last night. We're all taking turns picking people up at the airport."

"Good. Let me know if I can help."

She and Valerie exchanged smiles, and she glanced back at her dad. He was engaged in conversation with Carl Alexander, but she caught his eye and waved before she turned and headed for her car.

She started her engine, then eased into the line of cars, but turned left rather than right, the direction in which the other cars seemed to be traveling. Taking a few back streets to avoid the traffic, she started to ponder her motives for getting so involved in this investigation.

Because of the bottle and note. By accident or divine intervention, she had read the note and repeated it to people who had half convinced her the writing belonged to Marty, who was mysteriously missing. Christy had been the one to give the bottle and check to Big Bob, stirring up suspicion.

When she tried to stay out of the investigation, her aunt kept asking her to drive by the house and check on Marty.

And then, when she wrote about the bottle and note in her Beach Buzz, Sandpiper had called. And through her conversation with him, she'd led Big Bob to the house...and to Marty.

So how could she not be involved? Call it curiosity, or even obsession, but whatever had taken hold of her drove her on. Why had she asked to visit Big Bob, and what information did she have after all? She bit her lip, realizing too late she had acted on an impulse that she would probably regret; it certainly wouldn't be the first time.

12

At home Christy quickly changed from her dress to a comfortable pair of green Capris with matching T-shirt. Her sandals flip-flopped over the hardwood floor as she hurried to the kitchen. On another whim, she decided to make a pitcher of lemonade to go with a late lunch. The drink always brought memories of summer and picnics and good times. She considered it the perfect choice after a depressing funeral.

Hovering on the edge of her consciousness was a memory she kept trying to escape during the graveside service. Another funeral service, drastically different. Family and friends had filled the church and overflowed onto the sidewalk. She never again expected to see so many floral arrangements or so many tear-stained faces. None more haggard then her own. Chad's funeral.

As she squeezed lemons into a glass pitcher, she tried to push those sad memories aside. She forced her mind forward, in the direction of Dan Brockman and the way she had enjoyed the evening.

Where would this friendship, relationship—whatever it was—

where would it go? And did that really matter? She needed to prove to herself that she could have a healthy relationship just for a while, if not longer.

She glanced through the kitchen window to the neighbor's yard, watching as David and Drew tossed a baseball back and forth. And in the yard to her right, she could see Jenny Beth and her dad playing with her new black cocker spaniel puppy.

It was nice to see happy people. She poured cold water into the pitcher, added sugar, and stirred. Then she sat down on the barstool and dipped her fork into her microwaved casserole. She glanced at Roy's special Sunday edition, still rolled up and tossed onto the eating bar. She had nearly an hour to kill, so if she was going to discuss the case with Bob, she needed to reread the article.

She removed the rubber band and unrolled the paper.

Staring back at her were the faces of Marty McAllister and Dr. Peter Stewart. She studied Marty's face, and then her gaze moved to Dr. Stewart. He had a long thin face, narrow-set eyes, and tight lips. He was a baby step away from looking…well, downright ugly. Or maybe the picture didn't do him justice. One thing she knew, she'd never seen him before. She read the brief account, studying it more carefully than she had when Roy asked her to proof it. She had hardly paid attention to the words then, being angry with Roy and eager to flee. Now she read carefully.

> Peter Stewart was born and raised in Syracuse, New
> York, attended medical school at Johns Hopkins, then

trained in the field of plastic surgery. He opened a private practice in New York City and had worked there
for the past twenty-five years. After developing diabetes,
he had taken an early retirement. He is survived by one
brother, Lawrence Stewart, an architect. His parents are
deceased.

There was no mention of a wife or children. His brother had
been contacted and quoted:

Peter was looking forward to retiring in Florida. This
was his second trip to the state searching for a home
that suited him.

His body had been returned to New York and cremated, in
accordance with his wishes. Roy had suggested he'd get a quote
from Valerie and Bonnie, but these were missing. Bonnie was
grieving, and Valerie had probably been too busy. Or Roy was racing the clock to crank out his special edition.

Christy laid the paper down and reached for her lemonade.
The sweet liquid flowed into her dry throat, and she picked up a
slice of lemon and nipped at it. Strange how a report of someone
could cover the basics yet say so very little about him. She thought
of her special toy, an expensive Internet search engine that nosed
out details for her research. She had not used it for personal reasons, feeling it unfair to snoop into people's lives when her search

did not pertain to writing fiction. She'd been tempted, of course, but she'd never done it. Now she could and would.

She rushed through her lunch, drained her glass of lemonade, and hurried to her office. Hitting the button to pull the computer's brains from sleep mode to active, she sat down and waited as the monitor flashed to life.

Before she went to her favorite search engine, however, she opened her Favorites to the folder marked Newspapers. Then she began to scroll back to the first account of Dr. Stewart's murder in the Panama City newspaper. She wanted to read it again, to see if she had missed something that might give her an edge. The main points of the article were the same as in Roy's paper. Motive believed to be robbery.

"Et cetera, et cetera," she mumbled.

What she needed was more information about Dr. Stewart, to see if perhaps someone might have followed him here from New York.

With that in mind, she closed the file and went to her special search engine. Excitement tingled as she logged in and began another search, typing in the name "Dr. Peter Stewart." She sat back in her chair and waited as a long list of names began to roll down the screen of the monitor. There were three Dr. Peter Stewarts, but only one address matched his Park Avenue residence.

Feeling a rush of adrenaline, she punched a few more keys and waited. The recent account of his death in a New York City newspaper popped up, another small account of the murder with sentences similar to those in the Panama City newspaper, citing robbery as a possible motive.

Then she leaned forward, as another article, vastly different, unfolded before her startled eyes. It was an old article, dating back to 1989, detailing a jewelry heist and the fact that the suspected thief, Benny Salvatore, had not been apprehended. Dr. Peter Stewart's name was highlighted farther down in the article, and at the next sentences her adrenaline spiked.

> An anonymous tip led authorities to the office of
> Dr. Peter Stewart, noted plastic surgeon. However,
> Dr. Stewart and his staff denied ever seeing or hearing
> from Salvatore.

The article went into more detail about the jewelry heist and the thief, but there was no further mention of Dr. Stewart.

She sighed, wishing people wouldn't call in their "helpful" tips if they weren't sure about what they were reporting. It was precisely that type of tip that wasted investigators' time and taxpayers' money.

She left that article and went back to the account of Stewart's death. This time her focus jammed on a word that hadn't stood out before.

> …looking for a *home.*

The word jam slowly dislodged as her thoughts started clicking. If Dr. Stewart planned to buy a home, he would most likely consult a Realtor. What if Marty, whose business cards were scattered all over the Panhandle, had been one of the Realtors he consulted? A rental car with a Florida tag wouldn't have stood out among locals. Christy's instincts took over. Sometimes she seemed to have an inner radar that beeped when she was onto something. She felt that beep vibrate through her senses.

A quick glance at the clock told her she had five minutes to get to Bob's house for her appointment. Bob had no patience for anyone who couldn't be on time. She bolted to the kitchen for her purse and car keys, then shot out the door.

Five miles above the speed limit wouldn't warrant a speeding ticket in Summer Breeze, unlike some areas she didn't care to recall. She rode the pedal, accelerating to greater speeds where she dared. She ran a yellow light, telling herself it would be worse to stomp on the brakes, and in minutes pulled to the curb of Bob's two-story white frame house, right on time.

She hopped out of the car and dashed up the walk, glancing right and left for stray balls and kids. The front yard held only bare spots in the grass, testifying to kids' activities, but no children this afternoon. At the wide porch, she tapped lightly on the door. It flew back, and Big Bob filled the doorframe.

"Come on in," he said, leading the way into the first room on the left.

A wonderful smell permeated the house—Judy had something

divine in the oven, no doubt. She could hear the low thump of music overhead, and from somewhere in the distance, probably the backyard, a girl's voice rose in protest and a boy's voice retaliated, sweeping her back to verbal tussles with Seth.

Bob closed his office door and motioned her to a chair in front of his desk. Stacks of papers competed for space with his computer and telephone. The small room held a few family pictures on the wall, along with a couple of plaques he had received in the line of duty.

"Now what've you got, little gal?" His leather chair creaked in protest as he sank his considerable weight into it. "And you better have something solid to encroach on my precious time—and I only call my time precious when my family is involved."

Christy nodded. "I know, and I feel guilty—"

"No, you don't. So tell me what you've got." Bags and shadows underscored Bob's eyes. He looked overworked and exhausted.

She got right to it. "What about Archie Cynaubaum's wife? The next-to-last call on Marty's cell phone came from her."

A dark eyebrow jumped, then fell, as understanding registered in eyes that narrowed to slits. "You've been talking to Sherrie again, and I've already warned you about that."

"I have sources other than Sherrie," she replied, lifting her chin to fake a self-confidence that was deteriorating beneath Big Bob's scowl.

"Well, if you're suspecting Mrs. Cynaubaum, I'll put your mind at ease. Both Mr. Cynaubaum and his wife have alibis."

"And with their money, they could buy alibis faster than I buy shoes."

Bob merely shrugged. "What else you got?"

"Okay, Dr. Stewart was looking for a home, and Marty sells homes. Is there a chance the two of them got together? And did anyone see Dr. Stewart with Marty?"

He lowered his eyes, and Christy's radar beeped. Her random shot had scored a bull's-eye. "The investigators are handling this, not me," he said, looking back at Christy.

"I reread the newspaper article," she plunged on with new vigor, "and I figured out that he might have hooked up with Marty. Everyone knows she's got the most listings in the area."

"But not the most in Panama City, and that's where he was staying."

Then a thought struck her, and she scooted to the edge of her seat. "You know from the phone records that he hooked up with Marty, don't you?"

"Listen, little Mystery Lady, I know he hooked up with Marty because several people saw her driving around with a stranger that one person has identified as Dr. Stewart."

Christy gasped. "See!"

"See what?"

"They were both killed. The robber…" Her voice trailed off as once again she found herself at a dead end.

"Christy, you said you had something to tell me. You've told me nothing I didn't already know. My gut tells me you're just snooping and—"

She was saved by the bell or rather the ringing telephone on his desk. She began to bite the skin around the nail of her thumb, her mind working. There was some other reason for Marty and Dr. Stewart to be together; she knew it; she could feel it.

"*When?*" Bob shouted.

Christy jumped, staring at him.

Bob stood up, grabbed his pager and cell phone and shoved both into place on his huge belt. "I'll be right there." He slammed down the phone and stared across at her for a moment, obviously debating what to say.

"What? Come on, Bob. If not for me, you might not have found her. Not for a while, anyway."

"And now maybe we've found her killer," he said, coming around the desk. "This morning we got a search warrant to go through Buster Greenwood's house. The detectives just found her jewelry and wallet in a ski mask hidden under his sofa. They're reading him his rights now."

Christy froze, trying to process the information while Bob, in contrast, had sprung into action. He was already standing in the door, yelling down the hall.

"Judy!"

Upstairs, a baby began to cry.

Christy stumbled forward, peering around Bob.

Judy stood at the head of the steps, hands on hips, anger written all over her face. "You just woke Tara, Bob! Why can't you—"

"Explain it to her, Christy," he said and charged down the hall leading to the attached garage.

She explained as quickly as possible, then darted out the door to her car. Buster? Did he kill Marty? Did he kill Dr. Stewart, too?

Once she had wheeled away from Bob's house, she began to drive toward Shipwreck Island. Bob would throw a fit if she followed, but maybe she could get a peek at Buster from behind some trees. Somewhere.

Bob had jumped into the SUV and roared off, siren blazing. There was no way she could keep up, but she pressed the accelerator down, thinking no other patrolman would stop her if she stayed close behind Bob.

She lost him at the red light, which he sped right through while she was forced to stop. By the time the light changed, four cars had moved ahead of her, creeping along at a casual Sunday afternoon pace. Drawing a deep breath, she tried to keep her cool and be patient. When finally she reached a stretch of highway where she could pass, she darted around one car, then another. By the time she made the turn out to Shipwreck Island, she had lost them all. But what good had it done?

As her tires rumbled over the bridge, she looked straight ahead, and her spirits sank. Two cars were eating up gravel coming toward her—a detective car with a flashing blue light on his dash, followed by a sheriff's car. They roared past her, lights and sirens blazing. She quickly scanned the first car, then the second, where she caught a blurred glimpse of Buster in the backseat.

She whipped her car to the side of the road, threw it in park, then turned and watched through the back window as the vehicles streaked around the curve. Christy sat back in her seat, staring absently at a sea gull launching itself from the top of a signpost and sailing over the water. While the sirens faded in the distance, she took a deep breath and tried to line up her thoughts.

Buster's ongoing arguments with Marty were old news around town, and, of course, everyone knew about the threat he had made when she started developing the land on the island. Rumor was, he had told her if she set one foot on his property, she'd be sorry. Sorry? What did that mean? Had he finally seen an opportunity to get rid of her and make it look like Dr. Stewart's robbery? The answer, of course, lay with forensics. If the weapon matched, if Buster's fingerprints were in Dr. Stewart's car...

Everything she'd ever heard about Buster indicated he usually acted on impulse. But from her limited knowledge of the crime scenes, she believed the murders of both people had been carefully planned.

She doubted he had ever eaten at the exclusive restaurant where Dr. Stewart ate, but that wouldn't stop him from lurking in the parking area. But what would be his motive for killing Dr. Stewart? Obviously, she didn't have all the pieces to the puzzle, but apparently the detectives did. Otherwise, there wouldn't have been grounds for a search warrant of Buster's house.

She took a deep breath and reached forward to turn the key in the ignition. So Buster was the Big Foot on her chart at home, the less likely suspect…who had just soared to the top of their most wanted.

A horn beeped, and she looked across to see Frank perched high in his red truck, his window rolled down. "Where you headed?" he called to her.

"Did you know Buster was just arrested?" she asked without preamble.

Frank nodded, pulled his truck to the side of the road just in front of her, and climbed out. He was wearing faded jeans, a work shirt, and tennis shoes. Obviously, he wasn't going to the restaurant.

Frank began to wag his dark head. "I hated to do it, but after they found Marty, and I got to thinking about it, I called Bob."

"Thinking about what?" she asked, staring at Frank's square face. He was clean-shaven, and his thick, dark hair lay neatly in place.

"I bought a little house over there," he pointed toward the last subdivision before crossing the bridge. "I'm fixing it up as a rental. Anyway, last Sunday after the lunch crowd thinned out, I met a carpenter over here to show him what I wanted done. When I pulled back onto the road—just like I did today—I looked down the bay there and saw Buster heading out in his boat. I thought it was odd—you remember last Sunday afternoon turned stormy;

the waves were beating the shore. I wondered then why Buster would be going out in his boat like that, and in a hurry, too. Had to be around two thirty. After they found Marty, I got to thinking about it and called one of the detectives who ate at the restaurant. He'd left his business card with me."

Why hadn't Bob told her this? Because Bob wasn't supposed to tell her, she answered her own question. But how could he sit there listening to her theories, while knowing Buster might possibly be the latest suspect? What else, she wondered, had he known and failed to mention?

"And now they've found Marty's jewelry and billfold hidden in Buster's house," she said looking back at Frank.

Frank dropped his head, kicking at a broken seashell.

"Do you think he could have done it, Frank?" she asked.

Frank looked back at her. "I guess he could. He told me one time when we met up at the fish market that he hated what was being done to his property. Said he had that island to himself, to fish and hunt and live like he wanted." A grin tugged at his lips but never quite made it. "Then the—well, I won't say how he referred to Marty—but that she came over here and ruined his island."

Christy stared into space for a moment, digesting what Frank had said. No doubt the detectives had been quietly checking him out from day one. When Frank admitted he had seen Buster speeding out in his boat in choppy water, it gave them enough probable cause to request a warrant. Or perhaps forensics had given them something more damaging.

"So do you think Buster saw Marty and the doctor together? Maybe she brought him here to show him the house and Buster saw them. And being furious with her for developing his island, he hatched a plan: follow the doctor, rob and kill him. Doing this would distract attention from his real motive—to kill Marty."

Frank lifted his head to study the clouds, his big brow puckered in thought. "Yeah, I think you're right." He looked back at her, and his face relaxed as though he had settled things in his mind. "Ya know, we didn't think Buster was that sharp, but maybe that's what he was counting on."

A car passed with a pretty, thirty-something woman at the wheel. She waved, and Christy waved back.

"Who was that?" Frank asked, staring after the car.

"I don't know."

"But you waved at her."

Christy laughed. "Frank, sometimes I forget you're a Yankee. Waving at everyone is a Southern tradition."

Frank chuckled, shaking his head. "You guys do some funny things. Well, I gotta run," he said, stepping back from her car.

"See you later, Frank. Oh, by the way, Jamie, your new server, came to church today and brought her little boys."

"I know. She asked to have Sundays off to take her boys to church. I agreed."

"That was good of you, Frank." Christy wondered why he never came. She knew he had been invited by several people, but he always used work as an excuse. "I know you're a busy guy, but we do have a service at night."

His eyes drifted away from hers. "Never been in a church in my life, Christy. My old man was an atheist, and my mother…" His shoulders rose and fell in a shrug.

"But you're not an atheist, Frank." She made the statement before she thought about it, and yet she believed she was right.

He shoved his hands deep into his jeans pockets, rocked back on his heels, and looked off in the distance. "I believe in a Higher Power, and that's about as far as I'd go with it. But I'm all for Jamie trying to raise her sons right. I admire her for that."

Christy nodded. "Well, I'd better go home. See you later," she called as she started her car.

As she backed up enough to make a U-turn, she felt weariness creeping through every bone in her body. Between finishing the mystery she was writing and keeping up with the real mystery in her community, she had worn herself out.

As soon as she got home, she went straight to the television, hoping to catch the five o'clock news. She fidgeted through a couple of commercials, then waited impatiently until the teaser for breaking news filled the screen. She was looking into the scowling face of Buster Greenwood being led to jail. He was wearing jeans with a hole in the knee, a T-shirt advertising a local bar, and a base-ball cap that looked too small for his big, round head.

She hadn't seen him in a while, but time and booze had not

been kind. His eyes were swollen and puffy, his round face held a stubble of beard, and he was at least ten or fifteen pounds too heavy for his medium height. She never got a look at his feet, and she began to wonder if the investigators would be measuring his shoe soles to see whether they matched the smeared print on the paper they'd found.

"A local man has been arrested for the double murders of Marty McAllister and Dr. Peter Stewart. Stay tuned."

Another commercial occupied the television screen as she grabbed a sofa pillow and hugged it, waiting anxiously for the details on Buster's arrest.

The commercial ended, and a local newscaster appeared on screen. He was positioned on the street in front of headquarters in Panama City, where a curious crowd had gathered. He eagerly related the breaking news of Buster Greenwood's arrest and promised more news to follow.

Nothing he reported was news to her; in fact, she could have added enough details to give his story a real punch.

The designated time for this report had come and gone, and now the reporter switched to a two-car accident on Highway 98. "Fortunately, no one was seriously injured…"

She hit the Power button, and the newscaster disappeared. She stared at the blank screen, heaving a deep, long sigh. She felt like calling Sherrie or even Bonnie but resisted the urge. They needed time to themselves.

She pulled herself up from the sofa and headed to her office.

Now she could get something done with her novel. She might even make her deadline after all.

Taking a seat at her computer, she stared at the monitor. Her thoughts, however, were not on her own mystery. Her thoughts lingered on Buster's arrest and the mystery of Marty's death. The only thing that troubled her about justice being done was the knowledge that Buster came from a wealthy family. Even though there was no love lost between Buster and his family, she had no doubt that the best defense team would be brought in to clear the family name; for the family name, more than Buster, would be of utmost importance.

13

Monday, February 23

Christy had turned off the ringer on her telephone, as well as the sound on her answering machine, before going to bed last night. Now, as her head rolled on the pillow, she came awake with a renewed hope. The killer had been caught, and their lives could return to normal.

Feeling better than she had in days, she hopped out of bed and headed for the shower. Afterward, she pulled on jeans and a sweatshirt. She actually had an appetite this morning, and her thoughts drifted toward a real breakfast: bacon, eggs, grits... Her mouth watered.

She went to the kitchen and put on a pot of coffee, then glanced at the answering machine, blinking furiously. When she checked the caller ID, she reached for the daisy pad to write down names and numbers. Her mom, then her friend Susan, saying she'd be home on Friday. The last one was Bonnie.

This was the call she chose to return first as she propped the phone between her shoulder and chin and went to the refrigerator to inspect the contents. Two eggs sat in their plastic nests. She dialed and waited, reaching into the meat drawer, and saw, with relief, that two strips of bacon remained in a Ziploc bag.

"Hello." There was no music in her voice.

"Hello, Bonnie," she said, opening a cabinet and pulling down a box of grits. "Can I do anything to help?"

"No, but I wanted to thank you for the food." All the joy had been drained from her voice.

"When is...the funeral?"

"Won't be until Thursday. We got out-of-state people who can't get here till tomorrow. And I had to wait a day on reserving the funeral parlor. You take care, girl."

"You, too. And, Bonnie, please know that I'll be thinking of you."

"Thanks, honey. I will."

Christy hung up, shaking her head. Bonnie's heart was broken.

Christy had fried the bacon crisp and gently flipped the fried eggs to make them come out of the skillet soft. That way she could stir the eggs into her buttered grits, toss on the salt and pepper, and go to it.

And that's exactly what she was doing when she heard an engine pulling into her driveway. It was a dreary morning, and she wondered who had braved the misting rain to stop by her house. Probably one of the callers she hadn't bothered to call back. A door slammed, and she headed to the back door.

Peering out, she saw Jack, head down, charging up the sidewalk to her back door. He reminded her of a wet bird dog trailing a hot scent.

"Well, good morning," she called, walking over to unlatch the screen door.

"What's good about it?" Jack frowned, brushing raindrops from his shirt. He was dressed in clean slacks and dress shirt, a fact that alarmed her. He was clean-shaven and not even wearing his baseball cap. The thinning brown hair was pasted down with some kind of hair spray that reminded her to buy him something nicer, more subtle.

"What's good about it?" she repeated. "I'll tell you what. Bacon, eggs, and grits. And if you adjust your attitude, I intend to put a plate on the eating bar for you."

A twinkle lit the vivid blue eyes as he entered the kitchen and closed the door, shutting out the sound of the rain.

"I forget how much I miss a woman until I get a whiff of breakfast cooking."

"How long were you and Pat married before she died?"

As soon as she asked, she wished she hadn't. The eyes lost their light. "Twenty-four years. Chad had just turned ten."

She went to the cabinet, pulled down an extra mug, and poured him a cup of coffee.

He sank down on the stool beside her. "I'm not hungry," he said, staring at her bacon. "So you go on and eat your breakfast. Don't let me interrupt you."

She ignored that, knowing full well he probably hadn't had more than a couple of doughnuts or a bowl of cereal, his usual fare.

Placing the mug of steaming coffee before him, she returned to the cabinet and grabbed a plate, opened a drawer, and pulled out silverware. Then she tore off a couple of paper towels, her everyday napkins, and headed back to the eating bar.

"I told you—"

"I know. But I intend to share with you, unless you have something against eating after me."

He lifted the mug of coffee and took a big sip, then closed his eyes and breathed a deep sigh.

"There's nothing better than a good cup of coffee." He opened his eyes and focused on Christy. "When shared with a friend."

She tilted her head and grinned at him. "Well said." She took a seat beside him. "Come on, clog up your arteries. It'll make you feel better." She slid half her breakfast onto his plate, ignoring his protest.

She didn't look his way again until she heard the fork rattle on the plate.

"God, this is good."

"Glad you said a blessing. I don't always do that."

He had made an attempt to clean up his language, at least in her presence. At one point over the years, she had nagged Jack about his cursing. Then she gave up. Now she decided maybe it was time to try a different approach. "When are you coming back to church?"

He hadn't been since Chad's funeral.

He shrugged. "Been meaning to. I will…one of these days."

"I'd like you to sit with me when you do," she said, her eyes pinning his.

He looked at her and sighed. "The third worst thing that's ever happened to me is that I didn't get you for a daughter-in-law."

"Well"—she took a sip of coffee and turned to face him—"let's just agree that you get me for an adopted daughter. After all, there's enough of my delightful personality to spread around. And you seem to forget all that time I hung out at your house. And more than once you told me I should listen to my dad. But I always liked the way you gave advice," she said, wrinkling her nose.

Jack merely grinned.

They were both remembering her rebellious years, when Jack had sometimes given her a dash of advice while dispensing a bucketful to his son.

"Well, you know, anytime you need me, I'll be right there," he said.

"Thanks. I've always known that," she added gently. She had heard the mellowed tone in his voice and thought he might be about to get sentimental, so she jabbed him lightly. "I take it you lost the poker game."

"What… Oh, that was last week. Nah, we came out about even."

"Hmm. Well, then did you talk your way out of a speeding ticket in court this morning?"

"Now just what makes you think I've been to court?" he said, the old repartee starting between them.

"The way you're dressed." And then she thought of something else. "Jack, have you been to the doctor?"

"Nah, I haven't been to the doctor. Can't a fellow change out of stinking fishing clothes without you women thinking the worst?"

"Sorry," she said, forking her grits. And then a more pleasant thought occurred to her. Maybe Jack had a girlfriend. She tried not to smile at the idea that pleased her so much. She knew Dixie down at the coffee shop had always liked him. But before her mind followed that trail, he spoke in the same gruff voice that had greeted her at the door.

"I been down to the jail to see Buster," he said.

Christy almost spilled her coffee. She turned to face him, stunned by this announcement. "I didn't know you two were friends."

"I been knowing him for twenty years, Christy. I'm not sure I'd call him a friend, but since he doesn't have any…maybe…yes, maybe I'm his friend."

"I thought his family would have bailed him out by now," she said, pushing back her plate, the remnants of her breakfast forgotten.

Jack finished the last bite on his plate before he swiped the paper towel over his mouth and replied. "With half a million dollars bail on him, even the Greenwoods have to wait until the bank opens."

"Do you think his family will bail him out?" she asked, her mind working.

"Yeah, they'll bail him out and probably hope he goes home and hangs himself."

"Jack!"

"They don't care about him," he said, a frown creasing his forehead. "They say he's been an embarrassment to them for years. But being the society types, they care about what others think of them, so that's why they'll do it. But they'll probably take their time sending a lawyer."

She stared at him for a moment, saying nothing. Then she got off the barstool and went to get the coffeepot to refill their mugs. "Let's go sit in the living room."

He followed like an obedient dog trained to mind his manners. While she settled on the love seat, he slumped comfortably on the sofa. She looked at him curiously.

"What do you think?" she asked.

"About what?"

"Do you believe Buster did it?"

Jack snorted. " 'Course not. He's been framed."

She stared at him for a moment. "Are you saying you think someone planted the evidence?"

"H…heck, yeah. Buster may have done some things that weren't too smart in his time, but if he'd killed that woman, he wouldn't have stuck her jewelry and billfold inside a ski mask and pushed it up under the sofa."

Christy sighed. "That ski mask explains a lot of things."

"All it explains is that if forensics does their job right, they won't find Buster's hair or fiber in the ski mask." He hesitated, then slapped his palm against his forehead. It was a gesture of intense frustration, which she had come to know well.

"Now what?" She looked at him, concerned.

"If someone was smart enough to go down there and plant the evidence, then that someone went into Buster's bathroom and got a hair from his comb and stuck it in the mask." He sighed. "What's the use? Buster knew the day he walked up to see what was going on with the police cars and all, that from the way they were looking at him, he'd be a suspect. And sure enough, it wasn't long till they were beating down his door, hammering him with questions. Next thing, they roared up and stuck a search warrant in his face."

"Well, Jack, in all fairness, the detectives are supposed to question neighbors, business associates, clients, and certainly anyone who's ever had a disagreement with the victim." And she knew Buster had. "What kind of questions were they asking him?"

"Where was he between one and two thirty on Sunday afternoon? And did anyone see him out in his boat? Did he go out alone? Wel-l-l-l..."—Jack rolled his eyes—"Buster always goes out alone. He's a loner. That's who he is! And he always goes into Panama City on Saturday to buy bait and ice at Hal's for the next week. Or to turn in whatever he caught the previous week. Just because he was there, as usual, around the time the doctor was killed a block away, doesn't mean a thing."

"But what about Marty? He had threatened her."

"And it's on record. That wild-eyed woman went straight to the police and filed a complaint against him when he told her to stay off his property."

"Come on, Jack. I think he said more than stay off his property."

Jack shrugged. "He may have said if he caught her there again, he'd wring her neck or something like that. But that's just Buster. He's always going to wring someone's neck."

"Too bad he made a reference to her neck."

"Well, he didn't cut her throat. He told me this morning that he didn't do it. That someone was trying to frame him."

Christy folded her napkin over her plate, saying nothing. It wouldn't do any good to point out to Jack that any criminal who is caught with evidence claims to have been framed.

"Who does he think framed him?" she asked.

"He doesn't know. Maybe the shrimper he got in that brawl with. Well, that won't hold 'cause the guy packed up and left Florida. Coulda come back, though." Hope surged into his voice when he thought of that. "But here's the thing, Christy. As long as I've known Buster, he's always used that hawk-bill case knife of his. He told me and J. T. one day down at the wharf that it was the best knife made. Said you can use it for anything—to cut bait, to clean fish, to cut twine. Even cleaned his fingernails with it." He sidled a glance down at her. "Do you know what a hawk-bill knife is?"

She shook her head. "I'm not sure I want to know."

"Well, it's basically a pocket knife with a hooked edge on it. Fact is, he used that knife when he got in the brawl with the shrimper. If he had used that knife on the redhead, they'd be able to recognize the weapon pretty fast. It's not like a regular knife. If he'd used the hawk-bill…" He made a face and shook his head.

"The investigators believe robbery was the motive, Jack. I'll bet Buster could have used another boat. Maybe two."

"He didn't want another boat. You know Buster—well, that's the problem. You don't. If Buster cared about money, he wouldn't have stayed down there in that run-down shack. All he's ever cared about is having enough to eat and drink, going out fishing, poaching a deer every now and then. Mostly being left alone. Sure he got mad when she came in and tore up his island but not mad enough to kill her over it." He drained his coffee mug and stood. "I can see it's going to be hard for him to get outta this, mainly because he hasn't got enough friends to prove it isn't characteristic of him."

"Well, Jack, I believe in the justice system. Innocent until proven guilty."

He guffawed at that. "These investigators are acting like third-grade detectives. And the whole town's already convicted Buster! The fact that Frank La Rosa saw him going out in his boat on a stormy day doesn't mean a thing. He goes out every day. On that Sunday when he got to the deep water, he turned around and came back. But the police have it twisted to look like he went out to drop the evidence."

"His knife? The clothes he wore?"

"No, not his knife. It's been turned over to those eager-beaver detectives. They bagged his knife first thing." He paused, studying her face. "You think he did it too. I can tell."

"Now wait a minute, Jack." She placed her mug on the table and stood. "I'm not discounting anything you've told me. And it's possible Buster was framed," she conceded. *But not likely,* she thought. "Did you get dressed up like that to go to visit him in jail?" She asked suddenly.

"Nah, I got a dental appointment in ten minutes." He glanced at his watch. He took a deep breath and looked back at her, and this time the grin she loved began to work its way across his face. "How'd that fancy dinner turn out?"

She wasn't prepared for the change of subject, but she caught up. "The meal was great."

He waited, making a come-on-tell-me-more motion with his hand. "And the date?"

"He was okay. If you're interested, his name is Dan Brockman. Major Dan Brockman. He was involved in Operation Red Dawn. Went into the rathole with the other soldiers and pulled out Saddam."

His head tipped back. "You're kiddin' me."

"No, I'm not kidding you, Jack. He's since gotten out of the military and is spending some time with his parents over at Bay Point. And he's a nice guy," she added in a voice that she hoped sounded casual.

From the way his blue eyes flashed, she knew he had seen right through her casual approach. "Why don't you bring him out to Rainbow Bay sometime? Does he like to fish?" A hint of suspicion flared in his eyes.

Christy smiled. Jack was suspicious of anyone who didn't like to fish. "Matter of fact, he does. And he's looking around for some property to buy. Got any you want to sell?" She had tossed the words out carelessly, but suddenly their eyes locked, and she knew they were both thinking about the ten acres he had given to Chad and her to build a home.

"I have some I'd give to *you*," he said, reaching forward to give her a hug. "Thanks for the breakfast, sweetie. I owe you some more grouper."

"No," she caught up with him, "I owe you a lunch. Why don't you meet me after you get out of the dentist's office, and we'll go have a big plate of barbecue."

He shook his head. "I'll be on soup, more than likely. But thanks for the offer." He turned for the door, then stopped. "Oh, one more thing. Buster told me that nobody's paying any attention to what he told them about that woman. On the Sunday afternoon the redhead was murdered, he saw a woman up at that house around one o'clock. A tall woman with a tan coat and hood. Didn't see her face, just saw her back when she was out in the front yard snooping around."

"If he didn't see her face, how does he know it was a woman?"

"Men don't carry shoulder bags. Least the ones I know don't."

He laughed, then headed out to the door in his typical fashion: making an exit on a joke.

She watched, shaking her head at this lovable guy as he stomped down the sidewalk to his truck. The rain had stopped, but the air felt heavy and damp.

"Bye, Jack," she called after him, watching as he climbed in his truck, backed out, then gave her a final wave before roaring off.

She closed the door, leaned against it, and stared into space. For only a moment she thought about that stretch of property with the big live oaks and the blue strip of water. Then her thoughts moved on to what Buster claimed to have seen. A tall woman in a tan coat.

Sherrie had said the next-to-last phone call that registered on Marty's cell came from Stephanie Cynaubaum. Had she come to Summer Breeze to tell Marty to stay away from her man? More likely she would have given some important reason to get Marty to come to the ship house. But why would Marty go when she should be headed to Destin?

Then there had been another phone call from a pay phone near the bridge. She was certain the investigators had been there to lift prints. That was probably why they were so certain it was Buster. But Buster could have used that phone plenty of other times. It was the one closest to his house. She'd bet he didn't own a cell phone.

As she went back to the eating bar to gather up the dishes and take them to the sink, her mind replayed Jack's words. Had Buster been framed? From what she'd heard of Stephanie Cynaubaum, she might be desperate enough to do it, if she had seen Buster going out in his boat.

No, that didn't ring true either. She doubted the woman even knew Buster, or if she did, how could she be sure someone else wasn't in his house? And how did she get into the house to plant the evidence?

She shook her head. Her theory about Stephanie just didn't feel right. And just because Buster claimed to see a woman in a hooded coat didn't actually mean he did. But why would he lie to Jack?

Why *wouldn't* he lie if his life depended on it?

She sighed as she ran water over the plates, cups, and silverware, then placed them in the dishwasher. She had just closed the door of the dishwasher and turned the dial to the wash cycle when, out of the blue, a thought struck like a thunderbolt.

What had the lady from Pensacola said? The only time she'd seen Mrs. Cynaubaum was in a restaurant last winter. *Mrs. Cynaubaum was wearing a tan raincoat, but even with the coat on, I could tell she was quite thin.*

She began to pace the kitchen floor, tempted to call someone to get the phone numbers of the ladies in Pensacola. She wanted to ask if that raincoat had a hood.

She stopped pacing and began to chew the skin around her thumbnail. Why would Buster lie about a woman in a tan coat? There were all sorts of things he could have said. If he was lying, why hadn't he said he saw a man—maybe a ragged man who looked homeless? That would sound more believable. The odd thing was, she did believe him.

But Big Bob said they had checked out the Cynaubaums, and they had an alibi. Of course they'd have an alibi, but that didn't mean she believed it.

She wandered back to the eating bar and sat down. Planting her elbows on the bar, her mind began to chew on the facts. As usual, the cool logic that came to her in a clench took over. *Motive. Opportunity.* Maybe this woman had both. Maybe her smoldering resentment over Marty had caught fire. Maybe that fire had flared out of control one dreary Sunday. Crimes of passion were usually violent.

Christy sighed. Now that Buster had been arrested, it would be difficult to convince anyone to consider Mrs. Cynaubaum, particularly when they believed her alibi.

Her mind refused to let it go. She kept visualizing a tall woman in a tan raincoat. She could have called, pretending to be a buyer standing in the front yard of the ship house, wanting to see the house *right now.* Perhaps she had promised to pay cash if she liked the house. Cash would definitely have swayed Marty. Perhaps, as before, Marty thought she could hurry over, make a quick deal, and still get to Destin only a few minutes late. It would explain why she hit the brakes too hard when the red light stopped her in front of the Pancake House.

If Marty had never seen Stephanie Cynaubaum, and Christy

felt certain she had not, Mrs. Cynaubaum could pass herself off as a wealthy buyer.

But…another cold voice of reason shut down her theory. Marty would have asked for a name, and she would have put that name on the note. And…could a woman kick in that big heavy door? Overpower Marty and…kill her in such a gruesome manner? Maybe she had an accomplice, a hit man.

Christy stood and wandered into her office. She tugged the cord on her blue draperies and saw beyond her window that the rain had started again, a slow gray drizzle that seeped into the bones.

With a tug on the other cord, the drapes swished and shut out the rain. She sank into her chair and faced her computer. For a change, she was eager to get to her novel, to shut out the voices within. She had turned off the volume on the answering machine and was reaching forward to turn off the ringer when the phone rang. The caller ID showed the number of her dad's private line.

"Good morning," she said. "Well, I guess it's a good morning. Not a very pretty one, is it?"

"It'll clear up," her dad replied. His voice sounded strong and optimistic. She gripped the phone tighter, wanting to pull some of his profound strength and optimism over the wires and into her being.

She decided to voice her troubled thoughts. "Dad, what do you think about Buster Greenwood being arrested?"

A pause from the other end preceded a heavy sigh. "Well, I don't know Mr. Greenwood very well. I do know Big Bob, and from everything I've heard about the detectives working this case, I think they've arrested the man they believe to be the killer."

She sighed. "You could be right."

"It seems to me the investigators wouldn't have arrested him without pretty solid evidence," her father continued matter-of-factly. "However, I always say a man is innocent until proven guilty."

"Very fair of you, Dad. Do you think…" She hated to ask the question, but now that Jack had planted the seed of doubt, she knew it would haunt her.

"Do I think what, honey?"

"Do you think there's a chance that Buster might have been framed?" She started to quote Jack and then decided against it. A lot of people in Summer Breeze thought Jack was eccentric, though she knew her dad had always defended him.

Another long pause preceded his answer. "I suppose there's always that possibility. But who would do that? And why?"

"The real killer, of course."

"Christy, I'm afraid you're allowing your mystery writer's imagination to cloud reality. I'm inclined to disagree with the idea that he was framed."

"Tell me your thoughts."

"First of all, it wouldn't be that easy to get into his house and hide those things, from what I've heard about Buster. But before I get another call, let me move on to my reason for calling, other than to wish you a good morning. The nice young lady and her sons that you invited to church yesterday?"

She blinked, trying to clear her jumbled thoughts. "Do you mean Jamie? She works at Frank's Steak and Seafood."

"Well, since tonight is visitation, could we talk you into stopping by Jamie's house with your mom, since she taught the boys in Sunday school? Beth said they seemed eager to come back. In fact, I think your mom may have tried to call you earlier."

Christy nodded, recalling her number had shown up as the first call of the day. But instead she had called Bonnie. Her thoughts clouded again.

"I shouldn't think it would take too much of your time," he continued pleasantly.

"What?" she asked blankly.

"You must be deep into your novel. You and Beth wouldn't need to stay long at Jamie's house. Just show that we're glad she came and brought the boys."

Christy hesitated, thinking it over. She'd been pretty closed up in her own world. Why not?

"Sure. Is everyone meeting at the church at seven o'clock to distribute guest cards?"

"Yes, but I respect your deadline, so if you'll just meet Mom in the parking lot of the church around seven, you two can go in separate cars, and you don't have to stay long."

"Okay, Dad. Sure."

"Thanks, hon. By the way, guess who called us at midnight?"

"That would be Seth, since he tends to get the time differences confused."

She hoped her dad hadn't heard the cynical tone in her voice, but she couldn't help it. She was thoroughly frustrated with her brother.

"Yes, but we didn't mind being awakened for good news. He's coming home."

"He is?" Christy clutched the phone tighter, surprised by the tears that sprang to her eyes. "When?"

"He'll be here in a month. And he's saved enough money to pay his way through summer school. He says this time it won't be as easy to drop out when he remembers all the dishes he washed to pay tuition."

Christy sighed with relief. "Dad, that is so wonderful. Why didn't you tell me first thing?"

He chuckled. "I was saving the best for last. Your mom and I feel that our prayers have been answered this time."

"And he'd better be glad you haven't given up praying for him."

"We never give up—for him, for you, for all the people who need our prayers, and those who think they don't. Oops, Martha Ann is buzzing me on the other line, so I gotta go. Love you."

"I love you too, Dad."

She hung up the phone and felt a tear trickle down her cheek. After six long months, Seth was coming home!

14

Monday night

Christy had typed furiously on her novel, unsure if what she wrote was good or bad, but there was an ugly fear hovering on the edge of her thoughts. A fear connected to a tan raincoat and a jealous wife who had been scorned.

She had almost finished her novel, but she had a pretty good idea that she would have to rewrite every word she had written today. Nothing had been thought through clearly. It had been an act of desperation, keeping her fingers flying like tiny racecars over the keys of the computer, her mind spitting out an ending that was probably all wrong.

Finally, at six fifteen, she saved her work, dragged herself to the kitchen to drink a glass of juice, then moved on to the bedroom to change into navy pants and a white cotton shirt. Dressy enough to represent visitation from the church, yet simple enough to let Jamie know they were down-home folks.

Yep, simple down-home folks with a murderer running around slitting throats.

The thought literally screamed at her as she buttoned her blouse. She stared vacantly into the mirror of her dresser. Strands of butterscotch hair stood out in all directions around her pale face. Even her lips were pale, a sign that her emotions were churning. She dragged a brush through her hair, then sent a plume of spray around her head. She concentrated on her eyebrow pencil and lip gloss, then stepped back to survey herself. She looked perfectly normal, even though she'd killed pirates, hid bodies on Shipwreck Island, and…witnessed a real murder scene.

Mrs. Cynaubaum. Suspicion. It began to wind around her stomach again, reminding her of the rattlesnake she had once seen coiled by Granny's pond. The feeling, like the snake, would lie in wait, and eventually it would strike if she didn't deal with it. Or let someone else.

Steeling herself for his temper, Christy reached for the slim phone on her nightstand and dialed Big Bob's home phone. She hated calling him at home, almost as much as he hated her doing it, but she had no choice.

Judy answered on the first ring.

"Hi, Judy. It's Christy. Sorry to bother you, but I was wondering if I could speak to Bob."

"He isn't here, Christy. He went to Tallahassee today, and I don't expect him back until sometime tomorrow."

"Oh." Tallahassee. She could imagine all sorts of important reports from the FDLE in Bob's big hands when he returned.

"Would you like him to call you when he gets back? Or is it something that I should call him about tonight?"

"Oh no, not tonight. But I would appreciate a call when he returns. I just had something I wanted to mention to him. I know I've been a pest."

"Oh, puh-lease! Don't ever think that. You've been a tremendous help in this investigation."

"Thanks." Why couldn't she shut up and say good night? She just couldn't, that's why. "What do you think about the arrest of Buster?" she asked.

"The evidence against him is strong."

Like what? "Oh, right. Well, give the kids an extra hug for me, and I'll look forward to seeing you soon."

They said their good-byes, and Christy replaced the phone, trying not to feel guilty.

She grabbed her purse and hurried through the house, turning on a lamp here and there. She locked the back door, flipped on the porch light, then headed to her car.

As she drove toward the church, she knew her conscience, or maybe it was her writer's conscience, would give her no peace until she talked to Bob about Mrs. C, as she had begun to call her in her mind. If the deputy believed Buster did it, then maybe Buster did it, regardless of what Jack had said.

Still…she couldn't shake what Buster had told Jack or the nagging question in her mind: why would he say he saw a woman there if he was trying to incriminate someone else?

Jamie answered the door, an apron tied around her jeans, her T-shirt stuffed beneath both. She had a blotch of flour on her nose, and her hair was swept back in the usual ponytail. Her eyes flew from Christy to her mother and back, then she made a swipe at her nose.

"Oh, hi," she said, pausing in the doorway. Although she tried to keep the surprise out of her voice, Christy heard 'What are you doing here?' lurking in her tone.

"Hey, Jamie." Christy spoke up. "We just stopped by to drop off an invitation for the boys to Mom's Sunday school party."

"Oh, how sweet," Jamie said, the tension slipping from her face as she looked at the small basket of goodies in Beth's hand. "Come in, but please excuse the mess."

"You weren't expecting company," Beth replied smoothly. "And we can't stay long."

Jamie opened the door wider, and they stepped inside the small living room. The furniture was modern, showing love and wear. An overstuffed sofa was flanked by two comfortable chairs, and a scarred coffee table held comic books and one fashion magazine with the church bulletin resting on top.

"The boys are back in their room doing homework. I bribed them with peanut butter cookies afterward."

"So that's the wonderful aroma floating around," Christy said, sniffing the air. "Bribery is good."

"Reward, I'd call it," Beth put in, smiling the smile that put crinkles around her clear blue eyes and small mouth.

Christy glanced at her, always a bit amazed that wrinkles could look becoming on a woman. Not wrinkles, laugh lines. Life lines. Good life kind of lines.

The boys tumbled through the doorway and came to a halt, the smaller one stepping on the heels of the larger one. "Will-l-l-l!" Jacob yelled.

"Settle down, you two! Boys, you remember Mrs. Castleman"—Jamie waved a hand at Beth—"and her daughter, Christy."

The boys stared at Christy. "You're the Mystery Lady," Jacob said, looking her over carefully.

"Jacob!"

"At church I heard someone say, 'There goes the Mystery Lady.'"

"I write mysteries," Christy said, laughing. "It's a joke around Summer Breeze."

"Not your writing, hon," Beth defended.

"Well, maybe not. But the nickname I don't mind. Hey guys, you wanna go to a party?" Christy asked.

"We almost finished our homework," Jacob said, turning eagerly to his mother.

"The party is Sunday afternoon," Beth explained, extending the basket to them. "Our class is having a treasure hunt, so I brought you guys some clues, along with a couple of things for your mom."

"Wow-ee, a treasure hunt!" Will whooped.

Beth reached into the wicker basket, removed a miniature basket, and handed it to Jamie. It contained scented soap, lotion, and a sampler of herbal teas.

Jamie was clearly surprised. "For me? Well…thank you. How thoughtful."

Beth was handing out the clues for the party, and the boys were jumping up and down with excitement.

"Mom uses bribery too," Christy whispered, grinning at Jamie.

Jamie shook her head. "If I look confused, it's because we've never been so warmly greeted at a church. I come from city folks who don't know their next-door neighbors, and if there was a church around, I never heard about it."

Christy didn't reply that city churches were nice too. Jamie had obviously been through some hard times that had left her a bit jaded.

"Sorry," Jamie said, as though reading Christy's mind. "I must sound cynical. But I do appreciate your kindness." She looked from Christy back to Beth, still distributing her rewards.

Christy merely smiled. She felt sorry for Jamie, who obviously spent most of her time either working or taking care of her sons.

"Would you like to go for coffee or tea sometime?" Christy asked, surprising herself. Time was the one thing she didn't have.

Jamie looked surprised as well. Christy wondered if she was even conscious that she was reaching up to smooth back her hair, as though her appearance mattered.

"Actually, I would. The boys have been invited to a birthday party after school tomorrow, and I have a spare hour for a change. I could meet you for coffee. If you want to," she added quickly.

Christy tried not to hesitate. "I have an idea. Why don't you stop by my house after you drop the boys off? Coffee or tea?"

"I'm a tea drinker," Jamie admitted, her tone apologetic again.

"So am I." Christy wondered who had damaged Jamie's self-esteem so badly that she felt the need to keep apologizing, either verbally or by her body language.

Christy gave her the address, and Jamie nodded. "I know that street. I can be there around four o'clock. If that's okay," she added quickly.

"That's fine." Christy drew her lips into a smile, trying not to think about the deadline looming over her or the real murder mystery that wouldn't get out of her head.

Jamie turned to Beth. "Thank you so much, Mrs. Castleman."

"Our pleasure. And now we'd better get going. Wouldn't want you to burn the cookies."

Jamie's eyes widened. "I forgot! Oh well, the timer hasn't gone off, so I think I'm safe."

Everyone smiled again and said good-bye. The boys had already popped the little suckers from the basket into their mouths.

"You may have spoiled cookie time," Christy whispered as they walked back to their cars, parked at the curb. "They're already into the goodies."

Beth laughed. "The cookies will keep. Thanks for coming with me. And I'm glad you're befriending Jamie."

"No problem, Mom." Was there a note of cynicism in her voice? Who said moms and daughters had complicated relationships? There was truth to that statement. At least for Christy. Her mother always seemed so calm and perfect, which had been one of the problems between them during Christy's teenage years. But she didn't want to think about that now.

Beth gave her a hug, which she returned. "Maybe someday I'll grow up to be like my mom," Christy said.

"I know you're kidding, but that isn't funny. You are a unique and wonderful person. I admire you very much. I should have told you more often. I just always thought you knew."

"Yeah, I did." Now her tone had gone from cynical to flip, but her emotions were hovering near out-of-control, and she was trying to reel them in by reverting to her sense of humor. "So, Mom, it's great about Seth coming home."

"We're so excited," Beth replied. Beneath the streetlight that haloed her mother's face, Christy could see the tears forming in her eyes.

"Hey, it's okay," she said, reaching out to squeeze her mom's hand. "Soon you'll have all your little flock back in the nest."

Beth sniffed and smiled. "I can hardly wait."

"I know. Well, I gotta run." She turned and hurried around the back of her car. "Have a good evening, Mom."

"Thanks. You, too." Her mom turned back to her station wagon. The backseat was loaded with baskets, books, and a few gift items from the Treasure Chest. Christy had seen those things when they'd met in the church parking lot, but this was not a surprise. Her mom spent Monday and Tuesday evenings delivering stuff to people of all ages. The nursing home would be her next stop.

Christy slipped into the cool leather seat, slamming the car door with one hand, turning the key in the ignition with the other. Before she pulled away from the curb, she glanced back at Jamie's house and saw two small happy faces pressed against the front window.

The rest of the evening was surprisingly uneventful. The news of Buster's arrest was now old news, and to her relief, the phone had stopped ringing. The voice in her head that had been nagging her about Mrs. C had quieted down at last. Maybe it had something to do with stepping out of her own world and extending a hand to someone else. Her spirits had lifted after going to see Jamie and her boys. In fact, a warm sense of contentment had begun to settle over her.

Dad must have been right. Bob and the detectives had gathered enough evidence to convince them to get a search warrant, and then they had hit pay dirt. She had to believe in the legal system and mind her own business for a change. What a relief that would be.

After a warm bath, she was so relaxed she practically melted into bed, sinking deep. For the first time in several days, she reached over to the nightstand and picked up her book of Proverbs. Dad always referred to Proverbs as the book of wisdom.

The verses calmed and soothed, and for the ten-thousandth time in a lifetime, she wondered why that always surprised her. She had cut her teeth on memory verses from Psalms and Proverbs, with her dad spouting them off to Seth and her. Even now, after all the years, she could pull them out of her head as quickly as the little boys had plucked clues from the basket.

Come to think of it, verses were a bit like clues, providing pieces that fit in the overwhelming puzzle of life.

She didn't know until she awoke the next morning that she had fallen asleep with the lamp on and Proverbs lying open at her side.

15

Tuesday, February 24

She had finished her tea and toast and settled in at her work station, determined that today would be the day she finished her novel. She admired the thick stack of pages resting on her desk, hugged by a rubber band. It was her final draft, with the exception of her last chapter—a short one to tie up loose ends and explain the mystery for those who hadn't figured it out.

Pushing the button that would wake her computer, she settled into her chair. Her desk phone rang, and she jumped, then leaned over to read the caller ID. Unless it was someone important...

Dan Brockman's cell number showed up. She sat up straighter as the phone rang again. Taking a deep breath, she lifted the receiver and gave him a cheery hello. "How was your trip to Tennessee?"

"It was good. Mom had a great time seeing relatives."

"And you?"

"I did, but I'm glad to get back to the beach. This Gulf breeze works some kind of magic on me. I didn't realize how much until I got back. It makes me more determined to find a place of my own."

"You mentioned property before. Are you looking for a house or just a place to build?"

"Ideally, I'd like to build my own place someday, see if I'm any good at architecture. In the meantime, I'm open to a beach house that's not crowded in with a lot of other homes."

"I know what you mean. I like my little place, but sometimes I wish for more privacy. When did you get back from your visit?" she asked, kicking back in her chair and looping the phone cord around her fingers.

"Late last night."

Christy smiled, pleased that he was calling her so soon. "Then welcome back to the land of sunshine and friendly breezes."

"And a lovely woman who's intelligent and fun."

"Oh? Who did you meet?"

"I won't even dignify that with an answer. Have you finished your novel?"

"Not quite. I've been a bit distracted. Did you know Buster Greenwood was arrested?"

"In connection with the murders of Mrs. McAllister and the doctor? Yeah, Dad called us up in Franklin. So is everyone relieved over the arrest?"

"I think so."

"Think? Maybe I should ask, are *you* relieved?"

"Sure. But not all the forensic reports are back. I try to reserve my opinions until the technical stuff is taken care of."

"Sounds like a wise thing to do. So I gather I'll have to postpone our celebration for another few days?"

She glanced at the computer screen, torn between duty and desire. "I'm finishing it today. What do you think of that?"

"I think I like it. Is tomorrow evening too soon to celebrate?"

"Tomorrow evening sounds perfect."

"Have any special place in mind?"

"Why don't you surprise me?" she asked, loving the comfortable feeling they had begun to establish. This could get serious, at least on her part, but she was trying to proceed with cautious optimism.

"Okay, I'm good at surprises."

"Hmm." *I'll bet you are,* she thought.

"Only I'd like to pick you up at home, if you feel you know me well enough for such reckless abandon. This meeting in parking lots might not be the type of courtship your father has in mind for his daughter."

Christy threw her head back and laughed. "I must look younger than I am. Dad stopped overseeing my courtships years ago. But thanks. And yes, you can pick me up at home." She gave him the address, and they agreed on a time. To her slight annoyance, her heart was soaring, and she couldn't think of a way to settle herself down.

Neither said good-bye. She couldn't seem to wind up the

conversation, or maybe she didn't want to. He, too, seemed to want to hang on.

"So what are you going to do today?" she asked, wondering how he spent his days.

"I'm thinking of going fishing. Dad has a golf game, and Max doesn't care about fishing."

For a moment Christy's mind flashed to Jack and their conversation.

"Where are you going to fish?" she asked.

"Hadn't thought about it yet. One of the back bays, I guess. Dad left early, and I didn't have a chance to ask him."

Christy chewed her lip, wondering if she dared. She decided to take the risk. "Let me make a phone call. I know the perfect spot, but you need permission."

"Sounds enticing. Want me to call you back?"

"I'll call you. I have your number on my caller ID."

"Thanks, Christy. I appreciate it."

"Well, don't thank me too soon. He's a special friend of mine, but to some people he seems eccentric. Make that cranky. I'll call you back."

She hung up and leaned back in her chair, thinking. Why wouldn't Jack like Dan Brockman? She remembered that Jack had served four years in the army, so maybe they could discuss war stories.

Then she thought of something else, and she knew the time

had come. She got out of her chair and walked to her bedroom, looking into the face in the silver frame, smiling sadly at the grinning young man.

"You left *us*," she said, reaching for the frame. "We would never have left *you*."

She took a deep breath, picked up the picture, and opened the lowest drawer of her chest, the drawer where she kept her old sweaters and T-shirts. Carefully she laid the picture, facedown, on top of the sweaters. Then she closed the drawer and walked back to her office.

Admittedly a pack rat, she felt as though she had just put her cheerleading uniform in Granny's cedar chest. Or, more significantly, the house plans she'd forced herself to fold up and slip into a manila envelope. Those plans were also in the cedar chest at Granny's house. A precious, important part of her life had passed, and yet she had the keepsakes and three fat scrapbooks to preserve the memories.

But now her heart had opened up again, making room for another set of memories. Another guy who might turn out to be special in a different way.

She sat down in the chair, dialed Jack's number, and waited until he growled a hello. "Good morning," she said. "What's up with you today?"

"If I'd break down and get caller ID, maybe I'd sound better when my favorite girl calls."

"That's asking too much of you, Jack. Listen, I have a favor to ask but feel free to say no."

"Why would I say no to you?"

She thought about it and wondered if he might agree just to please her and later resent it. "Because I'd rather you be honest with me. We've always been honest."

"Hey, this is starting to sound too serious too early."

She laughed. "No, it isn't. I was just calling to see if you'd mind a friend coming out to fish."

There was a moment's hesitation. "Does that friend happen to be the one who dragged Saddam out of his hole?"

"It does."

"Well-l-l-l…"

Christy could imagine him slapping his pocket for the missing pack of cigarettes, then reaching instead for his coffee cup. "No pressure. Just say no."

"Why would I wanna say no? I've still got a long-lost dream of teaching a grandson to fish."

"Jack!" She refused even to explore the implications of what he was saying. "Just forget it," she snapped.

"Aw, don't get all riled up over an old man's attempt to be funny. Send him out. J. T., clumsy old guy, stumbled over my best fishing pole, and now I gotta try to fix it, so I'm stuck here for the day."

"Jack, are you sure it's okay?"

"'Course I'm sure. Tell him to bring a six-pack."

"I'll call him and give him your number. You two can work it out. I have a novel to finish."

"Thanks for not saying, 'Now be nice, Jack.' 'Cause I might not wanna be nice."

"That's up to you, Jack. Thanks. And bye."

By the time she hung up, she was already beginning to regret asking. Jack was sure to make too much of this. But then, what could it hurt—sending a nice guy out to spend a little time with a lonely man with a huge heartache? If Dan had been good for her, maybe he could be good for Jack. Or maybe not. That was up to them.

Before she had time to back out, she reached for the phone and dialed Dan. He answered on the first ring.

"Hey. You've got permission. But first I should warn you: Jack is…well, a little bit eccentric, as I said before."

"You also mentioned cranky."

"Well, in his defense, I should tell you that he lost his only son six years ago. It…changed him."

There was a moment of silence. "How did his son die?"

"His car…he raced cars." She really didn't want to get into it. "Look, I'm in a rush. He lives out at Rainbow Bay. Well, he owns most of it. His name is Jack Watson, and—"

"Christy, thanks. This is really generous of you."

She caught her breath. *He knew!* She didn't waste time wondering how she had given herself away; actually, she didn't think she had. He was just that perceptive. He had heard something in her voice or figured it out from what she had said that night as they ate dinner and watched the sunset.

She swallowed. "I think you'll like him, just…give him a chance to get to know you. Oh, here's his number. I told him you'd call and set up the time and all that."

"And I'll get his advice on bait. Well,"—his tone lifted—"I'm keeping the Mystery Lady of Summer Breeze from finishing her latest novel."

"Mystery Lady," she laughed. "How did you know?"

"People love to talk about you," he said. "So you gotta live up to your reputation. I'm looking forward to tomorrow night."

"So am I. Good luck with the fishing."

They said their good-byes, and Christy could feel a silly smile slipping over her face as she replaced the phone in its cradle. Swiveling in her desk chair, she looked back at the computer screen, her thoughts scattered. She could *not* let herself wonder what Jack would think of Dan, or vice versa. That was out of her control, but what she could control was the ending to her novel. And it would be a good way to keep herself from picturing Dan out at Rainbow Bay.

"That settles it!" She reached over and turned off the ringer. For the rest of the day, all calls could go to the answering machine, and she'd turn off the sound on that as well.

Lost in her special land of fiction, she had been typing fast and furiously, and now her right hand was aching. She turned toward the wrist brace with its splint and then laughed.

"Fine time to think of it," she said, flexing her fingers. But she didn't care about the ache, for she had just typed "THE END."

Lifting her arms over her head, she pressed her palms toward the ceiling, drew in a long deep breath, then slowly released it. Her eyes wandered to the icon for the Internet, and she clicked it to check her e-mail. To her relief, everyone seemed to have forgotten about her today. For no reason she could think of, Dr. Peter Stewart popped into her mind. Quickly she clicked the buttons again, speeding through the Dr. Stewart articles she had saved to a file. She pulled up the shortest one, the one that had interested her most.

She reread it and chewed an inside corner of her lip. A light bulb flashed in her brain. Last year when she had attended a mystery writers' conference in New York, she'd met a gal from the FBI. They had exchanged a few e-mails since then, because Erin was working on her first novel and had asked Christy for pointers. Christy had e-mailed her a list of reference books that she had found helpful, and Erin had sent some ideas about her plot. Christy had made a few suggestions.

"If I can ever help you," Erin had offered, "please let me know."

Impulsively, she closed the file on Dr. Stewart, opened her electronic address book, and found Erin's address. She took a deep breath. Did she really want to bother Erin with this? After all, the investigators had made an arrest.

But then she thought of Jack standing in her kitchen, frustrated over his friend Buster. She owed it to Jack to explore every possibility. Particularly since he was allowing Dan to fish in his beloved waters.

"Okay, can't hurt anything," she said to the monitor and proceeded to zip out an e-mail to Erin. She encapsulated the double murders, then asked about Dr. Peter Stewart, specifically his being questioned in regard to the jewelry heist. She then attached the short article that had spiked her curiosity. She hit the Send button, and her questions catapulted through cyberspace to her friend in New York.

Satisfied with her mission, she left the Internet on while she went to the kitchen to brew a pot of tea. She opened a Ziploc bag of roasted pecans from Granny's trees and dumped them into a china bowl that matched her special teacups handcrafted in England.

She rarely used the lovely tea set that had been a gift from her grandmother, but she wanted Jamie to feel special, to know that someone liked her enough to go to a little trouble for her. Christy doubted that Jamie ever sat down to tea that someone else had prepared for her.

Thirty minutes before Jamie was due, Christy detoured back through her office and saw that a letter had popped out of her electronic mailbox. Quickly she retrieved the e-mail from Erin and read over it.

Christy, sorry I can't help you very much. All that happened so long ago that I don't know anyone still working here who was connected to the case. I looked up the lead detective, and he happens to be someone my dad knows. He's now retired, but here's his phone number in case you want to call him…

Christy grabbed a pen and pad and jotted down the name and number. She glanced at the clock. She still had twenty minutes, so why not?

She dialed the number, and the deep voice of a man filled the wire on the second ring. She swallowed, having dialed before she'd framed a question, but she plunged in. "Mr. Edwards, my name is Christy Castleman. We have a mutual friend in Erin Fitzpatrick—"

"Yes, I know Erin. Nice young lady."

"She gave me your telephone number. I hope you don't mind my calling, but it concerns a jewelry heist in New York back in the eighties."

A heavy sigh. "The most frustrating case of my career. Could you tell me why you want to know about this?"

She explained that she was a writer and that a man in her community had been arrested in the double murder of Dr. Stewart and a local Realtor named Marty McAllister.

"Mr. Edwards, I was reading old news files on Dr. Stewart and found that he had been questioned in connection with a robbery suspect in the jewelry heist. If I may ask, why did you say that case was the most frustrating of your career?" She asked the question even though she thought she knew the answer.

"Well, because we never caught the man and woman."

"Man and woman?" she repeated.

"Yeah, always kind of figured it was an inside job. The woman —Libby she was called, I think it was Libby Lawton—worked at the jewelry store. A month after the thing went down, she quit her job and moved away. Or, to be honest, vanished in thin air. Just like Benny Salvatore, the boyfriend. Sal, he was called."

"And what did you think about this Sal being spotted in the plastic surgeon's parking lot?"

Another heavy sigh. "Well, I read in the paper about his recent murder, and...I hate to speak ill of the dead. However..."

"What is it, Mr. Edwards?"

"It wasn't the first time we'd had a tip about the good doctor. He'd gone to school with a guy we'd linked to the Mafia. Before Joey Palverone went missing, we had a tip he'd been seen having dinner at the Russian Tea Room with Dr. Stewart. Later Joey turned up dead in Greenwich Village. Died of a heart attack. And he'd had plastic surgery."

"Really?" Christy was intrigued.

"Yeah, but when we went back to Stewart again on Benny Salvatore, Stewart threatened to sue us for harassment. We backed off, because it was just an anonymous tip. Some of the guys thought it was a coincidence, but frankly, Ms. Castleman, I don't believe in coincidences."

"So…" Christy was trying to sum up everything he had said. "With all your experience and expertise, do you think Dr. Stewart did surgery on both men?"

"I can give you my gut feeling. Doesn't mean it's right."

"Go ahead."

"Joey got by us when he shouldn't have. Then when Sal and Libby slipped through the net, we knew they had to be well disguised. I'm talking a permanent disguise, as in cosmetic surgery."

Christy's mind zipped back to the woman involved, and now a startling possibility presented itself. "Tell me what this Libby looked like—and how old she was."

"Whew, that's tough. She was in her early thirties. That'd make her in her fifties by now."

Christy swallowed hard. "Was she a small woman with red hair?"

"Small woman but blond, as I remember. Or bottled blond, as my wife says."

"Mr. Edwards, if I faxed you a picture of a woman, do you think you could tell if this woman bore any resemblance to your Libby?"

"Not my Libby! But she did make a pass at me, and that's what got me suspicious. I've been happily married for forty years, Ms. Castleman. And I always wear my wedding band. Even if I weren't married, I'd never be attracted to a woman as flashy as Libby. And she wouldn't be attracted to me. My wife said she was flirting to try to distract me from questioning her. I don't tell her this, but my wife is usually right."

Christy scrambled through the box of business cards on her desk. "Mr. Edwards, do you have a fax machine?"

"No, but there's a place down the street where I can send and receive faxes." He gave her the number, and she quickly wrote it down.

"I'm going to fax you a picture from a business card. Could you call me back after you get the fax?" She glanced at the clock. Five minutes until Jamie arrived. She gave him her phone number, thanked him again, then hung up.

She went to work, taping the business card onto a sheet of computer paper. She copied the paper on her copier, then faxed the copy to Mr. Edwards.

What if Libby was actually Marty McAllister? What if she and her husband pulled off the bank robbery? Maybe her deceased husband had been Benny Salvatore. Maybe her nephew Bruce knew about the heist and the money, and in return for helping her get established here, she had signed everything over to him at her death. If she had called him about Dr. Stewart being in town, Bruce might have seized a golden opportunity to get rid of her and collect the insurance money.

Marty had made enemies, and she didn't make good choices

with boyfriends, either. Maybe Bruce believed he would be way down on the list of suspects.

Seconds after the fax went through, she heard a tapping on her back door.

16

Christy tried to settle her mind, shut off the wild dance of confusion in her head as she hurried down the hall to unlock the kitchen door.

"Hi, come on in." She opened the door and smiled as Jamie entered the kitchen.

"Hi, Christy. Hey, this is nice," she said, glancing around. She was still wearing the yellow and tan outfit from Frank's Steak and Seafood. Her brown hair was swept into a neat ponytail, and her makeup was subtle while complementing her fair skin and hazel eyes. "What's the flavor of that candle? It smells wonderful?"

Christy glanced at the fat candle burning low in its stand. "Something about spring, I think. You like it?"

"I love it."

Christy opened a cabinet and pulled down another one, still in the box. "I hit a two-for-one sale. Here you go."

Jamie looked surprised. "Oh. How nice of you. Let me pay—"

"Puh-lease! I'll never burn two of these. Let's have tea."

They settled in at the table, and she poured tea from her china teapot into their cups. "So how was your day?" she asked.

"It was okay. Mmm, this tea is wonderful," Jamie said, obviously enjoying the taste.

"Have some roasted pecans. My grandmother lives about an hour north of here. She has a pecan grove, and I get to enjoy the harvest. And no, I didn't roast them. She does that too."

"Delicious," Jamie said, sampling one. "I never had a grandmother. I was raised by an aunt and uncle after my mother took off... Well, that isn't something you want to hear about."

"Why not? I was fortunate to have two grandmothers and a mother who *didn't* take off. Someone needs to remind me how lucky I am." She looked at Jamie, feeling sadness and concern. "Your mother left you with relatives?" she asked gently.

Jamie nodded. "I was raised in a poor section of Atlanta. Born out of wedlock to a mother who liked her men better than me."

Christy tried not to look shocked. It was not the confidence Jamie had shared so much as the flat indifference in her tone that saddened her. Jamie had long ago accepted the injustice, and Christy suspected this was one reason she lacked self-esteem.

"Anyway," Jamie continued, "when I became a teenager, I made my own friends, so it didn't bother me too much that my mother took off. I shared a home with three cousins, and no one paid much attention to me." She set down her teacup carefully. "Actually, I guess I should be honest and say I liked it that way. By this time, I had met Donny and wrapped my whole world around him.

Donny is the father of my boys," she added, her eyes sliding over to Christy. "I didn't do much better than my mother. About the morals, I mean. We'd only been married five months when Jacob was born. And I don't know why in the world I'm telling you this." She sighed, concentrating on the dish of pecans.

"You're divorced from Donny?" Christy asked.

She nodded. "He worked the night shift at the plant, and we began to drift apart. But—will you tell me to shut up? I can't believe I'm yakking so much."

"Why not? My friends say I'm a good listener. And what they tell me goes no further. I'd like you to feel that way."

Jamie shrugged. "I don't really have any secrets. Everyone back home knew I was relieved when Donny left me for another woman. He drank too much and...I'm ashamed to admit it, but he was abusive, and I took it."

When she fell silent, Christy spoke up. "Most women keep those things to themselves. I doubt you had a chance to meet Teresa Dowling at church on Sunday, but I'd like to introduce you. Teresa was in an abusive relationship for ten years. She finally got out of it when she ended up in the hospital for the second time. Like you, she lived in another town and was alone, because her husband had isolated her from her friends. The bottom line to the story is that she came home to her parents and got counseling. She went back to college, got a master's in counseling, and now counsels women who have gone through abusive relationships. She offers free counseling to those who can't pay," she added gently.

Jamie stared at her, wide-eyed. "It's hard to believe anyone does something for free. But then, look how nice you've been to me. And I know you're an important person here in Summer Breeze."

"So are you," Christy replied. "And what you do is far more important than what I do. You're a wonderful mother; I can tell."

Jamie's eyes lit up. "Thanks. Jacob and Will are my life. I try not to spoil them too bad."

"I can see that you don't."

"Well." Jamie took a deep breath. "To change the subject, I was wanting to ask if you'd met that Dr. Stewart. I don't usually buy a Sunday paper, but I did this week with so much going on in town. Anyway, I saw both those pictures and the write-up, and I was really shocked. I waited on Mrs. McAllister and Dr. Stewart when they came to the restaurant."

Christy had just lifted her teacup but set it down in the saucer with a loud clatter. "You waited on Marty and Dr. Stewart?"

"Well, I didn't know who he was at the time. He was dressed casually, wearing one of our Florida baseball caps pulled down on his forehead. But I remembered his face. I mean, how could I forget him? He left the best tip I've had in all my years of being a waitress."

"Really?" Christy asked, staring at her, her mind working on something else. "So the two of them came into the restaurant together?"

Jamie nodded. "It's been bothering me ever since I read the article. I mean, Mrs. McAllister came in often and brought clients, but seeing the two of them together and knowing what happened… I'm so glad the police arrested the guy who robbed and killed them."

"Yeah." Christy frowned. "I wonder why Frank didn't mention seeing the two of them together."

"Well, they just came in together that one time, and we were real busy."

Christy nodded. "Was Frank there?"

"Yes, he was there. And he saw them. He probably forgot because, like I said, the man wore a baseball cap, and Frank never talked to him. Well, not directly," she added, staring into space. "As I delivered their coffee, I saw Dr. Stewart staring at Frank while Frank chatted with someone at the next table. As I was walking away from the table, I heard Dr. Stewart say, 'Hey, pal. You owe me.' Or something like that.

"Frank looked at him oddly and said, 'You must have me confused with someone else.' Then he headed out to the kitchen. I thought maybe something was wrong with the meal, and he was complaining to Frank. When I asked, he said his steak was overcooked. So I got him another one. That's another reason I remember him. After that, he didn't complain, and like I said, he left a fabulous tip."

The phone began to ring, cutting through their conversation. Christy started to ignore it, then remembered she'd been waiting on a return call from Big Bob.

"Excuse me," she said, getting up from the table. She stepped into the kitchen and answered the wall phone.

"Christy, it's Bob." The deep voice boomed into her eardrums. She held the phone back a half inch.

"Hi, Bob. Thanks for calling me back." She looked over the eating bar to Jamie. "Can you hold just one second?" she asked Bob.

"One second is all!"

She placed her hand over the receiver and met Jamie's curious glance. "I won't be long."

Jamie seemed to understand as she got up quickly from the table. "No, don't rush. It's almost time for me to pick up the boys."

"Are you sure?"

"Oh, yeah. Thanks…for everything."

"You're welcome. Don't forget your candle. And stop by anytime."

Jamie nodded and smiled back at Christy as she picked up the candle and hurried out the back door.

"Sorry, Bob. Listen, something has been bothering me, and I really hate bringing this up—"

"No, you don't, so just spit it out."

"I've got to get this off my chest. I know you've arrested Buster Greenwood and all, but…" She hesitated for a moment. "Well, Buster claims he saw a woman in a tan raincoat at the ship house around one o'clock. I spoke with two ladies from Pensacola who know Stephanie Cynaubaum, and she wears a tan raincoat and—"

"And has an airtight alibi, like I told you."

"How airtight?"

"They were both seeing a counselor that Sunday afternoon. But…"

"But what?" Christy pressed.

"Now don't get the big head about your detective skills. You know she made a call to Marty's cell phone around one that day. The truth is, according to Mrs. Cynaubaum, that she had driven over here to have a talk with Marty. Apparently, the Cynaubaums had a showdown the night before. She'd caught up with him, and this time she was gonna leave him. But first she wanted to see the woman who had broken up their marriage. She'd found Marty's business card with her address and phone numbers among her husband's things. She said she came over here, called her, and asked if they could talk. Marty refused, told her she had an appointment to show a house.

"After they hung up, Mrs. Cynaubaum thought she was showing the ship house. Her husband had actually mentioned it to her as a possibility for a second home. So she drove over, got out, and looked around. She didn't like the house, didn't see Marty anywhere, so she got in the car and drove off.

"About that time, Archie called her on her cell, begging her to come home. For the first time in their marriage, he promised to see a counselor. In fact, he'd already called and set up an appointment as soon as she got back in town. So Mrs. Cynaubaum sped back to

Pensacola. A neighbor saw her pull into the driveway around two, and their appointment with the counselor was at two thirty. The counselor said they were right on time."

"But she could have hired an accomplice, led him to the house…then raced back to Pensacola."

"You can't get from Summer Breeze to Pensacola that quick. Not on a Sunday, for sure. The coroner places Marty's death between one thirty and two thirty. Besides, if by some miracle she had been at the crime scene, the DNA would have nailed her. And it doesn't."

"Does it nail someone else? The accomplice?" Christy pressed.

"You know I can't answer that."

Christy heaved a sigh. "So I guess Buster did it." She was tossing out bait, but he was too smart to bite. She opened her mouth to tell him what she had learned from Mr. Edwards, but Bob cut her off.

"I got an important call coming in. Gotta go."

"And our conversation is *not* important?" she teased. "Okay, Bob. I'll let you have peace at last."

"You sound like I'm about to die and be buried."

She laughed. "You know what I mean."

"Yeah, but I doubt it'll be the last time I hear from you."

"Have a good evening, Bob."

She hung up and stood thinking about the conversation. If she'd been wrong about Stephanie Cynaubaum, then maybe she was wrong about Marty's real identity being the jewel thief Libby.

Maybe the call that interrupted their conversation had actually saved her from another blunder. At this point, she only had a hunch. Until she heard back from Mr. Edwards, she really had nothing to tell Big Bob.

And then she remembered a beep had sounded on her line while she was talking to Bob, but she had dared not put him on hold again. Now she checked her message and saw that Mr. Edwards had called back. She clicked on the recorded message and listened.

"Ms. Castleman, I picked up the fax and looked at the picture of the woman you sent. I can't say if this was the same woman or not. The picture you sent shows a woman with small features. As I recall, Libby had larger features. Still, if she had cosmetic surgery, who knows? Age and size are about right. Anyway, my wife and I are going out for dinner, but if you'll call me tomorrow, we'll discuss this further."

She hung up and felt the inner beep of radar. She wasn't sure just what was setting off her suspicions, but she was on to something. She wasn't even certain if her instincts were humming over the possibility of Libby being Marty or the gut feeling that the jewelry heist, the surgeon, and the double murder were all connected.

As she went to the table to gather the teacups and spoons, she felt a new undercurrent of tension bubbling like a stream beneath her thoughts. As soon as she sent off her novel tomorrow, she would be free to explore everything further. And she'd find a way to get the truth about the DNA from Bob…or Sherrie.

"Obviously, they have something on Buster," she said to the kitchen wall. "And maybe all I have is a silly theory."

To vent her pent-up energy, she decided to do some much-needed housecleaning before going to the market. After all, Dan Brockman would be coming here tomorrow evening. She opened the door to the utility cabinet, pulled out the vacuum cleaner, and whirred through the house nonstop, then went back for the caddie of cleaning supplies.

For the next hour she dusted, cleaned, and polished. When finally she was satisfied with her progress, she dropped down on a kitchen stool and stared into space, enjoying the love song that floated from her CD player. The only deterrent to her great feeling was a growling stomach and the still-nagging suspicions about Libby. Or Marty.

She headed for the bedroom closet to grab a sweatshirt and shoes. Food… The first thing that came to mind was a club sandwich from the deli at the supermarket before she did her shopping. Then she'd treat herself to a pint of Praline Pecan ice cream for a late-night snack.

"Perfect," she said, pulling a sweatshirt over her T-shirt. Her gaze dropped to her shoe rack, and she knelt to examine her new boots, the ones with the stiletto heels. She caressed the butter-soft black leather and tilted her head, studying the heels. She'd wear them tomorrow night on her date with Dan. From past experience, though, she knew she'd better break them in first. Lifting them from the box, she sat down and pulled one on, wiggling her toes. Yep, better break them in tonight. With feet in boots, she tottered upright and headed for the kitchen.

She removed her grocery list from a magnet on the refrigerator door, then shoved her little cell phone deep into her jeans. Purse and car keys in hand, she locked the back door and flipped the switch on the porch light.

The rain had stopped, but there was still a cool breeze in the air, with March just around the corner. Spring was a nice thought as she started the car and backed out of her driveway. Her neighborhood was quiet and serene. She loved winding through the streets at night, absorbing the comfort of lamps glowing in windows and children sleeping peacefully in their beds. And now everyone could sleep in peace if Big Bob was right about Buster.

She turned onto Front Beach Road, thinking about her visit with Jamie. Or rather trying to focus on their conversation about Jamie's life, because something was buzzing around in her subconscious like a worrisome fly in a food-filled kitchen. Her mind should be like that food-filled kitchen, loaded with good thoughts. She didn't want a fly...or another nagging suspicion about the double murder, but here it was, and she couldn't chase it out.

Dr. Stewart and Marty. Together at Frank's restaurant. Big Bob said they had been seen together driving around Summer Breeze.

She had reached the block that held the most expensive homes in Summer Breeze, with various styles of architecture, set in the midst of wide grassy lawns. As it happened, she was approaching Frank's Spanish-style house, profiled in night-lights. Slowing down, she saw that lights blazed in windows, and Frank's white Jaguar sat in the circle driveway.

Why not ask him about the day Marty brought Dr. Stewart into the restaurant? She wheeled into the wide driveway and cut the engine. Frank seemed to have sharp instincts about people. Maybe if he remembered the guy, he might offer some perception about Stewart and Marty.

At the restaurant, people were always yelling at Frank, and being the hyperactive type, Frank had probably raced on past Marty and Dr. Stewart after Stewart had called to him. The restaurant was crowded, Jamie had said. And Dr. Stewart was wearing a Florida baseball cap.

She thought of Seth. When he put on a baseball cap and tugged the brim low, he looked quite different. Also, the newspaper featured a guy dressed in a suit, looking very businesslike. Frank would have remembered a guy with a baseball cap and not made the connection. Jamie might not have made the connection had it not been for the generous tip. And the fact that she had looked him right in the face.

At the rear of the house, she could see the workshop where Frank created his masterpieces for parties and receptions. She cut the lights and got out of the car, glancing from the side of the huge home to the workshop out back. She'd bet her boots he was out there now, because she could see the door was cracked, spilling white light onto the concrete slab.

Overhead, perched on its tall pole, a floodlight funneled a pool of gold around the small building, which she remembered was a commercial-grade cooler for Frank's ice. A fifties rock-'n'-roll song now making a comeback drifted into the soft night breeze as she approached.

"Frank?" she called. She stepped onto the concrete slab, reaching for the stainless steel handle on the big door. It always gave her the creeps to touch those handles, because once the handle was shoved into the locking slot, a person would get locked inside.

Again she was thinking of Seth. When she and Seth were children, just watching the guy bolt the door to the ice-cream truck sent her curious mind into writer's mode, thinking up a story about a little girl and boy locked inside the truck.

She swung the door wide and peered inside. The fifties song blared from the radio on a shelf beside the door. The room was an eight by ten, with twenty-inch shelves running the length of each wall to hold equipment and tools. The end wall held a stainless steel worktable where Frank sat, his head tilted back to study one of the designs tacked on the wall above the table.

He hadn't heard her call to him; the music was loud, and he was lost in his creation. He was chiseling the pure crystal ice he special-ordered from Hal's Ice House, glancing intermittently from the design of a huge swan on the wall, to the hundred-pound block of ice that would yield the swan.

She was conscious of dampness beneath the soles of her boots, and she looked down. Chips of ice covered the concrete floor, melting into a trail of water that ran toward a drain underneath the worktable. Sidestepping ice, she opened her mouth to call out to Frank as she raised her eyes and looked toward him.

His name froze on her tongue as she stared at something she had never noticed. His head was bent over his sculpture, and a scar was clearly visible beneath the fluorescent light overhead. It was an old scar, the width of a hair, faded and scarcely noticeable except for the bright light and the position of his head.

But it was there. A telltale line that ran from behind his ear around his hairline to the other ear. The kind of scar that came from cosmetic surgery in years past.

She recalled something her friend Liz had told her when they were teenagers. "Mom got a face-lift. She looks great, but the scar never goes away," she had said. "There'll always be a thin line, but her hair will cover it, so she doesn't care."

Her breath caught. Okay, so maybe Frank had gotten a face-lift years back. He was vain enough; she knew that. Cosmetic surgery didn't automatically connect him to Dr. Peter Stewart.

Also from New York.

Who did all kinds of facial surgery, who even changed the appearance of a person, according to Mr. Edwards.

The music had ended, and in the split-second pause before the announcer came back on the station, Frank turned on his bench and saw her. "Christy! I didn't hear you come in," he said, laying aside his tools and standing up. He looked tall and broad here in his small workspace, as he smoothed down the black rubber apron that covered his shirt and jeans. "What's up?"

She couldn't seem to find a reply, because her mind was still locked on the scar. And something else.

The half smile disappeared from his face as his dark eyes bore down on her. "What are you doing here?"

"I just stopped by to ask you something," she said, the coldness settling over her now. The coldness of the room. The coldness of his eyes. Her mind raced down twin tracks—she needed light conversation, and she needed to ask him a question. "You're making a swan?" she said, walking toward the worktable. "Nice."

"What were you going to ask me?"

She froze for a moment as her gaze landed on the tan leather sheath on his worktable. It was an expensive pouch, designed with pockets to hold various chisels. The size of each blade was labeled under the pocket: 1", $5/8$", $1/2$", $1/8$".

And on the table beside the ice, the chisel he had just put down grabbed her attention and wouldn't let go. She stared with a horrid fascination. He had asked her something else, but she wasn't conscious of his words, only the sharp blade of the chisel.

"A sharp-force injury," the coroner's report read. And Big Bob had mentioned a knife.

There was silence now. He had turned off the radio, and she could hear his footsteps behind her.

"Why are you over here snooping around?" The words were as sharp as the edge of the chisel.

She turned around to face him, and suddenly the thing that had been hovering in a far corner of her mind catapulted forward, like a train jumping the track.

Hey, pal, you owe me…

Pal…or Sal as in Benny Salvatore?

"Sal." The word shot out of her mouth like a lump of chipped ice and struck him full force.

His jaw went slack, and his mouth fell open. But a quick reflex kicked in as he lunged forward and swooped up the chisel.

Her knees began to shake, and she felt sick at her stomach as she looked from the blade to Frank's hard face.

"How long have you known?" His dark eyes pierced her face. His big hand was turning the chisel over, pointing the blade toward her.

All she could think about was the door. She had to get to the door.

"How long have I known what?" The question was dumb and useless, a momentary stall as she began to back away from him. "Whew, it's freezing in here."

"Shut up." He raised the blade, in striking distance now.

She whirled to make a run for the door, but her heels began to slip and slide in a crazy zigzag over the wet floor. She felt like an ice skater out of control. She threw herself against the wooden shelf, grabbing its edge for support, but her feet slipped out from under her, and she went down.

"Don't move," he said, towering over her, the blade inches from her face.

She hugged her arms around her, trying to still the trembling so he wouldn't see how scared she was. All she had to bargain with was her brain. She couldn't tell him she had just now figured it out. She had to make him believe she still held some secret that would keep her alive.

"If I don't make a phone call to Big Bob by…"—her eyes shot to a clock on the shelf—"nine thirty, he's coming here. I talked to him before I left."

"You're bluffing." His thick lips curled in a snarl of disgust. "They got Buster. They're satisfied."

Christy's heart was banging against her chest. "Was Marty really Libby?" she blurted out.

Her question stopped him but only for a moment. "No! Libby was smart."

Did you kill Libby? she wanted to ask, but she kept quiet. *God, help me. Please help me,* she silently prayed. Her research on crime had taught her that most killers thought they were smarter than everyone else and couldn't get caught. Maybe she could stall for time by flattering him about his clever tactics. She could feel his hot breath on her now, and she forced her eyes to remain fixed on his, not to waver. "Okay, I can't outsmart you. Marty was onto you and tried, but you outsmarted her. How'd you do it?"

He lifted his chin, and the dark eyes burned with arrogance.

"She knew something was up when Stewart recognized me. After I killed him, she thought she could blackmail me. I offered her fifty grand that last day she came in the restaurant. After she left, I went to a pay phone and called her. She'd brought the Miami guy in for lunch one day; his voice was pure Bronx. I didn't have any trouble convincing her I was Ridge Cohen, and that me and my girlfriend wanted to look at the ship house first."

Christy tried to calculate her distance to the door, but she was trapped, and he held the weapon. Her teeth began to chatter, and her feet were frozen in her boots.

Her boots with their stiletto heels.

"How'd you get in the house?" she asked, while she tried to devise a plan.

"I catered a social occasion there. Knew where the key was hidden." He raised the blade, and she knew he was through talking.

"Frank, don't kill me. Please."

The eyes were cold, the lips set in a firm line. He would stab her before she could lift her boot. All she had left now was the God she trusted. She closed her eyes, and suddenly she was a little girl again, sitting in her father's arms, learning memory verses. She opened her mouth and softly the words began to flow—the psalm she had repeated many times in her life—but it had never been more appropriate than now. "God is our refuge and strength, an ever-present help in trouble. Therefore, I will not fear, though the earth give way, and the mountains fall into the heart of the sea—"

"Shut up!" Frank yelled.

Her eyes flew open. His arm was raised to strike, and in that split second, she had just enough space to dart under his arm and make a dive across the floor.

She felt as though she were swimming, but she was actually throwing ice chips and water behind her, although she wouldn't realize it until later. She heard the hard crunch of ice under Frank's feet and then a curse as he hit the floor behind her. He grabbed her foot, and in the next instant she heard the rip of her jeans and felt a stab of pain in her left leg.

Twisting around, she looked over her shoulder. As he was struggling to stand back up, she yanked her right foot free, swung her leg over, lifted her foot, and with all of her might slammed the stiletto heel into his chin. Blood spurted as he lunged backward, grabbing the shelves for support. She watched in dismay as an end section of the shelf broke loose from the wall and toppled forward, landing on him.

She scrambled to her feet, but just as quickly, her injured leg gave way, and she fell again. Digging her elbows into the wet mess, she pumped hard, crawling as fast as she could toward the cracked door.

Wood was breaking behind her; Frank was fighting his way out from under the shelf. She reached the door, grabbed the handle to pull herself up, and then swung the door wide.

The night air had felt cool ten minutes ago, but now it warmed her frozen skin. Gasping the air into her chest, she felt an extra surge of adrenaline and used it to pull herself outside and then throw her weight against the door, slamming it shut.

She stood on the concrete slab, gasping for air, while on the other side of the door, she heard what sounded like a carnival of disaster moving closer and closer. With trembling hands, she grabbed the steel handle and bolted it down. The lock clicked.

An instant later the handle began to jerk, and she could hear Frank ranting on the other side of the door. She had escaped death by seconds.

Dizziness swept over her. For the first time, she felt the searing pain in her left leg. Beneath the night-light, she could see her torn jeans, feel the blood flowing down the back of her leg. The knife had ripped veins, and she was losing blood fast. She had to bind the wound tight, try to slow down the blood flow.

She sank onto the concrete slab and rested her back against the building. A fist beat against the door, and an angry voice roared into the night. She threw her head back, gasping more air into her lungs as dizziness fogged her vision. The night suddenly grew darker.

Her phone…in her pocket. Her trembling hand slid deep into the pocket and found the phone. She couldn't believe she hadn't lost it in the scuffle. Her vision blurred on the numbers. She held it close to her face. Tried to stiffen her trembling fingers. Pushed all her strength into her forefinger. Punched in 911.

Her teeth were chattering by the time an operator answered.

"This is Christy Castleman."

"Who? Ma'am, you'll have to speak louder."

"Listen to me," she cried. "I'm injured. I'm out back of Frank La Rosa's house, and I'm bleeding badly. He just tried to kill me."

"Frank La Rosa's house?"

She was losing her vision now, and soon her voice would go.

"He admitted to killing Marty McAllister…and…Dr. Stewart. I need…an ambulance…and the police…as soon—"

The voice on the other end of the line faded. The blackest night she had ever seen settled over her. The voice on the phone clattered onto the concrete. Reality faded to a tiny wave in a black sea.

She and Seth were swimming in Granny's pond again. Something cold and hard slammed into the back of her head. She went under.

17

Tuesday, midnight

Christy felt a warm gentle pressure on her hand. Slowly she opened her eyes. A white blur filled her vision. Voices seemed to echo through canyons. Soft voices, distant canyons. When she tried to move, a dull pain shot through her left leg, equaled only by an ache in her head the size of Texas. She closed her eyes.

Wednesday, February 25

Something wrapped around her upper arm and tightened. She flinched.

"Christy, can you wake up?" A woman's voice.

She pushed against the weight of her eyelids. They opened halfway.

The woman was dressed in white, and she held something...a cuff attached to...

"I just took your blood pressure. You're doing better."

When she moved, pain hammered her head.

"Christy, you're in ICU at General Hospital. Please try to stay awake. I'm paging the doctor."

"Am I dying?" she croaked, not daring to move her head again.

"No, Christy. You're going to be okay."

She tried to swallow, but the sides of her throat were stuck together. She closed her eyes again.

The next time she awoke to a different sensation. Her vision had cleared, and she was conscious of someone examining her left leg.

"Doing much better." The dark head lifted, and she was looking into the familiar face of Dr. Wilkerson.

He leaned over her. "How's my star patient?"

She pushed her lips into a smile, or tried to.

"Christy, I'm going to ask you some general questions. They may seem dumb to you, or they may not. What's your date of birth?"

She frowned, then realized what he was doing. Testing her mental capacities. "On April 12...I'll be twenty-eight."

He grinned. "Want to give me some more statistics?"

"Christy Castleman. Grant and Beth Castleman, parents. Seth Castleman, younger brother." The rush of words had left her short of breath. She tried again. "My nickname is Mystery Lady."

"Very good. Nicknames are big around here. We've had some guy who calls himself Sandpiper pestering the nurses about you."

"Sandpiper," she repeated. "One found the bottle; the other found the body."

"She's still groggy," he said to the nurse. "Christy," he said, speaking louder, "we're planning to move you to a private room in the morning if you don't misbehave."

Dr. Wilkerson had always reminded her of an oversized teddy bear with light brown hair, a furry beard, and a big round chest.

"You've had a blood transfusion, and your leg has a bunch of fancy stitches. Your head where you hit the concrete worried us the most. But you've just proved that the concussion hasn't altered your mental state."

His large brown eyes held a mixture of relief and joy, and Christy took a deep breath. "Thanks." She was ready to get back on that cloud she'd been riding, when the doctor gently tapped her shoulder.

"Christy, hang on for a minute."

She opened her eyes to see Dr. Wilkerson staring through the glass cubicle of the ICU unit toward…something.

"Big Bob's behaving like a wild bulldog fighting the leash." Dr. Wilkerson chuckled. "Think you could answer a few questions? Just a few," he added emphatically.

"Okay."

She tried to think. Why was she lying in a hospital bed in ICU? And then it hit her like a tidal wave, as a sickening memory rolled over her bruised brain. Frank La Rosa. He had killed Marty and Dr. Stewart. And he had tried to kill her. Slowly she turned her head to trace the IV from her arm up to the stand. The IV in her arm would pump life back into her. She had been saved.

She heard whispering. A nurse entered, followed by Big Bob. Maybe he was attempting to lower his voice, but that voice just did not lower.

"Arrest that man," she groaned. "He's harassing the staff."

His big frame whirled in her direction, and his dark brows shot up. In two giant steps, he reached her side and peered down at her face.

"How're you feelin', hon?" The hazel eyes looked sad and worried.

"Great," she said, trying to focus on him. What, she wondered, were they administering to her through the IV?

"You don't look so great," he said, tugging at the end of his big nose.

"Thanks. Maybe if you guys would catch criminals…I could work on my looks." Her words dragged out in shaky half sentences. But Bob seemed to understand.

He shoved a big hand through his steel gray hair. She squinted. It looked like a gray porcupine sat on his head.

"I hate this," he said, teeth gritted. "I mean, I hate it happened to you. Christy, why did you go over to his place by yourself? Why in the world didn't you call me?" He didn't bother trying to lower his voice or hide his frustration.

She swallowed, trying to organize her thoughts. "I was headed to the market. Along the way I remembered that Jamie—his wait-ress—told me…Marty and the doctor ate at Frank's."

"Yes, I know about that conversation. Jamie called me as soon as she heard what had happened. She related what she'd told you. Makes me so mad." Anger flashed in his eyes, underscoring his words. "I questioned Frank right after Marty went missing. I knew he was one of the last people to see her. He lied, of course." He blew a disgusted sigh that quivered the sheet covering her arm.

"Uh, Christy. I have some questions to ask you, important ones. Do you feel up to it?"

Not really, she wanted to say. But she knew this was crucial. "Yes. What…"

"First, tell me the part about when you went to his house. Or to his workshop. How did you end up out there, anyway?"

"One question at a time." She lay very still, moving only her lips. A nurse handed her a cup of water with a plastic straw. She sipped slowly, relishing the moisture on her throat.

"Thank you," she said to the nurse, who put the cup back on the nightstand, then faded into the background.

"Let's see. I pulled into the driveway…saw his lights on in the workshop. The door was cracked. I heard music…went back there."

She could hear the whir of machines from other units, people fighting for their lives. God had spared hers, and now she must do her best to tell Bob exactly what had happened, even though it seemed like a lifetime ago.

"I opened the door… He was bent over the worktable."

Bob had whipped out a pocket-size notebook and his trusty pen and was writing furiously.

"In the fluorescent light…I could see an old scar…along his hairline," she continued. "Cosmetic surgery."

Bob's head shot up from the notebook; she could read the unspoken question forming in his mind, but she didn't bother to detail the cosmetic surgery. He could check it out.

"I saw his ice chisels…the size of the blades."

Her voice faltered. *Don't think about it. Just give him the facts.* She had plotted and written dramatic endings to her mystery novels, never dreaming that she would someday be fighting for her life with a real killer.

"The ice chisels, the blades…" Bob was trying to follow her train of thought. "How did you know about the weapon used?"

"The coroner's report." Big Bob's dark brows shot toward his gray hairline. At least he didn't ask how she knew what was on the coroner's report.

"When I looked at those blades…the one he was using…" She released the sigh that had been lodged in her chest. "I just knew. Without a doubt. It came to me in a flash…so fast that I couldn't think…how to get out. And watching me, he knew…I had figured it out."

She motioned for the water. Bob's big hand settled clumsily around the cup, then inched it toward her mouth, adjusting the straw for her. She took another sip, waited for the water to slide down her throat.

He said, "I know about the Benny Salvatore heist. But I just didn't think…" He lowered his head as his cheeks turned red.

Bob…embarrassed? She almost felt sorry for him.

"Actually, he thought I knew more than I did. Then…I called him Sal, and…he reacted."

"But, Christy," Bob said, staring at her with a look of dismay, "how did you get away from him?"

"I was scared. I started…reeling off a psalm I'd learned as a kid."

Big Bob's mouth dropped open, then he slammed his lips together and swallowed. "Was that before or after he knifed you?"

She blinked. "Before. We…struggled. Fell. He caught me in the leg. I kicked back."

"You landed a solid blow!" For the first time since he'd appeared at her bedside, a pleased grin broke over his face. "You aren't the only one who needed stitches. So…"—his pen went back to the notebook—"you got out of that cooler ahead of him and slammed the door?"

"Right. I…somehow my cell phone stayed in my pocket. Tight jeans," she answered her own question. "My leg was bleeding…I was about to faint. I called 911, and then…" She lifted a hand to her sore head.

"Then you passed out and slammed your head on that concrete slab. The 911 operator called the paramedics and me, told me what you'd said. I took backup. First we got you in the ambulance, then we pulled our guns, opened the door, and entered. Frank...or Sal...was slumped on the floor, bleeding and half-frozen. Now listen, Christy, you're telling me that he admitted to both murders?"

"Yes. Stewart was here... Marty showed him around. I think ...well, I'm sure...Frank never expected the doctor who'd changed his face so long ago to show up here. At his restaurant." She swallowed, took another shaky breath. "I don't think Stewart knew who Frank was...until he looked him in the face."

"And so," Bob summed it up, "the doctor recognized his own handiwork. And Frank thought he had to kill Stewart to protect his identity. But how did Marty figure it out? Surely the doctor didn't admit his part in Frank's escape?"

"No. I guess...Marty caught the look that passed between them. Heard him say...'Sal, you owe me.' She started asking Frank questions. He got paranoid...overreacted. That's what the argument was about...in the parking lot. Someone saw them."

"Yeah, he told me he was trying to warn her away from Cohen, and she threw a tantrum."

"He told me that too," Christy said, amazed that Frank had been so convincing to everyone. "After she left the restaurant that last day...he called her. Altered his voice to sound like Ridge Cohen."

"How...and why did Marty fall for that?"

"Both men...from the Bronx. A distinctive accent. Frank's

been away for years. But still remembered." She realized she wasn't making complete sentences, but it was the best she could do.

"So Frank told Marty that he and the girlfriend wanted to look at the ship house first? And he was waiting when she got there?" Big Bob was nodding, putting it together now.

Christy stared into space, trying to remember something he had told her. Then it clicked. "He had catered there…knew where the key was hidden."

It occurred to her that her words had begun to sound as though they were wrapped in cotton. She fell silent, totally exhausted from remembering and relating.

"Well,"—Bob cleared his throat—"you've taught us all something about catching a criminal."

"Have a criminal mind," she said, trying to smile.

Bob's big lips shot back in a wide smile. Then his hand swallowed hers. "You don't have a mean bone in your body, and everybody in Summer Breeze knows it. Speaking of bones, a few of mine may get broken by your buddies if you don't hurry up and get outta the hospital. They may never forgive me for letting this happen."

The smile wobbled on her lips. "You didn't let it happen." *It.* A small word to cover the magnitude of what she had been through. "Did he…confess?"

He looked down at his big hand wrapped over hers. "No, but he might as well. We lifted a print from the garage door at the ship house and got DNA from beneath Marty's nails. Or rather the experts got it. Didn't match up with Buster or the homeless man. I didn't tell you that over the phone, because we were sworn to secrecy. We needed everyone to believe Buster was the real killer, calm everyone down until forensics could do more work."

"Poor Buster."

"Buster's family had already posted bail, and we'd released him. But as soon as we arrested Frank for…what he'd done to you…we got busy. We fingerprinted him; that was routine. But the prints matched the one lifted from the garage door. They also identified him as Benny Salvatore. We've put a rush on his DNA. I have no doubt we can match him to the evidence from Marty's body. Apparently she scratched him. One of the waitresses noticed a little nick on his cheek. He told her he'd cut himself with the razor."

Big Bob grabbed a breath and continued. "So…the judge has denied bail. The double-murder charge would hold him, but he's a flight risk as well. He escaped before and managed to elude the authorities for sixteen years. FBI is on the way. But right now, he belongs to us!"

"Did you learn anything about the woman—Libby what's-her-name? Did…he kill her, too?"

"No. The guy from the FBI who's coming here—Monahan's his name—said last year an elderly aunt of Libby's called from New Jersey. Said her niece Libby Lawton had been involved in the jewelry heist along with Benny Salvatore. Libby gave the aunt a diamond necklace to hide her and Sal in a garage apartment but never explained why. The aunt always suspected they'd pulled off the jewelry heist in New York. Two months later Libby was driving the aunt to the doctor, met a truck head-on. Libby was killed instantly, but the aunt got out with a few broken bones. Said Sal took off as soon as Libby was buried."

Bob heaved a sigh and shook his head. "Too bad the aunt waited till she was dying to clear her conscience about Sal running loose. Said she was Libby's only living relative. It had been so long, she didn't remember much about Sal except he had brown hair and a brown beard. Again, the FBI hit a cold trail…until now. Until you!"

A nurse appeared with a blood pressure cuff, and Bob stepped back from the bed, stuffing his notebook into his shirt pocket. "I'm gonna get out of here so you can rest. Fact is, I could use some rest myself. You get well, little girl."

Christy closed her eyes, too tired to utter another word.

Something bumped the bed, and a voice said, "Sorry, Christy."

She opened her eyes and saw two nurses scurrying around her bed.

"Good news," the older one said to her. "We're moving you to a private room. You're doing great."

"Thanks," she said and closed her eyes again. Then she suddenly remembered that in all the excitement, poor Dan had been stood up. But there was nothing she could do.

18

Thursday, February 26

Nurses came and went. They felt, wrapped, soothed. The *whoosh* of blood pressure, the poke of a thermometer. She soon learned to smile and say that she was okay, then drift back to sleep.

During her wakeful moments, she admired all the flowers. Dozens of arrangements decorated her private room, and a couple of blue balloons swung from the ceiling. She could read the card on the closest one. Seth.

Tears stung her eyes. The reality of what had happened settled over her, along with a depression that she couldn't seem to shake. It had to do with Frank, the murders, and finally her writing. For the past four years she had written stories of danger and near death, but now that it had happened to her, she felt changed. Different. In fact, she wasn't even sure she wanted to write again. Sometime before dawn, she had awakened to the startling realization that her manuscript was due at the publishing house, but it lay on her desk at home and on half a dozen disks. The worst part of it was that she didn't care.

Her mom and dad had been in and out, happily relating bits of good news. After Seth heard what had happened to his big sis, he decided to catch a plane home. He would arrive tomorrow. Blinking as a tear slipped down her cheek, she studied the big blue balloons attached to the ceiling. Maybe she'd just goof off with Seth for a while, have no serious thoughts about anything.

Once again the man who had slipped in and out of her dreams throughout the ordeal now loomed at the center of her thoughts: Dan Brockman. Her mom had read the names on the flowers and mentioned dozens of calls. But Dan's name had not been spoken. She wondered why he hadn't at least called to check on her. Did he think that she had intentionally stood him up? Hadn't he heard by now all that had happened? She wondered when or even if she would see him again.

"How's my favorite daughter?" Her father's smiling face seemed to light up the room as he walked through the door. He leaned down to kiss her cheek.

"Your favorite daughter, your only daughter," she responded with the usual quip.

Grant was wearing one of his golf shirts with khaki pants, and again Christy felt a surge of pride that this handsome, kind man was her father.

"What's with the sad face?" he asked, pulling up a chair.

She breathed a heavy sigh. "Dad, when we had that conversation last week—right before I went to see Jack, you remember? You reminded me we have freedom of choice, and our lives are shaped by those choices."

"I remember."

She thought about the psalm she had learned as a child and quoted in desperation when she thought she was about to die. She was certain that psalm had saved her, given her the edge over Frank. But Frank...

"Frank had a choice," she said. "Right at the last minute before ..." She paused, swallowed hard. "He could have backed off; he could have let me go."

Her dad sighed. "Yes, he could have. But he didn't do that, Christy. And now he has to pay the consequences."

She closed her eyes, feeling the ache in her throat that threatened tears. She didn't want to talk or think about it anymore.

"Well," his tone lightened, "you look snazzy in that fancy pink bed jacket."

"Thanks. One of the nurses took pity on me and freed me from that awful hospital gown."

She still wasn't allowed to get out of bed, but a bed bath and some basic hygiene had done wonders. She had brushed her hair, even applied lip gloss.

"They've taken the No Visitors sign off the door. Who are you expecting?" Her dad grinned, and she knew he was trying to joke with her.

"Oh, the media. The FBI. You know, the usual."

He chuckled softly and patted her hand. "Honey, I'm so glad you haven't lost your sense of humor. Some people—"

A knock on the door interrupted his sentence. He lifted his eyebrows, glancing from the closed door to Christy. "So which is it? FBI or media?"

Before Christy could reply, he had walked over to open the door. She guessed from the expression on her father's face that the person he faced on the other side of the door was a stranger to him.

He stuck out his hand. "I'm Grant Castleman, Christy's father."

"How do you do, sir? I'm Dan Brockman."

Christy sucked in her breath, darting a glance toward the drawer of the bedside table. Where was her compact?

"I don't want to intrude. I just came by to check on Christy." His deep voice flowed into the room, and she felt a little burst of joy. What a relief. She had begun to wonder if the head injury had damaged the part of her brain that sent happy messages.

"Come in." Her dad opened the door wider and stepped back, glancing at Christy. A question mark was written all over his face as he turned from Christy back to Dan.

The man who had occupied her dreams stepped into the room, looking better than any dream. He was wearing dark trousers, a dress shirt, even a nice patterned tie. In his hand was the largest bouquet of red roses she'd ever seen in her life.

"Hi, Dan." She smiled as he hesitated beside the door.

"The nurse said you could have a visitor. I didn't know if—"

For the first time since she had met him, he actually looked shy and self-conscious.

"That nurse who told you I could have a visitor was trying to save me from Dad. Just kidding. Dad, this is Major Dan Brockman. He was in Operation Red Dawn."

"Of course!" Her dad had made the connection and gave Dan a broad smile. "We're glad to have you home."

Christy cocked an eyebrow and studied her dad again. What an appropriate thing to say. How could he know that home was more important than anything to Dan right now? Well, maybe not more important than...anything.

"Thank you, sir."

The two men shared a moment of silent assessment, and then Grant cleared his throat. "So, Dan, if you think you can watchdog for me, I'll step down to the cafeteria and get some much-needed coffee."

"I'll do my best," he replied, as her father nodded with approval and hurried out the door.

Dan placed the huge crystal vase on the only unoccupied space on the dresser.

"Looks like you have plenty of flowers," he said, glancing around the room.

"But none as pretty as yours. What's with the Sunday clothes?" she asked.

"I wanted to impress your parents," he replied, walking over to stand beside her.

"Oh." She pretended disappointment. "And here I thought you were just trying to impress me."

"I'm always trying to impress you." He reached over and touched her hand. "You look great. But how do you feel?" His gaze ran the length of the IV, then he stared at her head, free of bandages but still bruised.

"I'm fine."

He leaned forward and kissed her cheek. Just a peck, but it sent her straight to that cloud she had been riding for days. But this wasn't medication or escape. This was real.

He reached for her hand again, and for a moment neither spoke as their eyes locked.

"I've been worried about you," he said, the deep voice gentle. "When you didn't show up, I didn't know what had happened. And then I heard about it and came to the hospital. You were in ICU, and I didn't want to intrude on your family. Instead I pestered the nurses."

She grinned. "I bet they enjoyed it."

"I doubt it. But something wonderful did happen that first morning while I was hanging out downstairs. I met your grandmother."

"Yeah, Dad said she was here." Christy pushed up on the pillow, grateful she could move a little without a jab of pain. "She didn't stay long."

"I guess...well, to be honest, she was pretty upset. She said the best thing she could do for you was to go home and pray. I'm sure she'll be back today."

Christy's eyes roamed around the room, settling on a colorful arrangement of pansies that she felt certain had come from Granny's place.

"How did you like her?" she asked.

"I liked her a lot. Then *like* turned to *love* when she invited me up to eat fried catfish. I accepted and asked if you could tag along when you decided to shake the chains here."

The only chains Christy felt were the invisible ones shackling her in a vise of depression. But Dan had broken the chains, and she was mentally kicking free of the sadness and gloom.

"You'll love the farm," she said. "You mentioned looking for property to buy. You might just like something up in that area."

"Might. For a long weekend but not all the time. Unless you're moving there."

Again their eyes locked. She stirred nervously, trying to think of something to say. She came up with, "Have you planned a special celebration for finishing my novel?"

Slowly, a grin broke over his face, relieving the tension in his eyes. "Matter of fact, I have."

"And?"

"You'll just have to wait and see."

"So…how did the fishing go?" She held her breath, hoping Jack hadn't acted up.

"I had a great time."

Her eyes widened. "Did you catch a big speckled trout?"

"I did catch some trout, but they weren't as big as the ones Jack caught."

"He went with you?" she asked, amazed.

"Yep. I sensed he was a betting kind of guy, so I bet him I could catch a bigger trout. He liked that."

"And that means he liked you, Dan. Thanks so much."

"I should thank you. He's a great guy. I'm looking forward to a friendship with him."

"You are?"

"I am."

"And what about your friendship with me?"

"I'm looking forward to that, too."

What a nice smile, she thought.

Suddenly the door flew open, and a red cowboy hat peered around the door.

"We got past the nurse's station," Valerie boasted. Her hazel eyes sparkled as she looked from Christy to Dan.

"And this time they're not running us off." Dianna entered behind her, holding a basket of goodies.

They were in full costume—red hats and purple outfits.

"They wouldn't dare." It was Bonnie's voice as she sidled through the door. Her eyes looked weary, but a smile worked her lips when she saw Christy. She was out of costume, in a black pantsuit, but everyone understood why.

"Bonnie, it was good of you to come considering—"

"I wanted to see you, honey."

Dan came to his feet, obviously confused about whether to stay or go. Christy reached for his hand.

"Don't let them frighten you," she said. "They happen to be very good friends of mine."

"Not to mention detectives!" Dianna boasted.

Everyone laughed, and then Christy leaned forward as though peering into Bonnie's hands. "This hospital food isn't the best. I hope you brought it."

"I did," she said, holding a plastic container of sweet potato pie. "But before that, the girls asked me to deliver another gift to you. One I created just for you."

Lips twitched, eyebrows lifted, as the women shared their private joke.

Christy glanced at Dan, who had slipped into the mood and was grinning broadly at them, obviously fascinated.

Christy knew Bonnie had made an emotional sacrifice to be here, and she loved her for it.

Bonnie cleared her throat, opened her mouth, and the deep voice so accustomed to singing gospel burst into a happy lilting tune. Christy began to smile, then she started to laugh, and everyone in the room clapped while Bonnie's big body rocked as she belted out the message...

"Lookin' for a rainbow... We're gonna find a rainbow...after the rain."

About the Author

I hope you enjoyed reading *When the Sandpiper Calls.* This story began with a simple idea early one morning when I was walking a beach in northern Florida. I enjoy picking up interesting shells or checking what the tide brought in, and on this particular autumn morning, I did what many writers do when their creative nature takes over. I asked the familiar question: what if?

What if a bottle was half-buried here in sand—not an ordinary bottle but an antique green bottle like I had seen in a gift shop? And what if that bottle contained an intriguing note like…"Call the police. Someone is trying to kill me." I stood and stared at the damp sand, my mind catapulting forward with possibilities. At that moment a little sandpiper came as close as he dared, peering up at me with a question in his eyes. Ah, and what if a sandpiper led me to this bottle with the secret note?

That was the beginning of my story, which would be changed, revised, and changed again over the coming months.

I have been writing off and on for twenty years while raising a family and living in different parts of the United States. Writing is my passion, and nothing is more fun for me than stepping into a brand-new world, filling it with characters, and planning a life for these characters. I've written romances, historicals, romantic suspense, and mystery. The cozy mystery is, by far, my favorite, because this genre allows the reader to participate in solving the mystery.

My faith has been a fundamental part of my life, and I thank God for being richly blessed. One of the greatest blessings is the opportunity to write. I hope to show in my writing how God works in miraculous ways through the lives of people. I want my stories to portray themes of hope and forgiveness through his love. In this story I wanted to reflect through my characters the freedom of choice that we have in our lives and the blessing of a second chance when we "mess up."

My husband and I have reached a point in our lives when we can now pursue the dream of spending our summers in the Colorado Rockies and our winters near the Florida seashore. I draw inspiration from both places.

I love hearing from my readers, so please stop by my Web page, www.PeggyDarty.com, and sign my guest book.

Since my readers are my friends, I'll end this little note with a favorite Irish blessing: May the road rise to meet you, may the wind be always at your back, may the sun shine warm upon your face, may the rain fall soft upon your fields, and until we meet again, may the Lord hold you in the palm of his hand.